Augie, Here are 5 copies of Acre's Orphans. I hope you
enjoy it, and I will let you know when I'm coming to
Chicago and maybe we can set up a store visit. Meanwhile,
best to you and Tracy.

WWT

Acre's Orphans

(Part 2 of the Lucca Le Pou Stories)

WAYNE TURMEL

Published by Achis Press

Published by Achis Press, 2019

Cover design and layout by Kelly Lee Parry
Printed by Ingram Spark

Dedication

To the crew at the Naperville Writers Group. Thanks for 5 years of companionship, support and butt-kickings.

Typing is a solitary act, writing is social.

Other Books by Wayne Turmel

The Count of the Sahara

In 1925, Count Byron de Prorok was the toast of the archaeological world. By 1926 his career lay in ruins. What happened?

Based on true events, the Count of the Sahara is the gripping tale of an extraordinary man's obsession, of America in transition, and a naïve young man's first steps in the adult world.

"A well-crafted novel full of suspense, light humour and rich historical detail that explores human strength and frailty"

Published by The Book Folks (UK)

Acre's Bastard
(Part 1 of the Lucca Le Pou Stories)

Salah-adin is poised to conquer the Kingdom of Jerusalem. For 10-year-old Lucca "the Louse," it's life as normal. The streets of Acre—the wickedest city in the world—are his playground. But when an violent act of betrayal leaves him homeless and alone, he's drawn into a terrifying web of violence, espionage, and holy war.

Can one lone boy save the Crusader Kingdom from disaster at the Horns of Hattin?

"a top-notch historical adventure filled with memorable characters"
Published by Achis Press

For short stories, non-fiction books and more, visit
www.WayneTurmel.com

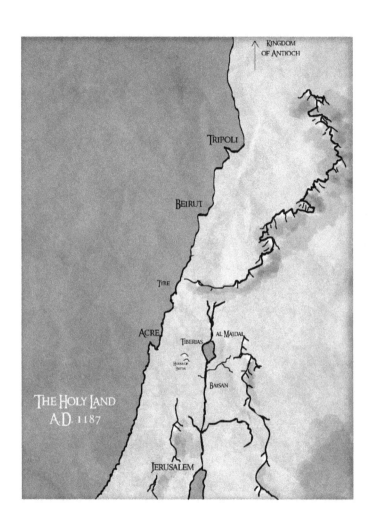

KINGDOM
OF ANTIOCH

TRIPOLI

BEIRUT

TYRE

ACRE

TIBERIAS   AL MAJDAL

HORNS OF
HATTIN

BAISAN

THE HOLY LAND
A.D. 1187

JERUSALEM

July 7, AD 1187

The City of Acre, Kingdom of Jerusalem

I knew I was dreaming but that didn't help much. I thrashed and turned in my narrow slat bed, sensing a presence—probably Sister Marie-Pilar or one of the other leper Sisters of St Lazar. Later she told me I slept for an entire day and night, but I really don't remember. I do recall voices muttering and my prying open sun-scorched eyes just long enough to make out friendly shadows and swallow a mouthful of cool water. Then I sank back into the blackness. The only faces I remember clearly were the dead. Those I couldn't forget.

When you roam the streets of a violent city like Acre, Death is not a stranger, exactly. He is always around, like the butcher's ugly dog—scary, but if you kept your distance and didn't get between him and his quarry, everything would be fine. Because I was an orphan—and had so few people in my life who cared about me—dying was always a distant possibility, but nothing to be concerned about until it was really my turn.

In the last two weeks, I'd made its acquaintance. First, I'd seen Charles the clerk murdered. I watched, useless, as the poor man had his throat slit by Al Sameen—the fat spy who'd kidnapped me. As for him, the last time I'd looked into his piggy eyes, my captor was falling off a mountain at Hattin, screaming to Allah for help that never came. Then there was Brother Idoneus, who'd tried to… But even my most awful dreams wouldn't show me that horror again. Instead, he appeared as I last saw him, beaten and in agony. He'd been wounded in battle, lying in the dark lee of a rock pile and crying for help and God's grace. Instead, Gilbert and I just left him there, at the mercy of the grave robbers and scavengers.

Gilbert, my fellow orphan, and more Idoneus's victim than I ever was, invaded my sleep as well. He too came as I'd seen him last, not dead but ashen-faced and mumbling too quietly for anyone but God to hear. We arrived home together, but I knew a part of my friend would never fully return. I kept straining to understand what he was telling me, but the droning never quite became words.

At last, I clawed my way up from sleep to wakefulness. My eyes stayed open this time and I sat up. All my thrashing nearly made Sister Marie-Pilar spill the bowl of broth she held in her lap. As she stroked my forehead, she cooed. "Well, you're back, Lazy Bones." I knew she was smiling because her eyes twinkled in the candle light. Her mouth, as always, was hidden behind the gauzy veil that concealed her scabby, tortured nose and lips.

I looked around the monk's cell that served as my home with its plain wooden cross and one smoky candle and managed to form words. "I'm home." She nodded and ran her fingers through my hair. She always enjoyed doing that, so I let her.

"Yes, thanks to God."

I smiled and sank back happily into my pillow, wrapping

the threadbare woolen blanket around me. Then I remembered something else. "The others who came with me, are they all right? Did the city fall?"

Sister didn't answer. She dipped a wooden spoon into the soup and brought it to my chapped, flaky lips. "Eat, Lucca. You'll need your strength."

Chapter 1

Even in a city as dirty, crowded, and generally stinky as Acre the smell of smoke stands out from the other odors. There are two kinds of smoke smells. The good kind promises a warm charcoal fire on a cold, rainy day—or a hot meal pretty much any time.

Today, it was the bad kind, and far more exciting.

My ten-year-old heart raced as I ran. After being cooped up for the last day and a half, being fed, cooed over by the sisters, and treated like an invalid, it felt exhilarating to be out on my own again.

After the harrowing events of last week and my return with the rest of the survivors, I was truly free. I picked up speed; whipping in, out, under and through the bystanders who couldn't move nearly fast enough for my liking.

Thick black clouds billowed up over the buildings, and flakes of hot ash stuck to my sweaty skin, so I knew I was close. It had to be the cotton warehouse, judging from how much smoke there was. Brick didn't burn well so it would take a lot of fuel to create that much of a blaze.

It was the biggest fire I ever saw. Hellish orange flames burst through the roof, and even from two blocks away they licked at the cloudless, sun-bleached sky. I rounded the last corner near the fruit market and ran into a huge crowd of screaming, angry people.

At first, I thought it was just the usual gawking mob, but something felt wrong. Rather than watching and joking, people were angry and shouting. Fists shook, and voices screamed hateful things in a babble of French and Turkish, and even a little Armenian.

"Death to Joscelin…" Lord Joscelin had been the big man in charge of the city before the battle. Some said he'd been captured with the other nobles at Hattin. I didn't know anyone who believed that. Most people assumed he'd fled and was cowering in Edessa. Brother Marco certainly thought so, and he was usually right about such things.

"We should burn the traitors, not their warehouses!" A young merchant I recognized from the market stood trembling with rage. Tears streamed down his cheeks, leaving muddy snail tracks. Shaking, he picked up a piece of paving stone, turning it over and over in his hands like someone else placed it there. Then he spun and hurled it over the mob towards the building. He took no aim, it was just a violent spasm of outrage. The jagged rock flew over the crowd and disappeared from sight. The merchant's voice croaked as he screamed, "You've killed us all, you bastards!" Then he put his face in his hands and sobbed. "You've killed us all…"

The people surrounding him cheered, and a few even reached down to pry up projectiles of their own. But before anything else got tossed, their eyes widened and they parted like startled goats, fleeing in all directions. A trio of ragged, exhausted, and humorless King's Guards pushed their way through the crowd. The biggest and meanest one I recognized. I always called him Three-Teeth, for obvious reasons. He shouted at the top of his lungs. "Which one of you motherless pigs threw that rock?" Spit flew everywhere from the gaps in his gums, and it sounded more like "motherleth pigth," but his mood didn't really allow for laughter.

Not surprisingly, his bloodshot eyes landed on me first. I shook my head violently and looked in the opposite direction from the real perpetrator, hoping to throw him off. I was no squealing rat.

Not everyone had my scruples. A dozen traitorous fingers pointed in the merchant's direction as guilt oozed out of the sobbing, pathetic figure. Three-Teeth grabbed him by the collar and shook him so hard, the poor man's feet left the ground, and he landed in a soggy, sad heap on the cobblestones. Several onlookers complained from behind the cover of much bigger people, but otherwise, the only sounds were the whip-crack of flames and the whoosh of smoke.

The other two Guardsmen pulled murderous-looking longswords and held them pointy-end towards the crowd, turning in slow, menacing half-circles. They didn't need to say anything, the panicky look in their eyes said they'd swing first and think later. The mob took two steps back, leaving the guards and the rock thrower in the center of a suddenly silent circle.

"What the hell were you thinking, lad?" Three-Teeth spoke to the man with surprising kindness—or maybe he was just tired. Either way, he'd never spoken to me in that manner.

The man was just a crumpled heap on the ground. "He's going to kill us all, isn't he?"

I knew—we all knew—who "he" was. Salah-adin was coming, but no one could be exactly sure when. After the disaster at Hattin, the entire Kingdom was ripe for the picking, and the port of Acre was the most important prize left, save for Jerusalem itself. Plus, he hated us for expelling all the Muslims a year or so earlier. Everyone knew payback would come. Nobody expected it to be this week.

Three-Teeth looked skyward and sucked air between his lips. "Not if we do his dirty work and go killing each other first, he won't. Get the hell out of here. Go home and await word." He pulled his longsword from its sheath and waved it menacingly over the merchant's head, shouting, "All of you, go home. Now. Any more burning or rioting, the Saracens will be the least of your worries."

Nobody moved. The crowd stared at the guards, who glared back. The only sound was the crash of charred beams from the burning warehouse as black flakes of ash drifted around us. I stood transfixed, not noticing anyone next to me, until a thick leather glove descended onto my shoulder.

"You heard the man, get out of here." I turned to see Brother Marco's haggard face. I'd only seen him once since my return, and it didn't look like he'd slept, changed clothes or bathed in the two days since. He probably hadn't eaten much, either.

My friend was still tall and imposing, but the normally icy

blue eyes were red and crusted. His neat, trimmed, brown beard was scraggly and matted against his chin and neck. Even when dressed in his beggar disguise he always appeared clean and inoffensive. Now his robes were mud-splattered and grey with sweat and dried patches I assumed were blood, long turned dark brown and crusty.

"What's going on?" I asked.

He sighed, as if answering took more will than he possessed, "Count Joscelin has surrendered the city to Salah-adin."

"So why are they burning the cotton building?"

Marco shook his head, like the answer could be found written in the clouds of smoke. "Some people are furious that Joscelin surrendered the city without a fight—mostly to protect his own businesses, like that warehouse. They can't get their hands on *him* so…" The older man shrugged eloquently. "A lot of folk are furious at the King and the Orders for not doing their jobs and protecting them, some want to fight to the death, and some want to run but have nowhere to go. They're frightened." He'd told me before, and I knew it to be true: frightened people seldom made good decisions.

"Salah-adin's already here?" My voice squeaked as I asked. For most, the Commander of the Faithful was a bogeyman—something people used to frighten children at bedtime or get citizens to pay their taxes for defense, as if their meager contributions were the difference between conquest and survival. Unlike those people, I'd actually met the man himself a few days before, at Baisin on the banks of the Jordan, and felt no hurry for a return visit. He had offered me the opportunity to convert to Islam and spy for him, and I'd refused. Politely, to be sure. Now I was just another Christian brat in a captured city—and one who'd refused him service. While he was not the monster many claimed he was, I suspected he wouldn't be as magnanimous or forgiving on second meeting. As Marco said, frightened people seldom made good choices.

"He will be soon enough. A tough old bastard named Taqi-adin is sitting outside the gates with a fresh army. The city's surrendered, Joscelin is safely north—my guess is Edessa but maybe Tripoli. I think Taqi's just waiting for things to calm down before he takes possession of his prize... Assuming there's anything left to claim." Marco's eyes scanned the crowd and winced.

"Are you all right?" A stupid question, but I asked a lot of those, and Marco never seemed to mind. How could he be all right? The man's friends had been slaughtered, the city he swore to protect was burning, he hadn't slept since Tuesday, and it was unbearably hot. Oh, and he was a leper to boot. He nodded anyway.

"Get out of here, Lucca." He leaned on me as he shifted his weight from one leg to the other, hobbling a bit. "Have you checked on your horse yet? Firan says you haven't been by and he hasn't been paid for three days' food and stabling."

"He's not my horse." Droopy (I had to call him something, and it fit) was a cantankerous old pony who, uninvited, had followed me home across half of Outremer after the battle at the Horns of Hattin. I'd left him with my friend's father, Firan, before I went home to sleep for a day and a half.

That just earned me another shrug. "Well, you brought the nag home, and that crotchety bastard thinks he belongs to you. And that's a battle you need to fight on your own. A man needs to address his debts." The Syrian carter was as mean a man as I knew. I certainly didn't want to be on his bad side. But where would someone like me find money to feed a horse?

Tired of my foolishness, Brother Marco steered me north and gave me a shove to send me on my way. "I'll see you at home, Lucca."

I would much rather have watched the warehouse burn than face Firan and his temper. Truth be told, I'd have rather been *in* the fire, but at least this would give me a chance to check on Droopy, as well as Firan's son, my friend Fadhil. I hadn't seen any of my friends since my return, at least anyone besides adults. Fadhil had been helping his father deliver water and supplies to the battle when disaster struck. We both had tales to tell.

The breeze off the docks pushed the smoke towards the King's Gate and up over the Tower of the Legate, so I followed it north and east. Anyone risking the midday heat was already gawking at the fire, so the broad main street was strangely quiet. I kicked a stone up the center of the road for a while, then heard angry young voices down a side alley.

I took a few steps into the narrow space between buildings, letting my eyes adjust to the sudden shadows. Three boys, a year or two older than me, stood in a threatening triangle around a tall figure.

"You're a filthy Saracen, aren't you?" I recognized that voice, even from the back. It belonged to Martin the tanner's son. He couldn't have been more than twelve, but his voice had already changed and rumor had it he already shaved. Twice. Whether or not he was really that grown-up, I had no idea, but one thing I—and everyone in Acre—knew, he was a terrible bully.

The subject of his abuse stood in terrified silence. The brown hair might have been cut in a boyish way, but there was no doubt that it was a girl. She stood a bit taller than the boys, almost a head taller than me, and was perhaps the skinniest creature I had ever seen, with bones like a bird. She fought back tears and bit her lip, shaking her head.

I knew from harsh personal experience that Martin was never more awful than when he had weaker prey cornered, enough friends to back him up, and his victim outnumbered. "You are, aren't you?"

"She's not wearing a veil," the smallest of the boys offered unconvincingly.

"She's not wearing a cross either," Martin countered in his thick accent. "So she's not a Christian. At least not a very good one. I think she's a heathen. They think they can do whatever they want because Salah-adin's coming." A terrible smirk crossed his face and he pointed his chin at her knowingly. "Yeah, a heathen…" He paused, not sure how to finish the insult. Then his dull eyes lit up as it came to him: "…whore." I suspected it was the first word he could think of, but he seemed awfully pleased with the choice. "Do you know what we do to heathen whores?"

While I was positive Martin and those boys didn't know the answer either, the girl's eyes flew open in panic. She took two steps back, right into the second biggest tormentor, who grabbed her by her bony elbows and held her tight. Martin stepped close to her, seeming to grow larger by the minute.

He stood nearly her height, but twice as wide. I'd been close to him, and it was no treat. He smelled like rotten cowhide and piss most of the time, hazards of his Genoese family's trade.

The third boy could tell things were getting out of hand. "Martin, we shouldn't…"

The man-boy reached for the girl and squeezed her face in one massive paw, making her lips pucker painfully. "Shut up, momma's boy."

The smaller boy obeyed and backed off. I wasn't as smart.

"Let her alone." As usual, my mouth responded before my brain, and by the time I realized what I'd done, four sets of eyes turned on me.

"Oh look, it's Lucca the Flea."

"Louse," I said, deciding that false bravado would have to substitute for courage. "*Le pou* is louse, not flea, you fat idiot. Where'd you learn French?" Martin turned his attention away from the girl, which was as far as my plan went.

Unfortunately, I now had his undivided attention, which I hadn't taken into consideration. Martin turned my way and crossed his arms. The smaller boy also stepped towards me, recognizing someone even he could push around. It was two to one. Almost three if you took size into account.

I stood facing the two unoccupied goons, while the third had a very hard time restraining the skinny girl, who thrashed around like a bonefish in a net. At the moment, she wasn't my main concern.

I recalled the voice of Jacques, the former sergeant and now occupant of the St Lazar Leper Hospital, who had tried so hard to teach me to fight. "Always attack, that way you're the only one who knows what's coming."

So I attacked. The sergeant was wrong, though, because as I approached Martin, my fists windmilling wildly, one giant, adult-sized set of knuckles caught me square on the nose, and shooting stars filled a suddenly black sky. I dropped like a bag of stones.

Flat on the ground, I made too good a target for them to resist. Martin shook his fist in surprise and pain, as if it was my fault he'd hurt his hairy knuckles. Worse, the other boy aimed a cowardly but effective kick to my ribs. I pulled into a useless, gasping, sniffling ball.

Overjoyed at having the advantage over someone for once, the runt pulled his leg back for another kick. I rolled away out of reach. This infuriated the little creep. He took a running start for the next attack. This time I was ready, and rolled far enough out of the way to grab his ankle and drive it upwards. He landed on his back with a grunt and a satisfying whine. Without thinking, I rolled on top and got two good shots in before I felt my tunic tighten around my neck. With one hand, Martin pulled me off his accomplice.

He shook me like a dog with a rag in his teeth, then

14

punched me again. I realized at that moment that no matter how much Jacques and his big friend Vardan kicked me around the training yard, they had hit me only as hard as necessary to make their point. When someone is punching you with seriously bad intentions, it doesn't just knock the wind and pride from you, it hurts. A lot.

From my crumpled position at his feet, I looked up into Martin's snarling face. His fists clenched to prepare for the beating he was about to administer. "You shouldn't have…" But he never got to finish his sentence.

From over his back, a black shadow appeared.

Before he could do anything about it, the girl landed on his back with an incomprehensible but soul-freezing shriek in Arabic. She leapt on him like a falcon striking a rat—nails first. Her skinny claws slashed at his skin, and she clung to his back as he spun around and around, trying desperately to shake her off. Her screams matched his. With Martin occupied for the moment I turned to the kicker. He scrambled backward in the dust to get away, his advantage now vanished. The boy who'd been holding their victim lay crumpled on the ground, rocking back and forth, cradling his walnuts in cupped hands and gasping for air. That left only Martin, who yelled furiously and spun one way then the other trying to shake off the harpy settled tenaciously on his back. With a confused shout, he lost his balance and fell face first into the dusty street.

The girl seemed unaware that he was down. She kept pounding on him and scratching with her now bleeding fingers, sobbing and panting between shrieks.

This wasn't my first street fight, and I recognized the chance to run for it. I turned for the open street, then yelled at the girl. "Come on, let's go."

If she understood me, it didn't help Martin. She continued flailing, scratching, and screaming. As satisfying as that was to see, we didn't have time for that nonsense. I grabbed her wrist. She turned on me, eyes burning with fury. I pulled harder. "Come on, we have to get out of here."

The girl seemed confused for a minute, then realized she sat astride a pile of shouting, writhing, very angry Italian. She jumped off and stared stupidly for a long second. I grabbed her arm, nearly encircling it with my small hand, and pulled. This time she followed.

Her legs may have been longer than mine, but I was quicker, so we ran side by side back to the main street and then towards the corrals, watching over our shoulders to confirm nobody was after us. She followed my cues towards the animal pens, where I hoped to find sympathetic grown-ups. Our sides ached, and as soon as it seemed safe, we stopped. I dropped my bum onto the bottom rail of a goat pen to recover, while she bent over a fence post, panting, crying, and finally laughing.

"Thank you," she said between gulps of air.

I tried to speak, but settled for nodding and waving weakly in response. Straightening up, she wiped her bare arm across her eyes. "I'm Nahida. Nahida *bint* Azzam."

"Lucca," I said. I was just Lucca, but I added, guessing she didn't speak French, "Lucca le Pou."

Before she said anything else, I heard a familiar harsh

voice. "It's about time you got here. You think I'm going to take care of that damned horse for you?"

For only the second time in my life, I was glad to see Firan the carter.

Chapter 2

"About time you showed up, you little demon. That godforsaken animal of yours is eating me out of business." Firan was huge, as wide at the shoulders as one of the oxen he drove, and his dark hair and thick black beard added to his fierceness. He lumbered toward me like a horse pulling a stone sled. "Come to take care of your bill?"

He stopped short, surprised to see me with a girl, particularly a Syrian girl. Although he looked like the Saracen of your nightmares, his family had been Christian for two generations, and he took his faith seriously. So much so, in fact, he pretended not to speak Arabic at all, which was nonsense, but everyone let him think they believed him. In French, he demanded, "Who's this?" He looked Nahida up and down, not at all thrilled with what he saw.

Nahida balled her firsts and scrunched her face, dark eyebrows nearly meeting at that huge nose. She didn't understand a word he said but didn't care one bit for his tone.

"Her name's Nahida."

"Where'd she come from? What are you doing with her?"

I shook my head. "She just…followed me."

Firan snorted. "That's what you said about that damned pony." He sneered at the poor girl. "And the horse is probably less trouble. Go home, girl. This one has work to do."

This was news to me. I expected to do a lot of things on my first day back in the city—at least my first day awake—but work wasn't in my plans. It never had been before, and I saw no good reason to start now. Firan wasn't taking no for an answer, though.

"Do you have any coin?" Adults asked stupid questions sometimes. "Well, feeding and sheltering an animal doesn't come free. You have to pay somehow, and Brother Marco said you'd work it off. Come on, Fadhil is over there now and he'll show you what to do." It wasn't a request, and I'd watched him backhand his own son—who he actually liked—for disobeying an order. He'd have no qualms about squashing me like a bug. Whatever sympathy he had for me when he rescued me on the road from Hattin had vanished, replaced with his usual sour meanness. I followed, defeated, with my head down. Nahida waited for only a second and trailed along. Firan shook his head but didn't say anything else.

The ugly mood that infested the rest of the city felt evident here too. The bitter smoke in the air poisoned everything in Acre. The usual good-natured banter and insults exchanged by rival carters and animal traders had a real bite to them today. People did really seem to hate each other's mothers.

Crossing the corral, I saw a weathered, bony old driver beating an equally ancient, unhappy-looking donkey. He cursed and swatted it with a leather strap. The poor beast brayed pathetically but stood there taking a beating meant for Count Joscelin and all the powers that had failed Acre.

We approached the shaky lean-to that served as shelter for the least important animals. Nahida's stick-thin shadow reached the hut long before mine did. My friend and playmate Fadhil looked up at our approach, beaming to see me alive and healthy. His smile faded when he saw my companion. "Who's she?"

"Nahida." She and I answered at the same time. The girl didn't bother to introduce herself to him; she just shouldered me aside and ran past Fadhil to the creature that was the source of my aggravation, Droopy.

He was tied to a post beside two ratty-looking asses in the filthiest, darkest corner, just chewing and staring. "Is he yours?" she asked in Arabic. She bent close to him, nuzzling his dusty neck and matted, nasty mane.

"Sort of," I said. "Be careful, he bites."

"Hard, too…" Fadhil showed us his arm where two blue and purple half-moons showed through the dried muck and dirt on his skin. Nahida didn't seem to care, though. She rubbed that snotty, velvety nose, then gently ran long fingers over his neck and back. Droopy happily shook his head and leaned closer for more. He never did that around me, and I felt a stupid pang of jealousy.

Without another word, she bent and picked up a simple metal comb from the ground, used her fingers to pluck the dirt out, and confidently brought it to Droopy's mane to groom him. On the second pass, she hit a snag and he turned to her with his big, square teeth bared. I thought for sure

21

he'd take a chunk out of her, but the big idiot gave a little "chuff" through his nose and turned away so she'd have room to work. Nahida continued, a little more gently now, whispering a little song in Arabic, so low we barely heard her, but the dumb old nag seemed to like it.

Fadhil's dark eyes bubbled with questions I couldn't answer, so I shook him off. There'd be plenty of time to talk later. He handed me a shovel. "Papa says you should know which end to use." He grinned and pointed to the flat end. Then he whispered, "It's this one," and laughed.

Sulking, I snatched it from him. His hand kept a grip on the handle, and I compared it to mine. My friend was developing real muscles. Even though we were of an age, working with his father had put him well on the path to manhood. I, on the other hand, was always smaller than him. Faster, sure, but weak as a girl. I looked over at Nahida and remembered her pummeling Martin the tanner.

Maybe weaker than a girl. Shorter, too.

"How much do I have to do?" I tried not to sound as pouty as I felt.

"All of it. That thing eats a lot." Fadhil wiped his hands on his tunic, sounding just like his father did when issuing orders. "I have to water the real horses. I'll come back soon." He left with purposeful strides, only turning back to sneak a surreptitious look at the girl singing to herself and lovingly stroking old Droopy.

I gawked at the shovel in my hand, then at the muck covering my bare feet. Putting the head against the floor I gave an exploratory shove. Poop was heavier than it looked, and I didn't relish working in this heat. The alternative was facing Firan's wrath, though, so I set to work.

Over the next hour or so the dung heap outside grew as tall as me. I started out shoveling quickly, taking small scoops and running them over the pile, dumping the shovel then scurrying back. It soon became obvious that was a poor strategy if I wanted to survive the afternoon. Eventually, I found a rhythm that worked, and while embarrassed by how small and pathetic each shovel-full was—and how my stinging hands could barely lift them—I eventually struck the stable's dirt floor.

As I worked, the turmoil in Acre seemed far away, although an occasional argument would break the calm. We heard at least two fights break out, and Nahida and I would look away, pretending not to notice. This dilapidated pile of sticks serving as a stall seemed like an oasis of calm after the morning we had.

While I slaved away, Nahida stroked Droopy and sang, somehow managing not to laugh at me, at least that I saw. She displayed confidence around the horse I'd never seen from a woman before. Of course, I couldn't recall ever seen a girl handle an animal at all.

"Where did you learn about horses?" I asked.

"My family. Papa traded…trades them. He even sells them to *Effendi* Raymo." She dropped the local name for Count Raymond of Tripoli like it was nothing. Her family must have a lot of money and connections. The contented smile slipped for only a second. Then, after patting Droopy's velvety snout, she seemed happy again.

"Where is he? Isn't he worried about you?"

Nahida bit her lip before answering. "We were on our way here with stock for your army and we…got separated. Bandits attacked us. "

"Bandits?" I heard the inappropriate excitement in my voice. I tried to sound uninterested, although I was bursting to hear all the gory details. "Who were they?"

She shrugged. "Scum. Sons of the Devil. Since *Effendi* Raymo went away, they've gotten worse. The roads aren't safe at all. They came out of the hills to take our horses." Her mouth snapped shut and she looked away from me. After a long moment, and in a softer voice she said, "Papa's going to meet me here and take me away from this terrible, stinky place as soon as he can." Her dark eyes dared me to argue with her but living in an orphanage you learn not to challenge people's stories, so I nodded like I believed her.

"That's good. But Acre's not so bad." Just then we heard a terrible shouting match and the sounds of a scuffle outside the stable. That didn't help my argument any, and I realized we were both holding our breath, hoping the fight didn't spill over to us.

When it was clear we'd be spared that piece of ugliness, she asked, "What about you? Where's your family?"

I gave her a mostly true version of my tale. How I'd lived in the Hospital orphanage for a while, had to leave, now lived with some friends. It was truthful as far as it went—Father Alex had long ago beaten the difference between sins of omission and commission into my skull. That I had to flee because Brother Idoneus tried to use me like a woman, or

24

that the friends in question were a bunch of lepers, despite my being clean of the disease—that could all wait until we knew each other better. Besides, it wasn't like she was spilling her guts either.

Discussing our families seemed a dead end, so I asked her how old she was.

She hesitated before answering. "Eleven summers. Almost twelve. How about you?" Only a year older than me. Would I grow that much in a year? Probably not, and I found myself resenting her.

"Ten. Nearly eleven though," I added. I didn't want her thinking I was a baby, and St Luke's day was only two or three moons away. Not knowing when I was really born, I used my name day to mark the years. Nobody but me cared anyway.

One more good scoop and I could finish the job, so I gave it a grunt and dumped a last super-heavy load on the heap, sending a thick black cloud of flies buzzing around my face. I lost my footing and nearly followed the manure onto the pile but managed to catch my balance. My hands were scraped raw and throbbed wildly. I leaned on my shovel, trying to appear satisfied with a man's work instead of just exhausted. I looked back just in time to see Droopy turn my way, offer a bored look and lift his tail. Three big poop-balls dropped onto my nicely cleaned stall floor. One of the donkeys brayed, appreciating the joke.

Nahida threw her head back and laughed. It was more of a loud, unladylike honk, but it showed her nice white teeth and a pretty-enough smile. I'd never seen a Muhammadan girl laugh without her hands over her mouth before. I knew the subject was a touchy one but as usual, my incurable curiosity pushed manners to the side.

Why aren't you wearing a hijab?" Not only was her hair short for a girl, it was uncovered.

She took a moment before answering. She thrust her jaw out and looked me in the eye. "Because I'm not of age yet. Plus, we're *Druzeh*. We don't have to wear it if we don't want to, although most of us do just so the Muhammadans leave us alone. Why do you live with the *Firangi*?"

"Because I am Firangi—at least my father was." I puffed my chest out a bit. Again, it was true as far as I knew, and she couldn't prove otherwise. I was all too aware that I appeared more Syrian than Frankish, except for my green eyes. It bothered me a bit that she couldn't see my superior Christianity, such as it was, written on my face. I felt for her, though. These days it was better to be demonstrably on one side or the other.

There was no envying her position. The Druze were a mystery to pretty much everyone—even those who understood religion, which left me out. They weren't any kind of Christian, even the wrong kind like the Copts or Greeks, but they weren't really True Believers either. All I knew was that not identifying completely with either religion during these latest troubles was bad news. Her people were mistrusted and abused by pretty much everyone. Like Jews, they were allowed to live in Christian cities—at least the ones up in the Lebanon, like Beirut and Tripoli. Count Raymond was known for being tolerant of them.

What would happen now that Salah-adin's armies controlled the coastal cities? It didn't seem like anything good was in store for her and her family. Especially without Count Raymond to protect them. I didn't want anything to happen to her. She seemed nice. For a girl, at least.

"You missed a spot," a deep voice informed me. I wondered again how someone as big as Brother Marco always managed to sneak up on me. "Get that last load and let's move."

I scooped up Droopy's last offering. His big shaggy head nudged me affectionately. I mopily shouldered him away and took my burden over to the heap. From across the stall, I watched Brother Marco run his hand over the pony's now shiny coat. "You did a good job on him."

"I did that." Nahida wasn't about to let me take credit for her work, even in a language she couldn't understand.

Marco raised an eyebrow but answered in Arabic. "Did you now? Well, good job, young lady." His blue eyes turned my way for an explanation I didn't get the chance to offer. She yakked and carried on as quickly as a camel-seller.

"Thank you, sir. Do you think I could do that for you? For your horses, I mean. Or the man who owns this stable, peace be on him, could…"

The knight held up his gloved hands to stop her. With a sad smile, he said, "Hold on there. I'm afraid I can't offer you any work, *saghirti*, although I can see you are excellent at it. Better than some people I could name, to be sure…"

My cheeks burned with shame. That seemed like an unnecessary comment to offer in front of a stranger, and he'd never called *me* anything like "little one," although that seemed awfully girly.

Nahida dropped her eyes in disappointment as he added, "You'd best scoot before Firan gets back. I can't imagine he'll be happy to have you hanging around. Come on, Lucca. Let's go home."

Nahida hid her disappointment pretty well. She paused, then with a practiced motion jammed the comb into a niche in the wall where Fadhil could find it. She nodded and followed us out with her head down but a determined scowl on her face.

None of us said a word as we left the shed. Across the crowded and tension-filled corral then out into the streets crowded with aimless wanderers and those desperate for news, Nahida followed us like a gosling until we reached the narrow lane leading to the St Lazar House.

"This is as far as you can come with us," Brother Marco said in a tone that wasn't unkind but left no room for argument. I knew that tone of voice all too well. "Perhaps Lucca will see you another day."

I saw the hurt in her eyes and wanted to say or do something useful. To offer her shelter or…something. Instead, I lifted a hand in a pathetic wave and muttered, "G'bye."

She raised hers in a silent farewell. Without another glance Brother escorted me home, limping the whole way.

Chapter 3

"Keep an eye out," Brother Marco whispered sternly. His eyes darted around at the bustling, muttering crowd. This was the first time we'd been out together since my return.

"For what?" I had to ask, even though I knew full well what he'd say. We had been playing "the game"—or what I used to think was a game—for weeks, and I was getting good at it. Mind you, the last time I got kidnapped, was held in Salah-adin's camp, and witnessed the slaughter of half of Christendom's knights, so maybe I wasn't as good at it as I believed.

I expected him to say, "For what shouldn't be there." It's what he always said. Instead, he clucked his teeth in frustration. "Look for signs of trouble. We can't have people stirring up shit today." His tone left no way to even pretend it was any kind of game. This was serious business. Then he made me promise to report everything I saw.

Determined not to fail, I looked around at what was there first. The citizens of Acre had gathered near what was once a mosque, had become the church, and would be a mosque again soon enough. They'd all come to witness the surrender of the city and learn their fates. Certainly, if there was shit-stirring going on, everyone seemed to be holding a spoon.

There had been more trouble overnight: two small fires and near-riots of varying sizes and degrees of seriousness. City guards fought citizens and bloodied heads in the name of keeping order.

Everyone seemed angry at everybody else. Newly converted Syrians fought with each other. Some feared the reprisals awaiting them when the Saracens took the city back and exacted Allah's revenge. Others stripped off their crosses and Firangi clothes as if they'd been awaiting rescue all along. Each called the others *khayin*—traitors—and infidels or worse. Knives were drawn, fists shaken, and vengeance sworn. All this and the enemy wasn't even inside the gates yet.

That would come in a few minutes, when Salah-adin's nephew, the general Taqi-adin, accepted our surrender and announced our fates. Nobody expected much in the way of mercy after the way the Christians had claimed the city; the only question seemed to be whether to accept death like sheep or make a fight of it and die with honor.

In a way, I had a choice. With my features, I could have passed for a Mohammedan—in fact, I had more than once—but that never felt quite comfortable. For someone like me, being Christian wasn't about religion so much as what I was born to—like poverty, being right-handed, or having green eyes. Being considered a Frank— Firangi— rather than a mere Syrian peasant, mattered a great deal, though, and you couldn't be one without the other. So, thanks to either my mother or father (God alone knew, and he was silent on the matter) I was more or less a Christian.

My fate hung in the same balance as everyone else's.

Of course, with the city's mood as it was, I got my fair share of dirty looks, and even the occasional kick, as I made my way around the square. I zigzagged through the quickly building crowd, scanning faces and looking for trouble. Nothing appeared out of the ordinary, but then trouble usually found me when I wasn't looking for it.

I followed the echoing of hammers on wood. At the far end of the square, workmen were putting the finishing touches on a low platform across from the mosque-chapel-mosque-again. Priests, monks, and acolytes scuttled in and out of the building, their hands full of icons, books, candles, and anything likely to be consigned to the flames. A couple of brave workers on a rickety ladder unbolted the cross from the top of the chapel and lowered it on a rope to the workers below amid a chorus of boos, jeers, and threats. Several city guards stood with their backs to the workers and their helmeted faces towards the crowd. They kept white knuckles on the hilts of their swords, eyes squinting against the late morning sun.

I shouldered my way closer to the riser. Two worried-looking merchants looked up from a piece of parchment to shout directions at the workers, then put their heads back together. The older one, a Venetian with a long, perfectly-oiled, forked beard and a wrinkled forehead kept barking at them. "For the love of Christ can we get this done? The General will enter the city at noon."

The younger man attempted to calm him. "They're doing the best they can under the circumstances, father. Who's actually offering the surrender?"

"Some Norman from England. Peter Brice," the older man said.

"Who?"

His father sniffed. "Exactly. Some toady of Joscelin's, I presume. Newly arrived, so he's not tied to the Orders or any of the Outremer families. Just a jumped-up clerk but speaks passable Arabic. He's supposed to do our groveling for us, then talk everyone into staying after Salah-adin takes over."

I'd never heard of this Brice—it might be something to take back to Marco, although odds are he already knew. I contented myself with catching snippets of the dark mutterings around me as I wandered aimlessly in a huge circle seeking crumbs of real information.

"...should burn the whole city to the ground rather than let the infidels have it." It was mostly older merchants and soldiers who held that opinion.

"Don't be daft. If there's no city left to claim he'll just kill us all." The smaller merchants and tradespeople—mostly born in Outremer without anyplace else to go—seemed to have a pretty good grasp on reality.

"We're probably all dead anyway." I couldn't argue with that logic but just the thought made me have to pee, so I tried to ignore those voices.

The higher the sun climbed, the thicker the crowd became. A small contingent of Templars and Hospitallers, the old and wounded who hadn't been able to march off to get slaughtered at Hattin, set up a perimeter around the platform. They stood close enough to prevent people from surging forward, but far enough back that they wouldn't be in direct sight of the Saracen general. Many of the civilians could expect mercy; the Knights of the Orders held no such hope.

I recognized some of them from my days at the orphanage. Brothers Samuel and Roger stood as tall as their aged and battered spines allowed, clasping their sword hilts. They were good men. I remembered them letting us children climb all over them, then throwing us off only to be gang-rushed all over again. There was no playfulness in their eyes today—only resignation and anger. I pitied anyone foolish enough to test them. Unable to strike against the enemy, they'd settle for lashing out at anyone—even fellow Christians—to ease their shame. I prayed nobody gave them an excuse.

Close to the stage, the crowd consisted of well-known merchants, clerks, and respectable citizens with businesses at stake. Farther back were ordinary townsfolk. The rest of Acre, with nothing to lose but their lives, would learn their fates the way they always had—through gossip, word of mouth, and when their doors were kicked in.

Once they'd found a spot in the crowd, most people stood praying or gawking around while jealously guarding their spot. They stood facing the stage. All except one fellow—an Armenian by the looks of him. Slowly and methodically, he made his way across the square from east to west but looking in the opposite direction from everyone else.

He looked like a successful merchant, so it came as a

surprise to see him approach a red-faced old drunk and whisper in his ear. I knew Dominic from the days when he'd sit at the port either begging for money to buy wine or looking for a fight once he'd gotten it. Nobody but me paid attention as they whispered to each other. The red-faced old coot grinned and nodded, patting the merchant on the arm reassuringly. In exchange, the Armenian reached into his pocket and handed something shiny to the older man, who palmed it, then staggered over to a place near the stage, checking back with his benefactor that he was in the right spot.

Why did it matter where Drunk Dominic stood? I hated not knowing something. I needed to know. That's how trouble always started.

The Armenian turned my way, scanning the crowd. I did my best to memorize his face. He was of middling height with nothing special about him except his eyebrows. Those were truly impressive, maybe the most awe-inspiring set of brows I'd ever seen. It was as if someone glued two horse brushes to his forehead. Despite the heat, he pulled a hood over his head and stepped nimbly through the crowd, bearing to his right, close to the stage but a safe distance from the wall of knights. He drew no attention from anyone except me, and he had no reason to pay attention to one nosy orphan.

My subject reached up to touch the shoulder of another man, a miscreant I recognized all too well. Big Paolo was a Genoese sailor who collected debts when the minor lords of Acre didn't want to be seen doing it themselves. I'd crossed trails with him myself a few times. One day he threatened to break my legs for alerting a family of tanners he was on the way to their house. It was the first and last time I ever got involved in his business. Unlike a lot of street toughs, Paolo never made idle threats. I liked my legs, even short as they were.

Eyebrows leaned close to Paolo and whispered something, getting a nod in return, then slipped something gold and glittery into that big hairy paw. Nobody just gave away bezants like that. What was he getting in return? I was pretty sure Marco would want to know. I know I did.

In my haste to keep my quarry in sight, I bounced off the broad backside of a fruit merchant, who immediately grabbed for the purse on his belt and gave me a filthy look. Any other time I'd have said something insulting to him for daring to suspect me. Either that or just taken the purse and run. Instead, I bowed and offered a quick "Excuse me, Monsieur" and continued seeking Mr. Eyebrows.

He slinked through the crowd quickly, but without seeming to draw unwanted attention to himself. It was impressive in its way; only the best criminals could pull that off. I certainly didn't have the knack. I may as well have just carried a sign that read "up to no good" whenever I tried to move that way. Not him. Nobody suspected a thing as he passed unmolested through the jostling herd of people. I didn't understand what he was up to, but I wasn't about to let him get away from me.

It was a little disappointing when my prey found a spot far off to the right of the platform and just dropped cross-legged onto the ground. He reached into his pocket, pulled out a date, and popped it into his mouth like he hadn't a care in all the world. He appeared to be the only person in the whole city not on the edge of full-blown panic.

What was I supposed to do? He wasn't doing anything except sitting in the hot sun with his eyes closed, completely relaxed. Whatever he was going to do, he'd done it.

I didn't have time to worry about it, though. Off to the east, the rumble of a swelling crowd preceded another noise. The thwomp-thwomp-thwomp of drums, then the clash of cymbals rose above the crowd's voices. The king's guards and a few Hospitallers cleared a path through the outer edge of the circle. At the head of them walked the biggest man I'd ever seen.

The knight wore a Hospital uniform but no helmet. His bare pate was all forehead. His hairline started so far back he only had half a tonsure. What hair he had ran halfway down his back, which violated half a dozen rules. His beard was square and long, brushing against the top of the cross on his chest. He was tall as a horse, but also broad in a way I'd never seen. I could have lain across his shoulders and still not reached each arm. There was no sword in his belt, but he carried a staff twice as long and heavy as the one Marco carried and looked like he knew what to do with it.

With shouted curses and threats, the giant and his mates cleared people back. Nobody argued; we just pulled back three or four steps, trying not to trip over the person behind us. Down the clear path, we heard the drums and gongs, then the shouting: Arabic whoops and war cries.

We were about to become a conquered city.

First came an honor guard of mounted warriors waving scimitars and lances and shouting, "*Allahu akbar.*" Then a dozen or so foot soldiers surrounded a man on horseback. I didn't care for horses, but even I could tell this was one of the most beautiful creatures God—or Allah in this case— ever made. It looked made of ebony and was lean without being skinny. Muscles rippled beneath a perfectly groomed coat and it moved as if *it*, rather than the rider, was the conquering hero.

The man astride the horse had to be Salah-adin's uncle, Taqi. His robes were immaculate, and his thick beard, oiled till it shone, reflected the baking noontime sun. As he passed through the crowd, the citizenry fell silent out of both awe and fear of doing something stupid. He didn't look like the forgiving sort.

Right behind him was a smaller but much more dangerous-looking soldier. While General Taqi looked straight ahead, this one's eyes never stopped moving—a bird of prey, always hungry. He wasn't even giving me a thought, and yet I felt like a mouse in an open field. Danger rippled like heat waves off of him.

The procession reached the riser and without assistance or fanfare the general dismounted. He turned to the crowd, hands on his hips, daring anyone to speak. No one took him up on the challenge. It was silent as hundreds of people held their breath.

A handful of Acre's most important merchants huddled on a corner of the stage, heads bent together in consultation.

Then the youngest and tallest of the lot took a tentative step forward. People grumbled and muttered as the man—it must have been that Peter Brice fellow—strode towards the general, slowly sank to one knee, and bowed his head.

This was the moment everyone knew was coming and still dreaded. All around me, grown men wiped tears of shame on their sleeves. I felt my own cheeks and eyes burn. My city, my home, was being taken away from me. I wanted to scream, or shout, or…do what exactly? I stood like everyone else—embarrassed, terrified, and mute.

Taqi-adin swiveled back and forth, examining the crowd, attempting but unable to hide a smirk. Everyone in Acre knew how long he'd waited for this moment. For years the Saracens had coveted the port city, fought battles outside its walls; and now they stood inside its gates as the undisputed victors. He took one last triumphant survey of the crowd, then turned to the kneeling man.

In poor French, just to show off, he shouted, "Does Acre yield to Allah and his servant, the Commander of the Faithful, the Sultan of Egypt, the Sword of Merciful Justice, Salah-adin?"

Brice nodded. His mouth opened, but no sound came out. He licked his lips, took a deep breath, and this time his reply was barely audible: "We yield the city and beg the Sultan's mercy on its people." A confused buzz rippled through the crowd as only those in the first rows heard anything. Brice took a deep breath and repeated it, louder and more clearly: "We yield the city, and beg the Sultan's mercy on its people." This time Taqi-adin gave a curt, satisfied nod.

The general said something else, but in such garbled French that by the panicky look on Brice's face it was clear he had no idea what it was. Taqi leaned over to his eagle-eyed second-in-command and conferred for a moment.

After an agonizing silence, he pointed at Brice and grunted. "You'll translate for me." Brice rose to his feet, nodding. In Arabic, Taqi shouted, "This city is now, as it always should have been, and forever will be, in the hands of the Faithful. You infidels have been shown the power of Allah, the Most Merciful." He nodded to the young merchant, who dutifully and accurately repeated it for the crowd. If the old soldier expected a response, he was disappointed. The pronouncement was met with stunned silence.

Brice passed the general's message to the assembly: "The Caliph himself will come tomorrow to worship at the mosque and offer thanks to Allah. He has no wish to rule over the ashes of his city or the bodies of the innocent.

"He has commanded me to tell you that if you lay down your arms and do no more damage to the Sultan's city, he will allow you to live. Only the enemies of Islam—the Knights of the Temple and Hospital—are to surrender. All others may live in peace, under the rightful law. Those who wish to leave will have forty days to do so and may go in the peace of God and with Salah-adin's guarantee of safety. Those who wish to stay and conduct their business are welcome to live under Allah's mercy and protection."

The members of the crowd who spoke Arabic already

buzzed like hornets, translating for their neighbors. A debate broke out about the exact meaning of "merciful." Throughout all of this, Eyebrows did nothing but watch the crowd, squinting and nodding.

I wriggled through the throng, trying to get closer to both the stage and my quarry. I didn't see Brother Marco, although I was sure he was there somewhere. Brice's strong voice rose above the babble to repeat the edict. Then he added, "Please, for the love of God, I urge you to listen. Let the city pass in peace so that your neighbors, your women, and children may be spared."

"Fucking traitor!" a voice called out from somewhere in the crowd. Soldiers on both sides reached for sword hilts, seeking the source of the disturbance.

Another voice, this time from the other side of the stage, called out, "Why isn't Joscelin doing his own dirty work? He's sold us to the devil!"

"I'll tell you why. Because he's hiding in Tyre with Raymond and the rest of the nobles who've sold us out. They're more worried about their money than the people." I knew that voice. It belonged to the old drunkard, Dominic. He swayed back and forth. Seeing he had an appreciative audience, he puffed himself up and continued, "Tripoli is in cahoots with Salah-adin. That's why they allowed him to escape. So he could betray us to Satan."

I wanted to shout, to defend Count Raymond. After all, I'd been at Hattin, he hadn't, and I'd seen... *but what was it I'd seen?*

All eyes but mine turned his way. I kept staring at

Eyebrows, who watched with a contented smile and popped another date between his lips.

On the dais, General Taqi hissed at the poor translator. "Quiet this crowd or we'll do it for you."

Brice held up his hands for calm, but the wave of anger that had been held in check for so long was swelling and about to crest. "Please, I beg of you, calm yourselves." Big Paolo elbowed himself some room, then shouted in a voice like thunder, "Calm my ass. Raymond of Tripoli, d'Ibelin, even Joscelin is safe, while our King is captive and our knights are feeding the crows. They should be here now, getting what they deserve. Instead, they've deserted us." The crowd roared its approval.

Several more voices joined in, shouting things like "Death to Tripoli and the traitors" and "Where is Raymond?" Paolo stood with his hands on his hips basking in their approval and very pleased with himself. Until that is, a solid oak staff cracked him across the back of his head and sent him sprawling into the dust.

The giant white-haired knight stood over Paolo's prone body. "Be quiet and stay down. Please," the brute said, in a surprisingly soft voice. Citizens all around turned on the Hospitaller, shaking their fists and screaming in outrage.

"He's right, They've killed us all..."

"Why silence him? Are you with them now?" Like a murder of squawking crows, the people turned on the small number of knights. The mob didn't seem to fear them, which surely meant trouble.

The unmistakable song of swords pulled from sheaths

quieted most of the rabble. All the knights drew their blades, brandishing them in front of their bodies, in hopes that a show of violence would help prevent the real thing. I had no confidence that would happen and felt very small among all these angry, unpredictable grown-ups. I began seeking an escape route.

By now Paolo had staggered back to his feet. He was used to being the bigger man, the aggressor, the winner. He rubbed the back of his scalp and shook his head to clear the cobwebs from his thick skull. Pulling sticky fingers away from the knot on his head, he stared in disbelief at his own blood.

"Who the devil did that?" the big goon demanded. He halted for only the briefest moment when he saw his opponent was one of the few people in his life he literally had to look up to. That didn't stop him from lowering his head and charging like a mad bull.

Several of us had to leap out of the way to avoid being trampled as Paolo's huge body struck the mountain of knightly flesh. The blond ogre took three steps back but stayed on his feet. He grabbed the ruffian's tunic and once again threw him to the ground. Again, he shook his head sadly and said, "Stay down. I beg you."

Paolo was in no mood to cooperate. He grunted and staggered to his feet once more but before he could launch another attack, three sword points waved in his red, puffing, ugly face. Briefly Paolo considered defying the odds, but finally spat on the ground and raised his hands. "All right, all right, I'll yield." The guards lowered their swords just a bit.

The thug addressed his audience of hundreds. "You see? They were useless to protect us before, and now they do the Saracens' dirty work for them. Tripoli is behind this. And Joscelin. You wait and see." As he spoke he was slowly backing up until he saw a break in the crowd, then he turned and made a run for it. Townspeople scattered like chickens to clear his path.

All the while, Eyebrows had come close enough to see and hear what was going on. He nodded and wiped the sticky date juice onto his robes. He offered a few half-hearted "hear, hears" along with the crowd but didn't draw attention to himself.

Brother Samuel stomped over to the big knight, shaking with anger, and spit between the man's feet. "Please? Why didn't you bother to kiss his arse for him too?" The giant looked away, unable to meet the older man's eyes. I'd never known Brother Samuel to raise his voice at anyone, but he unleashed his pent-up fury on the bigger man, who simply stood with his blue eyes downcast and absorbed the abuse. "Useless as teats on a bloody boar. A knight who won't carry a sword is no use to anyone. What in hell's name are you good for? Go back to the Hospital and make yourself useful."

I feared the giant might swat Brother Samuel like a fly. Instead, he sighed, nodded, and turned without a word.

So fascinating and bizarre was the scene I'd just witnessed, I momentarily lost sight of Eyebrows. I took a few panicky steps one way then the other, frantically searching. At last, I saw a hooded figure walking a direct line against the tide of people towards the dangerous-looking Saracen officer.

The mysterious Armenian removed his hood and bowed low in salaam. That just earned him a dismissive wave of the hand. I drew as near as I dared, then pretended to refasten my sandal strap. I bent low beside the wooden platform, straining to hear.

"That went well, don't you think?" Eyebrows asked like a child showing a mud pie to an impatient parent.

The Saracen snorted. "Well, the city's still standing, and your people did their jobs. I suppose that's the best we can ask for."

The Armenian bowed and scraped even lower. "Of course, *Effendi*. By tomorrow everyone will be talking about how Raymond of Tripoli betrayed them and can't be trusted. As promised."

In my shock, I inhaled a mouthful of dust and had to stifle a cough. That made my eyes nearly bug out of my head. By some miracle, I kept silent and refocused on the conversation. The tromping of feet and the taunts of the victorious Mohammedans at the demoralized Christians made it nearly impossible to hear anything useful.

"We must ensure…" then more muttering as the last of the Sultan's troops passed out of range.

"…You'd best be absolutely right…" I couldn't make out anything except old Eyebrows doing a lot of bowing and groveling. I crept as close as I dared.

"I told you, *Effendi*, the Lady will do her part as expected." If that was meant to reassure the soldier, Eyebrows was disappointed.

"Salah-adin may trust her, but I don't. She's a traitorous bitch with ambitions beyond her place."

Eyebrows bit his lip and bowed. "As you say, she has the Sultan's trust and every reason to succeed. She won't fail you."

The commander turned to leave without even acknowledging the Armenian, who didn't seem the least bit insulted or dissuaded. He simply fell in behind the soldier, staying within earshot.

"Forgive me, Excellency, but there is the matter of reimbursement. Today's work wasn't without costs."

The officer dismissed him with a sneer. "When the Lady's idiot son is Count, you can collect from her." If the spy— for that's what he was—was dismayed he didn't show it. Any disappointment was quickly replaced with a resigned, professional salaam.

"*Inshallah.* The Lady sends her regards." That didn't impress the soldier at all. He climbed onto his horse, gave a sharp whistle through his teeth, and rode off.

Who was the Lady? What did she have to do with Count Raymond of Tripoli? I burned with questions, and I knew someone else who'd want to know.

I had to tell Brother Marco right away.

Chapter 4

"Forty days? And where are we supposed to go?" demanded Sister Marie-Pilar. Brother Marco looked from her to me, then to the rest of the assembled residents of St Lazar. We gathered like all families did in a crisis, in the kitchen.

"Jerusalem. It's why we're all here," Sergeant Jacques said in his best don't-argue-with-me voice. "It's our duty. And if the noble bastards like Joscelin and Raymond won't defend the Kingdom, then it's up to us."

Brother Marco's eyes flashed. "Raymond will do his duty and defend the kingdom. Have no fear of that." His gloved hand clenched into a tight fist. This conversation had gone in ever-tightening circles for a while now and had finally reached the ugly stage where discussion became argument and things became personal.

There were perhaps fifteen people packed into the room. A few nuns, a couple of priests, and the healthier patients— lepers whose illness allowed them to move about. Most of them sat in stunned, awkward silence. As usual, my friends Vardan and Sergeant Jacques were not among the quiet.

Jacques was a grizzled old sergeant with bandaged feet who usually rested on a knobby wooden crutch, except when he was teaching me to fight. Or arguing. His anger drove him to his feet. "Then what's he doing hiding like a woman in Tyre? At least his wife faced Salah-adin. He didn't try to rescue her, he's not coming to rescue us, and he sure as hell isn't going to Jerusalem. He'll turn tail and run back to Tripoli like the coward he is."

Marco shook his head wearily, clenching his jaw. "That's not true. We don't even know whether he's still at Tyre or returned to Tripoli yet." He looked down at his feet, shifted uneasily, then said again, to his feet, "It's not true." I admired Count Raymond of Tripoli more than any man I'd ever met, but I'd seen him turn and run with my own eyes. Despite Marco's assurances to the contrary, I wasn't completely convinced.

Big Vardan the Armenian, one of the biggest, hairiest men I'd ever met, though far gentler than his hulking body indicated, laid a huge paw on Jacques's arm. "Hold on, my friend. Just a moment." He then addressed Brother Marco. "That's not what they're saying out on the streets, Brother. Everyone says…"

"But Sergeant Jacques says everyone's an idiot. So maybe they're wrong," I interjected, trying to lighten the mood. My attempt at humor failed, but at least their dirty looks were aimed at me and not each other.

"I'm not wrong." The Sergeant crossed his arms.

"You are," Marco replied, not half as convincingly.

"That still doesn't answer the question," Marie-Pilar barked from behind her veil. "We can't stay. You know what happens to nuns in captured cities. Even ones they can't touch, they can…they can…" Her head dropped into her

48

hands and she wept in big gulping sobs. Sisters Fleure and Agnes put their arms around her clumsily, muttering nonsense about strength and God's protection, which had been in short supply of late. Marco looked at the ceiling, seeking assistance from above that wasn't coming.

Sergeant Jacques turned to Vardan, who gave a quick nod of support. "Brother, you know this is horse shit, forgive me, Sisters. We're not going anywhere. If Salah-adin is true to his word—and I don't trust that heathen bastard an inch—what are we going to do? Hop to Jerusalem? Most of us won't last a day out there. No, we'll stay and fight. Or die. Probably both, but it'll beat getting picked off and left to rot by the side of the road. We're Christ's soldiers. I won't forget that even if God has."

Vardan just nodded, crossed his arms, lifted his eyes, and quietly said, "*Atavis et armes.*" "Ancestors and arms" was the motto of the Order of St Lazar. It made as much sense as anything grown-ups said, which meant not much, but they seemed to take comfort in it.

With nothing more to be said, the meeting broke up. The Brothers went to their cells, while sisters Fleure and Agnes excused themselves to escort the patients back to the sickroom. That left just Brother Marco, Sister Marie-Pilar, and me.

Marie-Pilar stroked my hair for the thousandth time that night. "Lucca, it's time for bed. Get along."

"Wait." Marco plopped down on a bench and stretched his left foot out in front of him. Sister grabbed a stool and tenderly elevated it. I always thought of the big knight as the most vital man I knew, but the lines on his face looked deeper, and his bloodshot eyes were buried deep in dark, bruise-colored bags I'd never seen before. "Lucca, you can't stay."

So the black cloud that had hung over everyone since I returned was about to burst. I felt drops sting my eyes, but it wasn't raining." Why not? I can help you...just like I have been. Haven't I been a help?" *Don't let me cry now, or he'll think I'm completely useless...* "Count Raymond said I was his best informant. You have to let me..." I felt Sister's small, cool hands on my shoulders and shrugged them off impatiently.

Marco bit his lip. "Yes, my little louse. You've been a huge help. God willing, you'll continue to help the Kingdom. It just can't be from here." He held up a hand to shut me up. Any other time, that would have worked.

"NO, I'm not a baby. I am old enough to fight. What I told you...about the Lady. Isn't that helpful? Did you know that? Do you think Jacques or Vardan could have learned that? No, because they're cripples and I'm the only..." I realized I was shouting at an adult and my hands flew to my mouth to stop the words, but they'd already escaped.

Sister's hands tightened on my shoulder, but she didn't scold me. "Lucca, Acre will be a charnel house, and you can't stay here forever. You know that..."

"But where will I go?"

She snuck a look at Brother Marco before answering. "Tripoli. You'll go to Count Raymond. He'll protect you." *Would he? Or would he turn his back on his friends like he had on his king and his fellow nobles?*

"And then I can bring messages back here and help you. See, I can help." The only two people in the entire world I cared about were in that kitchen and I had no intention of leaving them for long, no matter what they said, or how good an idea it was.

The normally stoic soldier slapped the wall. "For Christ's sake, for once just do as you're told, you little shit." In the months we'd known each other, Marco had never truly yelled at me before, and his words stung worse than a whipping. He winced as much as I did when he saw me flinch.

"Stop it! Enough of this! Marco, tell him." Sister Marie-Pilar was shaking now. I didn't know her gentle soul contained so much rage, but she shrieked like a fishwife. "Tell him the truth. Show him."

Marco nodded. He sat forward with a grimace and took a deep cleansing breath. Then he turned those icy blue eyes on me. They were clearer now but darted around, looking more towards me than at me. "Lucca, you can't stay with me…us…here." I tried to interrupt, but he held up his hand and I somehow shut my big mouth. "First, every day you're here, you risk becoming sick yourself. You must leave us sometime. When the Saracens have full control of the city, they'll let us live only as long as we stay out of the way. Time will come they'll want this building, and us, gone… And they won't just turn us out into the street. You know that, right?"

Of course, I knew it. In my time at St Lazar I'd learned a lot about leprosy and those who suffered from it While the libraries of Baghdad and Damascus supposedly teemed with scholarly books on how to treat lepers and other sick people, the reality of life in those countries was very different. My friends would be put to the sword, or stoned if the soldiers weren't brave enough to come within arm's length. Most likely killed by ruffians while soldiers looked on. I wouldn't give up. "So come with me to Tripoli. We can all go, can't we?" Sister's eyes brimmed with tears and she put her head in her hands.

"Marco," she whispered.

Brother Marco leaned forward and tugged at his boot. It didn't want to come off, but with a lot of grunting and swearing, he managed to remove it. That revealed a second layer of grey, filthy bandages. They were also wet, I saw with horror. The cloth was full of something oozy and smelly.

"It's back," was all he said. It's all he needed to say. His leprosy had flared up again. He unwrapped the bandages to reveal red welts and swollen skin similar to the scabs on his hand. But it was the bottom of his foot that revealed how sick he was. A huge ulcer, the size of my fist, covered the instep of his foot. Blackened scabs outlined oozing grey flesh. It reeked of the offal behind a tanner's shop.

I couldn't help myself. I threw up a little in my mouth but somehow kept it in.

"Lovely, isn't it? I told you God had a strange way of showing his appreciation for my service, didn't I?"

"Marco!" Sister hissed at him like a cat and quickly crossed herself. He ignored her.

"You see, boy. I can't go with you—I'd be useless and just as likely get you all killed. No. I'll stay here and do what I can for as long as I can. But you... I need you to do something for me." Unable to tear my gaze from his misshapen foot, I said nothing. "We'll gather as much useful information as we can for Count Raymond. And then you'll take it to him, wherever he is. You can do that for me, yes?"

Hell no. I'm a useless little boy who will get them all killed and it will be all my fault and I'll like as not die in the process. I nodded obediently. Marco gave a grateful sigh.

"Good lad." His gloved hand tousled my hair, and I let it rest there. "We'll learn as much as we can before you have to leave. Maybe we'll even find out who this mysterious Lady of yours is, eh?"

I nodded and sat on the bench beside him, letting my head fall against the wall behind me. *And then I'll come back and take care of you.*

Beside me, I felt Sister's reassuring presence and we all sat, not quite touching, in silence for the longest time.

Chapter 5

All of Acre was in the streets the next day. Some wanted to see the great and terrible Salah-adin with their own eyes, maybe to see if he would eat a child or defile a whole convent single-handedly like the legends said. I'd met the man face-to-face once, and that was enough for me. So, while I anticipated his arrival like everyone else, I also kept a keen watch out for a specific set of eyebrows.

Most of the action centered on the former chapel, soon to be a mosque again. A small crowd of people sweltered inside. Most were camp followers of Taqi-adin's army, waiting to worship with the Commander of the Faithful. A smaller group were *conversos,* local Syrian Sunnis who'd converted to the Holy Mother Church to work and live in the city and now found the Christian religion inconvenient. These traitors were mocked and jeered by the locals. Many of them returned the shouts with their own obscene gestures, the waving of shoes, and elaborate curses. Nobody's mother, on either side, got spared from abuse.

I checked over my shoulder again and again for the Sultan's procession. That would be hard to miss. I squinted and searched for a familiar face. I found one I recognized, but not the one I was looking for. Nahida spotted me a second before I saw her. She was on me before I could escape.

"There you are. Where have you been?" She asked like she was my wife. I tried ignoring her but that proved hard to do. She poked at me with a bony finger. "Hey, aren't you going to say hello?"

"Hello." That didn't seem to appease her, not that I thought it would.

"What are you doing? Waiting for Salah-adin? What do you think he looks like? I hear he's tall as a horse."

I shook my head. "No. He's just a normal-sized man," I said, still looking around.

"And how would you know? Did he invite you to dinner?" In reality, I was chained to a tent peg, but I didn't have time to explain that to her. From her tone and that smirk it was obvious she wasn't likely to believe anything I told her, anyway. In my limited experience, girls were like that. Of course, most of the time I *was* lying to them, but it irked me anyway.

Her Arabic nattering attracted unwelcome attention from the Frankish crowd. I tried shushing her with frantic gestures, but it was useless. Whatever fight we were about to have got interrupted by the swelling roar of the crowd and the clatter of horse hooves striking stones. A few brave souls ignored the Christians around them and shouted, "*Allahu Akbar*," and those wild ululations that sounded like fun when the Muhammadans did them, but I could never mimic.

In a crowd of noble-looking soldiers, it was easy to pick out Salah-adin, the Defender of the Faith. He was dressed in simple desert robes but wore a snow-white turban with a huge peacock feather, and a big purple gemstone in the middle.

"You're right, he doesn't look so big. He's not so scary," Nahida admitted.

"He's scary, he's just not that big," I corrected her. She gave me a look like she almost believed me, which I took as a victory. I didn't have time to gloat, because as impressive a sight as Salah-adin was, my gaze fell on the tall, lean figure dressed in dusty black robes and the giant black horse he rode on. I recognized that animal, and the man riding it.

It was Ali bin Yusuf bin Ali—the spy who had dragged me from Acre to Salah-adin's camp at Baisin before the battle. True, he'd carried me away, but he also advised me and helped me stay alive. Despite everything, I liked him and thought he liked me. But then, I'm always surprised when someone doesn't succumb to my charm. I get surprised a lot.

The death of his employer, *al Jassus*, had been a good thing, at least for him. It was clear he'd risen in the Sultan's ranks. If his improved circumstances pleased him, one couldn't tell from his face. He wore a worried scowl and his head swiveled from side to side. Hopefully, he couldn't pick one small, brown face out of a crowd of hundreds.

The procession stopped in front of the mosque. Through gaps in the mob, I saw a short, bobbly-headed Imam in white robes and *kufi* skullcap emerge from the building, salaaming and groveling, exactly like our priests did in the presence of nobility. Salah-adin gave a polite but restrained response, then leaped off his horse. Ali stayed atop his ebony mount.

That eagle-beaked face swiveled back and forth, using the height to search for troublemakers.

The Sultan appeared both victorious and humble. He bowed his head and entered the small *musallah*, or prayer room. The crowd, visibly disappointed at the lack of drama, milled around, not entirely sure what to do with themselves. Mostly they entertained each other with tales of cities laid to waste, the women and children sold as slaves, the men turned into crow food.

I searched the sea of frightened faces and noticed Big Paolo before I found Eyebrows. The huge goon bulled his way through the crowd. Hot on his heels was the same old drunkard, Dominic, and my mysterious Armenian. They were swallowed by the mob for a moment, but then I spied them moving west towards the far side of the mosque. I couldn't let them escape again, so I ignored Nahida and ducked around some bystanders.

"Where are you going?" That girl was a burr on my tunic—there was no shaking her. I felt her behind me but did my best to focus on the three men. They'd managed to find the only shade on the upwind side of the crowded and noisy mosque. The sounds of chanted prayer wafted defiantly out the windows into the streets to assault Christian ears. The good citizens of Acre were too defeated and cowed to do anything about it, though. They grumbled and waited in the hot sun for the Sultan to reappear.

"Where are you going? Wait up…" Nahida was impossible. In my young life I'd shaken off plenty of city guards, Hospital Knights, and even Saracen spies, but there was no eluding one tall, skinny pest of a girl. Finally, I wheeled around.

"Will you shut up? I need to hear what they're saying."

Her honking voice dropped to a whisper. "Why, who are they?"

"I don't know."

"Then why do you care what they say?"

Girls.

I grabbed her arm and pulled her behind two empty water barrels. From between the splintered wooden kegs, I had a decent view of the three men deep in conversation.

"If you're going to stay, be quiet." It was obvious I meant it so she ducked down behind me, trying to make sense of what we'd seen.

So did I. Paolo was laughing very loudly, draping his arm over the old drunk as if they were great friends. The skinny old man laughed along. Eyebrows smiled with the bottom half of his face, but he was faking it; his eyes were crinkled and hard-looking.

At last the Armenian held out a small flask, which the old man snatched and lifted to his lips in one greedy motion. Whatever it was must have been strong, because half of the mouthful sprayed everywhere and made him cough violently. As soon as he recovered, he took another swig. Paolo gave him another playful pat on the shoulder, which almost sent the smaller man to the ground.

Eyebrows feigned friendliness. "Relax, Dominic. There's plenty where that came from. My Lady is very generous when she's in the mood. And you did a good job yesterday.

Both of you." The old man grinned, showing all five teeth.

Paolo scowled. "Do you have anything else for us?"

Eyebrows smiled. "Perhaps, although this is a job for our more…experienced friend here." He pulled a small rolled-up parchment out of his sleeve and held it out to Dominic. "Do you think you can deliver this?"

"To who?"

"Does it matter?" A shiny coin joined the scroll in the old man's gnarled hand.

"Not overly." Both items disappeared inside the old sot's filthy tunic.

Eyebrows seemed to reconsider. "No. On second thought this might be too dangerous for you. Give it back and I'll let our big friend here do it." He held out his hand, but Dominic just took a step back and stiffened his spine.

Whether it was wounded pride or the fear of missing out on a payday, the old sot shook his head. "Don't think I can do it, do you? Let me tell you, I fought at Montgisard…AND Jacob's Ford when you were still sucking at your mother's tit… I remember I once took a Turk's eye out with one swipe of my knife. Used to be quite good with a blade, back then."

Paolo and Eyebrows exchanged glances. Paolo turned to the old fellow. "I've never seen you with anything sharper than your tongue. Do you have one now?" Dominic had to admit he didn't.

"No, I…lost it. I forget things sometimes."

The Armenian stroked his chin. "Paolo, give him yours." The big man looked as if he'd been asked to surrender a child or a vital organ.

"But it's my knife." This earned him a silent rebuke, and those Eyebrows lowered impatiently.

"Our Lady needs this message delivered safely, and if he's as good as he says..."

"I am," Dominic spit. That satisfied Paolo, who shrugged and handed over an old, well-used, but wickedly sharp dagger. The old man took it by the blade, tossed it in the air, and caught it by the very top of the handle, barely managing to keep his fingers attached to his hands. Then he tucked it up his sleeve with a nod.

Paolo managed not to laugh, and Eyebrows appeared satisfied enough. "Good, now here's..." I couldn't hear the rest as the crowd began to roar and then fell silent. The mosque door was thrown open and Salah-adin and his entourage emerged, having given Allah all the thanks for letting them take back the rat's nest and the cesspool that was the city of Acre—or "*Akko,*" as it was about to be renamed.

Nahida and I watched from behind our barrels. I'd never heard such a massive crowd stand so quiet as the Sultan, flanked by four huge bodyguards with white turbans and massive scimitars on their hips, made his way towards his mount. The only sound was the clopping of hooves and the flapping of his soldiers' banners at the top of their lances.

Suddenly a voice in Arabic shouted, "*iḡtāla...* Murder... He's going to kill the Sultan." I knew that voice. It belonged to Eyebrows. Everyone turned. Most didn't understand Arabic, so the crowd strained to see what all the noise was about. Paolo had cleared an empty circle around Dominic as the Armenian pointed and shouted again in French, "Assassin. He's trying to kill Salah-adin."

A thousand eyes looked to see who would try such a stupid thing. Among those looking around was Dominic himself, who wanted to see who the potential assassin was. He was more surprised than anyone to see an accusing finger pointing his way.

"Who, me?"

The crowd might not know Arabic, but Salah-adin's guards certainly did. Two of the Mussulmen forced their way through to the source of the chaos, sending civilians sprawling in the dusty street.

The drunkard was clear-eyed now, and fully aware of the trouble he was in. He put his hands up, forgetting one of them held the knife. "No, no I'm not…" His eyes darted to Paolo for help, but the big man just bit his bottom lip and looked up to the sky, then shook his head and faced his friend.

"I'm sorry, Dom." The thug drew back his fist and punched the old man square in the face with a horrible crunch. The skinny body flew through the air then landed in a sad pile at the guards' feet. We all heard an "oomph" as the air left his body, then the "crack" of a skull against stones, and another sound. It was the unmistakable tinkle of metal striking the ground as the knife fell from Dominic's hand.

Eyebrows strode forward salaaming to the guards, who made no answer. Their full focus was on the shivering, mousy figure in front of them. Dominic's eyes widened. He couldn't understand what Eyebrows was telling them, but knew it wasn't going to help him at all. "I heard him plotting to kill the Commander of the Faithful. I'm only glad I was able to stop him in time…"

"No!" Dominic shrieked, unsteadily rising to his feet with veins throbbing and his face turning purple. "No, I… Why would I? No, I'm…" He looked to the crowd, then back to Paolo, who had stepped back, blending into the crowd.

Eyebrows shouted in Arabic, and again in French just in case the crowd had any doubt what was going on. "He's in league with the traitor Raymond of Tripoli. Look, he carries a note…"

Dominic realized at that moment he was a dead man, but his legs believed he still had a chance to escape. He took three long steps before a flashing scimitar blade caught him on the shoulder and sliced clean through his body on a diagonal. His head and upper chest landed on the ground a step and a half before his bottom half. Blood spurted everywhere, running between the stones in the street.

The crowd screamed as a dozen more Mussulman troopers arrived, shoving people out of the way. For a moment it looked like the situation might turn even uglier. Eyebrows turned to the crowd, raising his hands for calm. "Good people of Acre, be calm. This is Raymond's fault. He's abandoned us and doesn't care if he gets us all killed." He then handed the note to the soldier with a salaam.

Happy to have someone to hate who wasn't there and armed, a few others joined in. "The hell with that coward. They've all abandoned us…" Then the whole crowd began yelling, shouting, screaming at each other or just to Heaven, where God seemed to be hiding out and not aiding the Christians of Outremer.

I heard the tortured sound of retching beside me and looked to find Nahida on her knees, shaking and puking up what little was in her stomach. Squatting there like a dolt, I tried to offer comfort but didn't know how. Awkwardly, I patted her back two or three times. "Are you going to be all right?"

She looked at me with wide brown eyes. "They killed him…"

I nodded.

"He wasn't… it was those other men, wasn't it?"

I nodded again, trying to keep one eye on the murder scene. I couldn't make out anything but the sounds of shouting and vomiting, but one guard bent over Dominic's body. After a quick search, he pulled out the parchment roll. I had a pretty good idea what it said.

Eyebrows wanted to leave no doubt exactly who was to blame for this catastrophe. He asked Salah-adin's man if he could translate the note for him, then he turned to the stunned citizenry. "It's from the Count of Tripoli. Raymond offered this poor soul ten bezants to do what he himself wouldn't dare."

The crowd turned even uglier. They shook their fists and shouted, "Death to Raymond," and "Kill the traitors," and a lot of other, far more obscene things. Then they started screaming at each other, and fists flew. The sounds of so many languages shouting and hooves scraping on paving stones told me this was not a safe place to be.

"You need to get out of here," I said to Nahida, who staggered to her feet, wiping her mouth on her sleeve. She took my arm to steady herself.

"Me? What about you? Where am I supposed to go?"

Was I supposed to think of everything? "Go to Firan's stable. Where my horse is. I'll meet you there." It was the only safe place I could think of at that moment. At first, I thought she'd do as I told her, but I should have known better. She towered over me and asked, "What about you? Where are you going?"

An excellent question. Eyebrows—and whoever he was working for—was going to a lot of trouble to make it seem like Count Raymond had abandoned the Kingdom. Marco needed to know. But I knew someone else who might be interested. "I'll meet you there. I have to go find a friend."

At least I hoped Ali the spy was still my friend.

Chapter 6

I checked that Nahida was really headed toward the stable, then took off in search of Ali. After the scene at the mosque, Salah-adin's party had headed for the main docks. I knew wherever the Sultan was, Ali would be close at hand.

I zigzagged through now half-empty streets, trying to figure out exactly what I was going to say in a way that made any kind of sense. I wasn't even sure what I knew, only that someone was trying to blame Raymond for the troubles in the city, and he wasn't responsible. Knowing what it was like to be accused of things I hadn't done; my childish sense of justice couldn't let that stand. But what difference would it make? Acre—in fact, the whole kingdom—was now in Saracen hands, and the Count of Tripoli was holed up in Tyre (or Tripoli, or Sidon, or back in France; the stories varied with the teller) and may as well have been on the moon for all it mattered. We only knew he wasn't here to help us.

I expected them to be at the public docks but was surprised to find a huge crowd near the Templar port. The Acre headquarters of the Poor Fellow-Soldiers of the Temple of Solomon had its own private docks, a huge training ground, and underground tunnels that led from the water to the bowels of the building.

It was unsettling to see two Saracen ships tied up where previously Venetian and Genoese boats ruled. I knew nothing about boats—I'd never even been on one and had no great desire to—but I could see these rode lower in the water, and were much wider than the Italian seafaring craft. Each of the big oars had two or more galley slaves chained to it. Slaves who had once been free citizens of captured cities. People like us.

The usually busy Templar House was quiet as a tomb. The few surviving Templars were holed up inside, trapped like rats awaiting final—and inevitable—judgment. Saracen soldiers chanted, wailed war cries, and shook weapons, shoes, and their bared behinds at the building.

Slowly I elbowed my way through the crowd, hoping to catch a glimpse of Ali. There were warriors from every region there; Damascenes, of course, as well as Kurds and midnight-black Mameluks. I was surprised to see tall, pale, white men, in Saracen garb. It seemed there were as many kinds of infidels as there were Christians. The only true Christians in sight were three merchants. One was Peter Brice from the day before. They squirmed like rats at a cat meeting. Brice stood, hands flailing wildly, explaining something to an impatient and bored-looking Taqi-adin. Salah-adin himself stared off towards the water, paying little attention to mere administrative matters.

Half the Muhammadans were engaged in mocking the Templars, while the other half kept worshipful eyes focused on their leader. I scanned the crowd for a figure in black and finally found what I was looking for, the one man facing away from everyone else.

Now I'd found him, I had to somehow get his attention. I ducked, wove, and shoulder-rolled my way to the edge of the inner circle. Frantically, I waved my arms and shouted, "Ali. Over here, Ali…," but my voice got swallowed up in the babel around me.

Several more tries to get his attention failed, and I was jostled around by the sea of people who shifted left or right every time Salah-adin took a step. A sudden pain shot up from my foot to my brain and back as I stepped on a pebble. I picked it up and prepared to toss it away in anger when I came up with a better use for it.

Every pigeon, rat, cat, and King's Guard in Acre knew I had a deadly aim with small projectiles. The number of days I'd spent on rooftops trying to hit a target with stones now proved useful. Confidently, I took aim at Ali's black turban, cocked my arm, and let fly. The stone flew in a perfect arc, right past my intended target and onto the ear of a huge, scary-looking soldier to his left.

My unintended victim grunted and swore, clutching his ear. Ali's eyes immediately followed the pebble's trajectory and turned my way. A second, slightly larger stone bounced off the neatly wrapped pile of cloth on his head, and his eyes settled on me.

"Ali, it's me…" My joy at gaining his attention evaporated like spit on hot cobblestones as his eyes narrowed and he let out a roar. I feared I'd again miscalculated how happy he'd be to see me—something that happened a lot—as he ran towards me, brows furrowed, black eyes squinting against the sun. Huge, callused hands grabbed me. I scrunched my eyes closed, fearing for my life.

My feet left the ground, and then two wet kisses on my cheek left a slimy trail. All the air left my body as I was crushed against his black-robed chest. "Is it you?"

I nodded, since talking required breath. He released me and held me at arm's length. "Lucca, Son of Fleas. Allah is great, I never expected to see you again."

Enough breath had returned that I could squeak, "I didn't either, I…"

Ali rattled on, and I remembered that listening wasn't his defining feature. Maybe it was all those years in the desert with just that big black monstrous horse of his, who wasn't much of a conversationalist. "I feared the worst when we saw you'd left with al Jassus…"

The code name of the fat spy who'd taken me from Acre to Salah-adin's camp, then dragged me to the top of the hill to watch the battle at Hattin, shocked me. A cold chill and shivers scaled my spine as I thought of that terrifying day. It ended with a round, black stain on the rocky ground at the bottom of the mountain.

"God is great, you are alive. But why did you come back here? Are you all right? Where are you living?" I didn't have time to answer any of his questions, they came at me so fast.

Finally, he was forced to breathe and I seized my opportunity. "Ali, I have something important to tell you… It's about the man who tried to kill Salah-adin today…"

His hands fell from my shoulders. He grabbed my elbow

and pulled me behind him as he took long strides through the crowd.

"What are you doing…?"

He said nothing, which frightened me, until we reached an empty corner of the Templar training ground, away from the throng. Then he wheeled around and dropped to one knee. His eyes at the same level as mine, he spat out a question. "Why are you still playing these games?"

"I'm not…"

"Allah has spared you, for whatever reason I don't know, but you are a little idiot if you don't take the chance he has given you. Either someone will kill you, or you'll…" Or I'd kill someone else. It was a little late for that warning. I knew it, and he suspected it. I was lucky he didn't consider me his enemy.

"This isn't a game, Ali. The man who tried to kill Salah-adin… He didn't. I mean, he wasn't the one, and they're trying to blame Count Raymond, and…"

Ali held a hand up to shut me up. "Are you still working for Raymo?" He used Raymond of Tripoli's Syrian name. "And *al Mjardam*—the Leper—he is still your master?" *Was he?* I didn't really know, and that wasn't the point. I shook my head violently.

"No, it isn't like that… I saw something. You need to listen." Ali cocked his head to the side, and with that huge beak of his, resembled an eagle studying prey from the top of a tree. He said nothing for far too long.

At last, he stood up putting his hands on his hips. "So…tell me what you have to tell me, my little flea."

"Louse," I said, unable to help myself.

"What?"

"Louse, not flea. I'm Lucca the Louse, not Flea. Lucca bin le Pou, not..." I felt foolish. Like it mattered what particular type of vermin I was. "It doesn't matter, please, Ali, please hear me out..."

He gestured for me to go ahead. I took a deep breath *and tried to picture how I'd tell this story to Brother Marco.* No embellishment, just the facts. I reported everything I could recall about Big Paolo and poor skinny, drunken Dominic. But mostly I told him about the man with the eyebrows.

"I'm sure he was Armenian," I concluded.

"And you say he had big eyebrows?" I nodded. He drew a line over his eyes with his finger. "Like two caterpillars fornicating over his nose?"

I burst out laughing at that image and nodded. "Yes, do you know who he is?"

This just got me a shrug of his shoulders for my trouble. "Armenians are all hairy as dogs. Like Allah had hair left over and used it all on them." That was true. But he was also avoiding the question, like adults do.

"And he said he was working for The Lady." Ali couldn't control the flare of those humongous nostrils. He knew who she was.

"Who's the Lady?" I asked.

Ali stood, wiping the dust from his robes, more to kill time than for cleanliness. I wouldn't stop pestering him. "Who's the Lady? And why does she want everyone to think Tripoli tried to kill Salah...?"

"Stop it, you foolish boy." Ali's finger jabbed me in the chest. "This is no longer a game you should play. It's not about Acre. Or one man. Whole kingdoms are at stake, and one useless orphan more or less won't matter. Stop now, or you will not live to tell about it. Just pretend you saw nothing."

I could see he meant well. But if his intention was to frighten me, it didn't work, at least not enough to stop me. An embarrassing rush of affection for the big Saracen washed over me. Ali worried about me. He was like Brother Marco in so many ways. Except that they'd kill each other on sight, of course.

I worried about me too, but not enough to stop asking questions. Once I poked my nose into something, I was like a stray dog with a bone. Nothing could make me stop gnawing until either the bone splintered, or my teeth did. "Who's the Lady?"

Ali looked away. "I don't know, but if it is a woman behind all this, you Christians should learn to control your females better. Look at all the trouble your Queen Sybilla has caused. She married who made her happiest in her bed, not who the men decided was better for her. And how has Allah rewarded you?" I wondered if it was a fair assessment of the situation, but enough people thought that way—both Christian and Muslim—that it had taken on the aura of gospel.

"But who…"

Ali took me by the shoulders and shook me until my teeth rattled in my head. "Stop it. This is not one of your Leper's games. And Raymo, or Guy, or your God no longer rules here. This is Salah-adin's city. You must leave, although God alone knows where you'd go. Jerusalem will fall next, Tyre and Sidon are already under attack." He realized how hard he was shaking me and released my shoulders. "Forgive me, my friend."

I felt myself building up a childish pout. "I needed to tell someone. What they're saying isn't true…" This got a dismissive sniff through that mighty, curved nose of his."

"Here's what is true. Salah-adin now controls this city; soon he'll control everything from Egypt to Damascus. And Jerusalem. Accept that. If you have to play spy, you could work for me…" The answer was as plain as mud on my face, and he sighed heavily. "*Inshallah*. Thank you for telling me this. I will consider it."

"What if I need to find you again?" I asked.

"It is best you don't. But if you do… Can you read or write?" I shook my head, convinced once again I needed to correct that flaw. He raised an eyebrow. "Not even that chicken scratch the Firangi call writing?" Another sad shake of my head.

Ali stood up, bent over me and placed two dry kisses on my cheek. "Then I don't know what to tell you. Goodbye, my little flea. Allah protect you, because if you keep this up, I cannot. Thank you for the information." He turned away from me, then looked back over his shoulder and said, "I would stay away from the sugar plant tonight if I were you."

I had no intention of going anywhere near the sugar mill—they had the meanest guards in the city. Furthermore, it was in the part of the city already firmly in Salah-adin's hands. But something interesting was obviously happening there—or about to. "Salah-adin said there'd be no more burning, and he's in control."

Ali shook his head. "Salah-adin is in *command*. Only Allah is in *control*. Stay away from there tonight. It's too dangerous for you…and anyone else." In other words, I was to spread the word.

I nodded, but he didn't see it. Ali strode towards Taqi-adin, Salah-adin, and the other Saracen leaders without looking back.

I had done all I could. I needed to talk to Brother Marco tonight. And Nahida. With all the excitement, I'd forgotten she was waiting for me at Firan's stable. Who knew what the old grump would do to her if he caught her hanging around again? I ran as fast as I could.

If I was worried about Nahida, I needn't have been. I arrived sweating, panting, and a little panic-stricken. She sat placidly on a stool, singing to Droopy and nibbling on a crust of bread.

"This Firangi bread is really good. I didn't know," she said, by way of greeting.

"Where'd you get that?" I asked her.

"Firan. When I first got here, he got all mad and threatened to call the Guards. Then he said he'd beat me." I could see that. "Then he told his son… What's his name? The good-looking one? Fadhil?" I honestly hadn't ever given a single thought to my friend's looks, and her statement bothered me a bit, but she prattled on. "Anyway, his father told him to bring me something to eat." She seemed happy enough. And she was safe. Witnessing Dominic's death hadn't affected her appetite at least. That bread did look good, and my stomach growled like a bear, but she popped the last piece into her mouth and rubbed Droopy's nose some more.

She finished her song, and the pony shook his mane in applause. Then she asked, "Did you finish your important business?"

"I think so, but I need to get home."

She nodded. "Will I see you tomorrow?"

I offered a noncommittal shrug. "*Inshallah.*" It really was a useful phrase when you had no idea what else to tell someone. "Do you have somewhere safe to sleep?"

She gave me a smug grin. "I have the perfect spot. Safest place in the whole city." I turned to leave. As long as she was safe, she didn't need me. "Aren't you going to walk with me?"

"Arggh. I guess so but come on. Let's go."

She rolled her eyes at my impatience, gave Droopy a kiss on the nose, and strode away on those long legs, leaving me behind. "Firan said you need to come muck out the stable again."

"Again?"

"Well, it's not like horses stop pooping just because you have important, mysterious work to do." She was right.

Chapter 7

I had the nightmare again.

The bad one where I'm on top of the hill at Hattin overlooking the battle. The fat spy, al Sameen, grabs me as he topples backward, only instead of letting go, I fall over the edge with him—plummeting to the ground. He laughs as we fall, but halfway down his fleshy face becomes the skinny image of Brother Idoneus, who laughs even harder, then changes back just as we hit the ground.

I woke up screaming.

Fortunately, night terrors and screams weren't rare in a leper hospital. I opened my eyes in the dark, crying, very much alone and ignored. At least I was alive.

I knew there'd be no going back to sleep, so I slipped out of bed and wandered the dark halls of St Lazar for a while. I strained to hear anyone else moving about, but the only sounds were what you'd expect to hear in the quietest hours before dawn; soft moans from the infirmary, snoring from the men's cells. There was deathly silence interrupted by one long, rattling fart from the sisters' cells. I barely stifled a laugh that would have given me away. It was probably Sister Agnes. She did that once in a while and blamed it on Sergeant Jacques, who heroically took the blame.

Still shaking from the dream, I grabbed a handful of contraband dates and pondered my next move. While I wanted nothing more than to speak to someone—anyone—it wouldn't be right to disturb them. Instead, I shoved too many of the sweet fruits into my mouth at once and headed into the tunnel that led to the alley.

I was used to the dank, dark passage by now. There was nothing in the rough-hewn earthen tunnel scarier than awaited me in my own room. I walked the length without any need to touch the walls.

I pushed the cellar door open a crack. Cool, pleasant air washed over me, and I took a deep breath. When I lived in the orphanage, I'd often take midnight rambles out of boredom or just because I wasn't supposed to. It had been a while, and my spirits rejoiced at the freedom. The night fears crumbled away, replaced by the exciting possibilities of an entire city where I was the only one awake to enjoy it. Or I should have been. On the breeze there came a rumbling noise and the clang of metal on metal I couldn't identify. My natural nosiness took over, and I made my way towards the sounds.

Something was—or had been—burning. The air didn't smell of charcoal so much as something over-sweet like a plate of honey-cakes left too long in the oven. Now there was the possibility of food involved, and I became even more interested. I followed my nose a few blocks until the air was thick with the cloying, sticky odor of burning sugar.

The fumes and the noise both increased as I neared the sugar mill and its warehouse. Ali had told me to stay away—

he knew something bad would happen. Drawing nearer, I figured out what the metallic noise was. Swords clanged and clashed. A small but growing crowd gathered to watch the fight, but it wasn't anything I'd have expected.

Yes, the City Watch and several pairs of Hospital Knights menaced the crowd of onlookers and kept them away from the fighting. The odd thing was that *they* weren't the ones swinging swords at each other and swearing at the top of their lungs. The combatants were all screaming in Arabic— all of them. A group of women in hijabs and niqabs, children and the older, poorer Syrians, screamed obscenities at Saracen soldiers who were fighting other Muhammadans in town garb.

It made no sense at first. What looked like local Syrians and some of Taqi-adin's men squared off against Salah-adin's uniformed, more disciplined soldiers. Men in rags and poor clothes with rusty swords, sticks, and farm implements swung with bad intent at trained fighters holding wicked-looking scimitars. The locals who weren't fighting scurried away from the scene, their arms full of whatever they could pick up—tools, lumber, and especially buckets or small bags full of sugar from the warehouse.

One rioter was so intent on keeping his treasures, he didn't see the big soldier standing directly in front of him. A single punch dropped him to the ground, where his bag split open and spilled several bezants worth of sweet, brown goodness. He made a half-hearted attempt to salvage it but had to dodge a vicious kick from the soldier and scurried sideways like a crab, until he was safely out of danger, then took off running with only a single panicky look over his shoulder.

Apparently, despite the Sultan's orders against looting, a group of locals and the less disciplined troops decided to claim some of Acre's spoils for themselves. They raided the sugar mill and storehouse. After years of being under the Christian boot, they seemed to feel that there was little point in capturing a city if they weren't getting something out of it. They weren't at all pleased with the Commander of the Faithful's restraint (or cowardice, depending on who was shouting and how far they were from a soldier). Smoke from one of the back rooms told me that somebody'd made a pathetic attempt at a fire, but it hadn't amounted to much.

Peter Brice and a couple of the other rich men in town stood arguing and gesticulating wildly at General Taqi and some of his officers. I couldn't hear them, but I was pretty sure there was a lot of crying about lost money and promises to protect businesses. The Christian residents stood outside the ring of guards and soldiers, bewildered at the sight of Muslim infidels fighting Muslim infidels and leaving the supposed enemy completely unmolested. Occasionally one of the Christians got too close or too rambunctious, and a guard shoved back or whacked them with the back of a gloved hand, but that wasn't at all unusual.

After a firm nod from Taqi, Brice and the merchants waved frantically, shouting for water and buckets to help put out the small fire in the back and save as much of the sugar mill as possible. A few brave souls took tentative steps forward, watching the scimitar-wielding fighters for signs of trouble. Some of the Sultan's troops cleared a narrow path and waved to the King's Guards and Hospitallers to make way for the quickly forming bucket line.

Several brother knights, including the huge blond giant I'd seen earlier, moved the Frankish citizens away from the fight scene, which was easier now that the looters and their supporters realized they'd been beaten—or betrayed—by Salah-adin's support of the Christians. A few pathetic buckets of water got splashed on the building, and a fat Venetian (probably the mill's overseer since it was actually owned by Count Joscelin) ran around pointing and shouting as if that would suddenly increase the amount of water arriving, or the accuracy with which it was thrown. Of course, the knights and guards didn't help much. They were content keeping the city's residents out of harm's way while watching their enemies beat on each other.

Just when it looked like things were winding down to a disappointingly nonviolent conclusion, a loud crack tore through the night from the back of the mill, accompanied by a searing flash of orange light. Whatever had been smoldering in there had finally ignited. The crowd oohed and ahhed, the Venetian groaned in agony, and a high-pitched scream came from inside the mill. Someone was trapped inside, but I couldn't tell who it was. It was probably a looter, which meant they had it coming for causing trouble. But as the fire doubled in size, then redoubled again, the crowd's sense of justice turned to real concern.

Whoever it was screamed in Arabic. The mysterious person sounded like a young person, maybe even a girl.

Whoever it was waved wildly from the second-story window. People shouted for her to jump. A few called for someone—anyone—to help, and a few of the citizens shouted for her to burn like all her kind should. They were quickly shushed.

The few people trying to put out the fire backed away from the heat and the thick, nauseatingly sweet smoke. Whoever was on the top floor was now alone. Saracen soldiers looked at each other helplessly, as Acre's troops pushed the growing crowd further and further back from what was now a full-blown conflagration.

Shouts turned to full-throated screams in both French and Arabic. The figure at the window put one leg out as if deciding to leap for her life. Then she stopped, frozen in place, unable to make the leap to possible survival although certain injury.

From behind me, someone let out a bellow, nearly a war cry, in heavily accented French. I narrowly leaped out of the way as the huge blonde Hospitaller ran past me towards the flames. A cheer went up from the crowd as the enormous knight approached the building. The heat scorched his face. He hesitated for a moment, dropped to a knee, crossed himself twice and muttered a quick prayer. Then he stood, lowered his head like a bull and ran into the burning building with a shout that sounded like "St John and the Hospital," but I couldn't be sure.

The young woman in the window either didn't see her rescue coming or was too paralyzed by fear to move. She stood, one leg in and one leg out, ignoring the shouts of the mob below to jump and save herself.

I watched, as transfixed and horrified as everyone else. The flames grew, and waves of heat pass over my face. Arab or Christian, everyone stopped fighting with each other to watch. The only sounds were the crackling of flames, the snapping of charred beams, and the shouts of the trapped girl.

I heard myself whispering along with the rest of the mob, "Jump, curse you! Come on, jump!"

The terrified figure looked up for a moment as if she heard me. She straightened her body and shifted forward, bracing her legs to launch herself into the air. Everyone gasped as one as she stood tall, leaned forward toward the street below, and then suddenly, miraculously, flew backward into the burning mill and disappeared from sight. The crowd groaned, fearing the worst.

We all stood staring in open-mouthed silence for what seemed forever, but could only have been a few seconds, then a townsman shouted from near the building.

"There he is!" he yelled, pointing.

The giant man, with a stick-thin figure slung over his shoulder like a bag of flour, stumbled out of the smoke and flame. He made it maybe two dozen steps then dropped to his knees. The girl rolled off his shoulders and fell flat in the cobbled street. The giant knight leaned forward on his hands, alternately gasping for breath and coughing wildly. Several of his fellow Hospitallers ran to his aid, but he shook them off.

"How is she...the girl? Is she...?" he asked between hacking breaths.

"She'll be fine," someone assured him.

All eyes turned to the skinny, smoke-stained girl crying in the dust next to him. Nahida rolled onto her hands and knees, struggled to stand for a moment, then thought better of it and fell back on the ground.

For minutes nobody approached her, until one woman in a hijab inched towards her. Jabbering in Arabic, she switched back and forth between thanking Allah for his protection and cursing the girl as an idiot. Then several more mother hens arrived, each one more concerned than the last. Nahida pushed them away and managed to stand.

"I'm fine, please, aunties... I'm all right." She turned back towards what remained of the sugar mill and its storehouse, now engulfed in flames. Then she remembered the blond enemy knight beside her. She fell to her knees, wrapped her arms around his neck, and wept into his shoulder. I couldn't hear her very well as she sobbed, "*shokrun laki... shokrun laki.*" What else could she say but "thank you?" It wasn't enough but said everything.

The Hospitaller looked at her, confused, then raised a huge hand and awkwardly patted her shoulder. He dropped his head into his hands and wept longer and harder than Nahida did. Nobody bothered them for several minutes. Finally, two Syrian women inched their way closer. They urged Nahida to stand, tugging her to her feet. She shrugged them off and offered her hand to the knight. He shook his head and waved her away. Maybe it was the embarrassment, maybe he was afraid he'd crush her, but she stood with her hand out until he stood on his own, towering over her.

By that time, I'd pushed, ducked, and weaved my way

through the crowd. Without thinking about it, I ran up and gave her a hug. Then I realized what I'd done and pulled my arms back as quickly as I could. She didn't seem to mind though and hugged me back.

"Lucca, what are you doing here?" she asked. Like nothing had happened and my arrival was the big news of the night.

"Me? What were you doing in there?"

"I was sleeping until those people showed up trying to steal everything that wasn't fastened down. I ran upstairs to hide from them…"

"You slept here?"

She looked at me like I'd just told her she had a second head growing out of her bum. "I told you I had a great hiding spot."

"But why here?"

She shook her head at my stupidity. "Because it was quiet, warm and…" she offered me a sooty grin, "it's where they keep all the sugar." She put her hand into a pocket and pulled out a sticky handful of brown goo. "Want some?"

Before I could answer, or even take any, Brother Samuel stormed over to us. "Brother Gerhardt, are you finished playing with the children?"

The giant nodded. The old man sniffed, "Shame you aren't as good at rescuing Christians as you are heathens; you might actually be useful."

I expected the big man to respond, maybe even punch Brother Samuel in the nose. I was disappointed. He simply nodded and rose to his feet.

"Are you wounded?" Brother Samuel asked, more from polite habit than genuine concern. This drew another silent shake of that shaggy blonde head. "Get back to the Hospital, then." The commander snapped at one of the other knights, "Let's get these people out of here before something worse happens." As he turned to go, he looked at Nahida and me. "What about you?" he snapped in passable Arabic. "Are you hurt?"

Nahida shook her head. "No, sir. *Inshallah*, I'm fine."

"Good, then go home." He was already three strides away before he finished the sentence.

Nahida turned to the burning shell of the sugar mill and gave a single sniff. Home wasn't a possibility.

"You don't listen very well, do you, Son of Fleas?" Ali stood over me, hands on hips, shaking his head sadly.

A different voice said, "Not worth a damn, actually." I looked over my shoulder to see Brother Marco, dressed in street clothes a little better than his beggar rags, but leaning heavily on his heavy oak staff.

The two tall men appraised each other silently. Finally, Ali gave the slightest of salaams. "My name is Ali bin Yusuf bin Ali. I am guessing you are…"

"Yes, I am," Marco said, placing his hand over his heart and offering the meagerest of bows. "I see you've met this one already."

"Indeed. Lucca and I had a lovely conversation yesterday about how he should find somewhere to play that isn't the sugar mill. Yet here he is."

"Yes, he has a habit of playing his games where he

shouldn't." My head swung from one man to the other, but neither deigned to look at me. Their eyes were locked on each other's faces, neither willing to look away first. Marco shifted his weight to his good foot and grimaced. "No harm was to come to the city if they surrendered it."***

Ali's eyes crinkled a little bit, but otherwise, he was perfectly calm. In fact, the corners of his mouth curled up the tiniest amount. "You know how it is. Warriors need to feel like they've won something. To risk your life and receive nothing for it... It was best they were allowed to claim a little something for themselves. Just for show."

Marco frowned, "A bloody dangerous game."

"Perhaps, but a far better response than when you Firangi took Acre the first time, no?" Marco's eyes dropped, but he said nothing. When the Christians had captured Acre, there had been hundreds of civilian deaths—women and children as well as fighting men. The city fathers, of course, never spoke of it, and bards didn't sing the tale, but it's one reason everyone was so worried about handing the city back over to Salah-adin. They feared the same or worse.

Ali cast his eyes on Nahida. "And, of course, no one was to be hurt. The mill was supposed to be empty. Are you well, little sister?"

Nahida's eyes widened in fright. She took half a step behind me and said nothing.

"Come with me, we'll find you a safe place to sleep." He offered his hand, but Nahida jumped back as if he'd tried to give her a live asp. "No? I pray you stay safe." Ali pointed at me, his eyes returning to Marco's face. "This one can't stay here."

Marco nodded, then sighed. "I know. He'll leave tomorrow."

They were talking about me as if I wasn't there, and I couldn't take it. "I'm not going anywhere. And what about…" I was cut off as each of the men held up a palm, telling me to shut my big mouth.

"Has he told you his news about the…trouble yesterday?"

Brother Marco nodded. "Yes, do you believe him?" Ali said nothing—which answered the question. Marco continued, "Someone needs to let the man know what's happening in his name, don't you think?"

"I think that's an excellent idea." Ali's voice dropped to a whisper: "As to the Lady in question…"

Marco frowned. "You know who she is?" My ears perked up. I certainly didn't and burned to know.

"Not with a hundred percent certainty, but I have my suspicions. As do you, I am guessing. "Marco hesitated before finally admitting, "The same suspicions, and about the same degree of confidence." He used to be a much better liar. Maybe it was his illness.

"We would both benefit from knowing the truth, I think. If only there was some way for men such as us to get word to each other. Such a thing can be difficult." One thick eyebrow arched.

"If only there were. I'm sure we can think of something." Marco touched his fingertips to his heart again and bowed ever so slowly. Whatever these two were talking about had been decided, and I was left completely confused.

"But what about me...?" They each raised a warning palm to shut me up. Grown-ups.

Chapter 8

Dawn was crawling over the eastern wall when I got home and went to sleep—for a while, until the dreams came. This time it was a new nightmare.

The sugar mill was on fire and Nahida was trapped inside. What was different this time was there wasn't any big blonde avenging angel to rescue her; it was all up to me. She kept crying for help, and despite my every effort, I couldn't reach her. First, I was trapped by a wall of tall grown-ups shrieking at each other. They ignored me as I threw my body against them, unable to break through. The next time, the path was clear, but my feet kept sticking to the stones which had melted into a kind of black tar that stuck me in place. The third time the flames reached out to me, and I was too afraid to move. Meanwhile, Nahida screamed and screamed, and I called out for help that never arrived.

I woke up hot and sweaty, but nothing was burning except the candle by my bed. The soaked sheets were the normal result of sleeping in a stone cell in the depths of a boiling, arid summer night. No one died, and Nahida was fine (no thanks to me) although I hadn't any clue where she was or if she was safe.

I recalled every word of the conversation between Ali and

Marco. They insisted I leave Acre today—and go where, exactly? Everything I knew was here, but with them both in accord, there was no appeal.

I lay in the stillness for a while, but closing my eyes only invited the dreams back. I'd had enough of them, and rose, pacing back and forth running my hand through my hair. As always, when I didn't know what to do with myself, I followed the advice of my grumbling belly and headed for the kitchen.

With half a hallway to go, I heard the voices from the kitchen. Adults were arguing. Their voices were angry, weary, and loud. I could pick out Marco, Sergeant Jacques, and sisters Marie-Pilar and Agnes even from this far away.

"He can't stay." That was Brother Marco.

Sister Agnes piped up in a quavering voice, "None of us can. You know what will happen to…us… Especially the women."

"The same thing that will happen to you if you try to leave. There's no protection outside these walls, and nowhere for any of us to go." Sergeant Jacques was trying to be as protective and encouraging as he could. It sort of worked, as Sister Agnes sighed quietly. His voice dropped to a determined whisper: "We'll die protecting this House if we must." Then he paused and added, "And I fear God thinks we must."

I stepped closer, trying to see around the corner into the kitchen without getting caught. Clinging to the wall like a short, skinny shadow, I leaned sideways and caught a glimpse. The two nuns sat on the bench, and part of

Jacques's body loomed over Sister Agnes. Brother Marco stood in front of them out of my view. Through her veil, Sister Marie-Pilar tried to sound hopeful. "But what about the other Houses of St Lazar? Surely some of them still stand?"

Brother Marco snorted. "And which are those? Jaffa? Gone. Sidon and Nablus? Gone. Even Jerusalem herself will fall any day, if she hasn't already."

"God will at least preserve the Holy City," Sister declared. Nobody believed that, including her.

"The latest we've heard is that Salah-adin left to join the siege. The Queen, the Patriarch, d'Ibelin, and a few men are holding the city, but they can't last."

"Balian d'Ibelin is a good man..." Jacques offered.

"He is a good man, and he'll negotiate the best surrender he can. Salah-adin respects him and doesn't want a slaughter either, but in the end, they are all civilians and nonreligious folk without an army to fight for them. The rich they'll hold for ransom, the others—at least the women and children— will be sold into slavery. As for us, how much of a bargaining chip is a handful of lepers without even a Grand Master to plead for them?" Marco's voice was becoming more ragged and bitter the more he spoke.

Since Grand Master Bernard died a few months ago, there hadn't been a formal head of the Order of St Lazar. That's why Marco had free use of the big office at the top of the stair. Each House was on its own. As for the other Orders, the leaders of the Templars, Hospitallers, and King's Guard were just heads on poles by now.

"What about us?" Agnes asked. "Perhaps we can appeal to Taqi-adin… At least for our sick."

"The less he thinks about us, the better," said the sergeant. For now, he'll leave us alone until the city is resettled and the worst is over. Besides, there isn't anyone to represent us. We have no Master."

"Yes, we do, and a good one, if he'd just take the job," Jacques growled. Marco would have none of that.

"No, God curse you, we don't." The big knight's staff struck the floor, ending the discussion. A gloomy hush fell over the group. The only sound was Sister Agnes sniffling loudly, trying to hold back tears and appear brave. I was doing the same thing where no one could see me, my back pressed against the sweating stone wall. "I can't…and all of this is beside the point. We need to get Lucca out of Acre."

"And go where?" I'd never heard Sister Marie-Pilar raise her voice, and with the sores and scabbing around her mouth, her speech was less clear than usual. "He'th jutht barely returned to us." She paused to wipe the corner of her mouth with her veil. I almost caught a glimpse beneath it, but she dropped it again quickly. "He'th jutht a little boy."

My throat felt like it would burst from the lump in it, and I couldn't take anymore. The words, "I'm not leaving you…ever," erupted from my mouth and I ran to her, throwing my arms around her tiny shoulders and burying my face in her wimple. "I want to stay with you."

Shameful, childish tears scalded my eyes, but I couldn't help myself. For the first time since my return, I wanted to cry, but I tried to hold it in, which just created the kind of ugly, hiccoughing noises you'd expect. Huge, body-wracking sobs made my shoulders bob up and down. Marco couldn't even look at me and turned away, adding to my self-loathing. Still, Sister's cool, birdlike hand gently stroking made me feel better. A very tiny bit.

"You see, he's only a child."

I opened my mouth to protest but nothing came out. As if to prove the point, a huge snot bubble formed in my nose, and I quickly wiped it away with my sleeve. "No, I'm not," I mumbled. "I have been to war, and I want to fight with you all." A real man wouldn't be blubbering like a baby though. *No wonder they want me gone. I'm useless to them and everyone else.*

From the corner of my eye, Brother Marco drew a deep breath and averted his gaze. He must have been as ashamed of me as I was myself. "The lad's been more of a man than I've been these past few weeks, but there's nothing to be done. There's one more thing I'll have to ask him to do and, God willing, he'll be safe after that."

With a last monumental sniff, I stifled the bubble in my nose and took a slow, deep breath. *Another job? What could I do?*

"Someone has to get word to Count Raymond in Tyre. We know he hasn't yet returned to Tripoli, and won't until the matter of Jerusalem is settled. He needs to know what's going on here."

"Brother, no…" Sister Marie-Pilar's grip was going to leave bruises.

"Blast you, do you think I like this? What choice do we have? The lad can't stay here…and he can't stay out of trouble. Salah-adin's people already have an eye out for him. Where else is he to go? Jerusalem is as good as dead. He has no people anywhere else. At least there's a chance he can make it to Tyre. Raymond will take care of him after that." Marco stopped, attempting to regain his composure. "He owes the boy at least that much."

If she felt his rebuke, Sister didn't back down. "He could go back to the Hospital. Now that…that man…is gone, it's surely safe now."

"No," I said, panic-stricken, "I'm not going back there. I want to stay here, with you…" I looked directly at Sister. The other nun, Agnes, "tsked" in sympathy. I did want to stay with them all. If I would die, I didn't want to be alone.

"You will do as you're told, damn you!" I—and everyone else—fell into a shocked silence. "Please, lad. I need you to do this. No one else can. And it's your story to tell. Who else?"

I shook my head stubbornly, arms crossed over my chest. This drew a disgusted "uck" from Sergeant Jacques, along with something about following orders and something else about paddling my arse that I didn't quite hear and he didn't quite mean. Sister hugged me tighter against her.

I wasn't going anywhere if I had a choice. I just didn't believe I had one.

Marco finally broke the silence. "There's nothing to be done. Lucca, I need you to do this for us…for everyone. Tripoli is our only chance now. Will you take a message to him?"

When Marco and I had looked at the map I stole from al

Sameen, Tyre was the next dot on the coast. How hard could it be to get a message to the next biggest city and come back in one piece? I'd faced armed spies, walked across war zones, stared down Salah-adin himself, and I had...gotten awfully lucky. There was no earthly way I was up to this job. I didn't answer, just sat there sniffling like the stupid, useless baby I was.

"That's pretty wild country, and not easy going. Mostly mountains and goat trails." Jacques wasn't encouraging, but he wasn't trying to be. To my surprise, he didn't want me to go either. "It would be easier to go by boat."

Easier to fly, too, but I didn't have wings. I did have something a lot slower and stupider, but it had brought me home safe once before. "I have a horse," I said.

For the first time in days, I heard Marco laugh. "Yes, such as he is, you do have a horse. And Firan will be glad to be rid of both of you. Maybe you can join a Caravan..."

"No, I won't let him." Sister Marie-Pilar's eyes hardened and she stood up, her hands tightly gripping my shoulders. Brother Marco shook his head in exasperation, but it didn't slow her down at all. "Not alone. I'll go with him."

"Don't be ridiculous."

"Is it so impossible? That I want to do something besides sit here and let you men take all the risks? Leave a boy to die alone in the wilderness doing something incredibly stupid?"

Brother Marco's eyes flashed with the fire I hadn't seen since I got back. "I forbid it."

Sister Marie-Pilar locked eyes with him "I...I am a bride of Christ. Not anyone else's. Christ alone, and even He can't stop me. You can forbid me nothing…Brother."

Hell itself broke loose then. Each of us had perfectly good reasons why Sister shouldn't even talk such foolishness but were drowned out by the equally strident arguments from the other people in the room.

At last, Marie-Pilar had had enough. She slapped her hand on the table. "Enough!" She raised a finger and pointed it at Marco. "You say we'll die if we stay, yet we're doomed if we leave. I can't sit here uselessly and wait for someone else to determine that. And I won't leave a child alone on the road on some fool's errand. I'll go with him and deliver him to your precious Raymond. Maybe I'll even plead for the sick here, since nobody else seems willing to intercede on our behalf. And if the Lord Almighty wants me dead, it won't matter whether it's trapped here like a rat or at the side of some road. At least the poor boy won't be alone, God damn you."

We were all in shock from hearing her curse. For lack of anything to add, she just said, "I'm going," and sat down.

Jacques blew his lips together like a horse. "Fine, I'll go with her. Vardan, too; he'll want to…" Marco held his hand up to silence him. Jacques clicked his teeth shut but obeyed like the good soldier he was.

"No, we'll need both of you here. Let's be honest; a flock of lepers traveling together won't help Lucca reach Tyre any faster. You stay here with me, Jacques. Vardan, too. I know just the man for the job of escort—if he'll do it."

Sister Marie-Pilar squared her shoulders. "Fine. Who do you have in mind…Brother?"

Brother Marco shook his head. "First, let me see if he'll accept, then I'll let you know. He's the best man I know. If he can't keep Lucca safe, then God doesn't mean for this to work."

Chapter 9

I've heard that when rich people pack for a long journey, they agonize over how much to take with them. Which tunics and what coat and how many pairs of shoes? I didn't have that problem. I slipped my tunic over my only pants, put my one pair of sandals on my feet, and reached under my pillow for the only other thing I possessed—the soldier's dagger I brought back from Hattin. It had lain untouched under my pillow since I'd returned. Vardan had tried to teach me to use it, but I hoped I never would. I was hopeless with it, but I picked it up, balanced it in my hand, and took a couple of swooping swipes at the air. It was heavier than I remembered.

Weeks ago, I'd been terrified to stay alone in this room, scared to death of the silent stone walls and the disease-stricken people who inhabited them. Now there was nowhere else in the world I wanted to be, and yet I was leaving again. The last time, I knew—or at least hoped and sort-of prayed—I'd be back. This time, there was no guarantee that the building, the people, or even the city of Acre would still be standing if I were ever lucky enough to return.

I took one last look around me, tucked the dagger in my

belt, and cracked open the heavy wooden door. It was still early, and the dawn streaming through the windows only made lighter, greyer streaks on the wall. The sun wasn't fully risen. Early morning noises—cheery greetings and muffled groans from the infirmary, the scuffle of bare feet on stone, and the clanking of pots in the kitchen—made me smile.

What little of the sun that managed to climb the walls shone into the kitchen. I was about to walk in when I heard Brother Marco cough. "Lucca, could you come here for a minute?" I followed him upstairs to the abandoned Grand Master's chambers.

He closed the door behind him and turned to face me. I waited for him to say something, but he coughed again, and looked as if he were trying to speak, then cleared his throat with a big braying noise. I waited patiently, but he still didn't say anything and I grew fidgety. Finally, I barked out, "What? What are you trying to say?"

That little bit of rudeness seemed to put some steel back in his spine. He lowered those eyes to mine and softly said, "It's a lot I'm asking of you. And now you have Sister…"

"But you said I needed to leave Acre. That Count Raymond was depending on me." His hesitation made no sense.

"You do, boy. You can't stay, but you don't have to do… the other. Perhaps you can join a caravan to Jerusalem, or up to Antioch, or just about anywhere else. Firan is taking his family near Nazareth. He says you could go with them." His eyes were cloudy with what looked like, but couldn't possibly, be tears.

"But Count Raymond…" I began, and he held his hand up.

"…is cowering in Tyre and will be under siege by now. He can't ask any more of you than you've done for him already…" I'd never heard him say—or even tolerate—a bad word about the Count of Tripoli.

"But…but you said we had a duty…" *Why was he trying to stop me from doing what I had to do?*

"You're just a child, curse it. You don't have a duty—not to Raymond, or God or anyone else." I started to answer back, but he continued, "Including me. Lucca, I was wrong to bring you into this. It was foolish…"

Why was it so foolish? I thought I'd done pretty well until now. God knows I was trying my best. "But didn't I do good? I won't mess this up. I'll do better, I promise." My own eyes brimmed with scalding water now and I wiped my snotty nose on my arm.

"He looked away for a moment and then dropped to one knee so we were face to face. "Lucca, forgive me. I should never have made you part of all this. You have done more than anyone ever expected—certainly more than I've done. You must take care of yourself."

"And Sister?" I reminded him. Had he forgotten Sister Marie-Pilar was going as well? "Someone has to look after her." He let out a snort, but I knew he didn't think it was funny, despite his halfhearted attempt at a smile. "Ha. Yes, I suppose someone does have to look after her at that. Once I thought I could… Well, you can look after each other, yes?"

I nodded. This was more like it.

He'd obviously decided to stop whatever foolishness he was thinking. He brought himself up to his full standing height and assumed a military posture. "So, you're ready to do this?"

I nodded and stood straighter and as tall as I could. "I'm ready, Brother."

He smiled. For real this time. "Very well, Monsieur le Pou. What are you going to tell Count Raymond when you see him?"

"One, Acre has fallen and Salah-adin has the city. So far, everyone is safe and has forty days to leave with safe passage..."

"Thirty-eight now, but yes. What else?" *Thirty eight days. Surely that was time enough for Count Raymond to come back and free the city while Salah-adin was in Jerusalem?* Maybe this wasn't such a fool's errand after all.

I counted them off on my fingers, but I had to start over. "Thirty-eight days and safe passage. Two, someone is trying to stir up trouble and slammering..."

"Slandering"

"...slan-dering his name. Especially this Armenian with the bushy eyebrows. And three, he should be on the lookout for The Lady, whoever that is." This earned me a very satisfying nod.

"And Sister?"

"I'm to deliver her safely to the convent at Tyre, and if I fail, it's my ass." I saw his confusion. "Sergeant Jacques told me that part."

That finally earned me a real laugh. "I'll bet he did. One last thing." He reached over to the plank desk beside him and picked up a vellum sheet with lines of writing all over it. Checking that the ink was dry, he rolled it tightly and tied it with two different ribbons—one blue and the other green. Brother Marco hesitated only a moment and handed it over. "This is for only Count Raymond to see. Don't go reading it to your friends at bedtime."

He knew very well I couldn't read a word. I gave him my famous adorable-orphan smile. He rewarded me with a wink.

"Are you ready for this?" Of course I wasn't, but nodded as bravely as I could manage.

I wasn't nearly ready for what awaited me in the kitchen. Everyone was there to see Sister and me off. Even the two grumpy, non-leprous priests who never acknowledged my presence the whole time I was there had come. One pressed a small wooden rosary into my hand and muttered something about it keeping me safe, although I suspected the dagger in my belt would serve better. I wrapped it around my wrist like a bracelet. The other priest, a thin man whose skin was as sad, grey, and lifeless as his hair prayed over me until both I and the Lord Himself wiggled impatiently.

I expected the nuns to overreact, but I wasn't ready for the open weeping from Sister Agnes, who crushed me so far into her chest I thought I'd pop out through her back. "God keep you, little man. God keep you safe." I didn't know what to say to that. He'd done kind of a halfhearted job so far, but maybe he'd listen to her. I nodded.

Sergeant Jacques held his hand out. "It's been a pleasure,

lad. Remember what Vardan and I taught you. Let me see the blade." I handed him my knife, handle first like he taught me. That earned me a grunt. "Take care of yourself...and her. Or you'll answer to me."

I could see he was as serious as I'd ever known him, and I didn't have the heart to tease him. I just stood at attention, shook his mangled hand, and gave a simple "Yes, sir." Then I turned to Vardan, who wrapped me in his giant furry arms and hugged me tighter than Agnes had, landing a sloppy kiss on each cheek. I squirmed away, wiping my face on my sleeve but smiling.

Sister Marie-Pilar endured the same torturous goodbyes, hugging and kissing and praying with everyone until Brother Marco called a halt. "It's time."

The grey priest demanded one more blessing, then Sister picked up a bag I hoped was full of dried meat, biscuits, and fruit in one hand. She took my dirty hand in the other, and we followed Marco out of the kitchen, down the hall, and out the front door of the House of St Lazar into the hot, dusty street.

My eyes burned as we stepped out into the heat and brutal sunlight. I made the mistake of looking back at the door full of bandaged, scabby people who had been the most beautiful I'd ever known. No one said anything, although one young soldier raised a cloth-wrapped stump in a final goodbye.

Brother Marco, Sister Marie-Pilar and I stood silent which was fine with me. My brain was too full of questions to worry about carrying on a conversation.

What if I get us lost?

What if we're attacked by bandits—could I really protect her?

What if the nunnery wasn't there? Or they wouldn't admit her? What am I supposed to do with a sick nun?

What if Count Raymond didn't come back with an army? Could I come back? What would Sister do with an orphan boy in a strange city?

We weren't the only ones on the streets that morning. In fact, a steady stream of people in small groups made their way toward the corrals. Time was running short, and those most eager to leave were getting out while they could. There were families; exhausted women with long, blank faces clutched babies to their chests while their men lugged sacks or pulled wagons or pushed wheelbarrows full of whatever was most precious. Christ alone knew where they'd end up.

A short distance from the corrals, caravans formed. Big, scary-looking men with dark beards and darker eyes called out for people wanting to travel together—offering protection for a reasonable fee. Everyone knew those promises were useless against a Saracen army, but at least somebody made them. The people sworn to protect Acre had failed, and any hope was better than none. Still, where were they going? Jerusalem? Yes, it still stood but was under siege and nearly a hundred miles away. Sidon? Nablus? Nazareth? I hoped for Fadhil's sake that city remained in Christian hands. Tyre was the closest Frankish city—thirty miles or so by land and surrounded by Saracens seeking blood. And that was the *best* option.

Mules and camels clogged the streets, screaming and honking even louder than the people. Some families stood dumbly gawking like they'd used all their energy making the choice to leave their homes and now couldn't decide where to go next. Frustrated elbows flew, along with curses and cries for children who'd gotten separated from their parents in all the chaos.

For a blood-freezing moment, I thought I saw Big Paolo standing by a hay cart, but it was only a Turkish caravan master—his eyes much livelier and his neck thicker than the big criminal's. I sought Eyebrows and thought I glimpsed him for a moment but couldn't be sure. I was convinced I saw al Sameen behind a crowd of water-sellers. The tall, bald figure of Brother Idoneus turned out to be a fencepost with a guardsman's helmet perched on it. I knew neither of those two could really be there, so maybe I'd imagined the Armenian as well.

She must have felt me shiver. Sister Marie-Pilar gave the bag of food to Brother Marco and reached for my hand. Her fingers were cool despite the already hot morning, and reassuring. She gave a little squeeze as I guided us through the crowds.

"It's this way, over here." I picked up speed, and she had to hurry in a most un-nunlike way to keep up. She attracted a lot of looks, but most people got out of our way, so that wasn't a bad thing. I slowed down—a bit embarrassed— when I saw Brother Marco struggling to keep pace. He limped along, his eyes scanning the crowd.

Eventually, I saw Firan's roughly built stable. I also learned who our traveling companion would be. In the entrance to the stable the mysterious giant, blond Hospitaller knight stood at ease, but vigilant. He held his thick wooden staff in front of him like a banner pole, and his eyes looked straight ahead. Brother Marco offered a sigh of relief.

"Thanks be to God, there he is," The two knights greeted each other with the kiss of peace while Sister and I stood there like big dumb stumps.

"So, they gave you permission?" Brother Marco asked.

The blond giant nodded. "Of a sort. They seemed glad to be rid of me."

Marco shook his head. "I doubt that."

"I don't. A Brother Knight who won't swing a sword isn't much good to them or anyone else. At least this way God has a use for me." Marco offered a sympathetic smile. If he understood what the man was talking about, I sure didn't. I'd seen this ogre knock people out with that staff, and he'd run into a burning building to save a little girl. *Why couldn't he use his sword? Maybe it's his shoulder or something.* One thing I knew, a bodyguard who couldn't use a blade wasn't going to be much more useful than a ten-year-old boy or a skinny nun. At least he had two horses.

A bony grey palfrey stood at the door, reins loosely lashed to a post. Droopy didn't look like much compared to a real warhorse. This grey was not the great destrier of the bards' tales, but it stood tall and arrogant, with a blanket and saddle strapped firmly in place and ready to go to work. I looked quickly—all boys do—and realized it was a mare. She didn't seem likely to support such a big rider, but looked like she knew her business. Next to her was a black pony, smaller, less impressive, and loaded with three bags of supplies. I saw two bedrolls strapped there but wasn't sure what else was it carried.

Then there was my brave mount. Mud-brown, shaggy, and short, Droopy came to about her shoulder. He looked like he would drop dead ten minutes from town. Perfect.

"Brother Gerhardt, I commend these two to your tender mercies. Lucca, come here... This is Brother Gerhardt." The giant made a small, polite bow.

"'Tis an honor, Master Lucca. I've heard vord of you...at the Hospital." I couldn't place his accent. "Word" sounded like "*vord*". I hadn't heard of him, but then he wasn't famous like me and my friends. It seemed rude to tell him that, so I said nothing and nodded until one of Marco's palms smacked the back of my head.

"Manners, lad. He's a Knight of the Hospital."

"It's a pleasure to meet you. Sir Knight." I offered, rubbing the sore spot on my scalp. This got me another bow, although he chuckled as he did it.

Marco put his good hand lightly on Sister's shoulder. "And this is Sister Marie-Pilar. She is to be delivered safely to the Cistercian convent at Tyre...or Sidon...whichever will accept her." Both Sister and I looked at him and then at each other in surprise. It was the first we'd heard of that part of the plan.

Gerhardt nodded, smiled at the little nun, put his hand to his heart, and bowed deeply. He crossed himself. "Ja, it is an honor, Sister." He looked from her to Brother Marco and cocked an eyebrow. "This is..."

Brother Marco cut him off. "The Sister who is going to negotiate haven for the rest of the people in St Lazar. She's, uh, tougher than she looks."

Gerhardt smiled a big horse-tooth grin that made him look like a humongous overgrown child. "They usually are. Shall ve?" He gestured to the horses. He offered his cupped hand to Sister, whose eyes got huge. I don't know if she'd ever been on a horse before, but she gamely climbed up onto the grey horse's back and sat awkwardly side-saddle.

"Ve'll valk out the gates. I'll ride vith you once ve get on the road north, ja?" He turned to me. "Get your horse, boy. It's time."

While he took both his horses' reins, I grabbed Droopy's bridle off the peg on the wall and slipped it over his nose. He only nipped once—a gentle reminder that he tolerated me and little more. At least he stood still while I struggled to get the job done. It only took me three tries to get the bit into in his mouth and escape with all my fingers. I was learning.

Brother Marco nodded. "I've paid Firan for the board, but you'd better get going before he decides you need to clean the barn one more time." My eyes flew wide open. "I'm not joking. And it wasn't cheap. Get out of here."

Straightening my back, I took the reins and dragged Droopy out into the blazing sun. I led him past Brother Marco with a soft "goodbye." Marco didn't respond. I snuck a look over my shoulder to see him speak softly with Sister, who wiped her eyes with her sleeve.

I was unsure what to do next—I didn't even know which gate we were supposed to leave through. From behind me, Brother Marco snapped. "You're in charge lad. They're waiting for you to give the word." *I'm in charge? We're in more trouble than I thought.* Brother Gerhardt stood beside his mare, waiting for me to say something. Sister looked down at me from atop her horse.

"This way?" I pointed. Gerhardt nodded, and I took two steps forward and stopped suddenly. Droopy bumped into me, but halted as well.

Nahida stood in front of us, bedraggled and filthy. She wore the same smoke-stained clothes she'd worn the other night. Muddy tracks on her face told me she'd been crying. A lot.

"Are you leaving? Where are you going?" She asked.

"Tyre… I have to…take Sister to Tyre."

"Take me with you. Please?" I looked over my shoulder. Neither sister nor Gerhardt spoke Arabic, so they just looked confused.

I knew Nahida spoke no French, but she saw the giant knight and smiled. She put her hand to her chest and greeted him with a shy salaam. He grinned and nodded back. "Hello, *Schatz.*"

"Where are you going?" I asked, although it was a dumb question. The answer, I knew, was "anywhere but here."

She crossed her arms in front of her. "Beirut. My uncle is there, and a lot of *Druzeh* live there."

I knew Beirut was far up the coast in the Lebanon practically to the kingdom of Antioch. "We aren't going that far," I said weakly. Her face fell, and her lip quivered.

"I can't stay here, and I have no money to join a caravan. The Christians think I'm Muslim, and the Muslims will kill me for being… I can't stay." She was as frightened and lost as I'd ever seen her. "Can I at least walk with you as far as Tyre? I have my own food…" She pulled some dried meat and nuts from a deep pocket. There wasn't enough there to last me half a day, and I knew it wouldn't be nearly enough for the three or four days it would take.

"Decide, boy." Marco's impatient voice came from over my shoulder. I wanted to say no. I should have said no. I did say no. "No. I'm sorry, but…"

A huge shadow fell over me. Gerhardt had stepped up behind me. "Vat's the problem?"

"She wants to come with us," I explained in French. Nahida frowned, not understanding a word.

"An infidel girl? Vhy doesn't she stay vith her people?"

I sighed. "She doesn't have any. She's *Druzeh*, whatever that is, and the Saracens hate her as much as the Christians. Maybe more."

Gerhardt grunted. "Druze? She's right. She can't stay here, they'll kill her." Without another word he reached out to a startled Nahida, who screamed as he grabbed her waist and hoisted her up. She kicked and squirmed wildly until he placed her on his grey horse's back behind a shocked Sister Marie-Pilar.

"He's a good man, Lucca, maybe the best I've ever known, but it's still your choice." Brother Marco had come up to us by this time. His glove rested on my shoulder, leaning on me for balance. My choice. I saw a sickly, bewildered-looking nun; a skinny, wild-eyed Arab girl clinging to her; a huge blond knight, and three horses; only one of which looked happy to be there. It didn't feel like much of a choice. I guess when you're the one in charge it often doesn't.

I did my best to look in command. I looked at Brother Marco for what I was sure would be the last time. "Which gate?"

His lips turned up ever so slightly and he pointed north. "The Gate of Flies, then the Damascus Road 'til the first turn north. Gerhardt knows the way."

I gave a harder than necessary yank on Droopy's reins. "Let's go," I said, as much to myself as anyone else. It didn't matter; they all fell in line behind me. I was in charge, God help us.

Chapter 10

We wound our way through the crowd until there was no more winding to be done. Then we stood among the moaning, groaning mass of people waiting to pass through the gate and out of Acre. Camels, horses, mules, and oxen voiced their impatience, along with all the people desperate to get to wherever they were going.

My mission was clear, so I was spared having to make a devilishly difficult decision. Many people still dithered over which way to go, even at this late hour. Most were convinced the easiest trip would be north to Tyre, assuming that city hadn't fallen yet. Everyone knew it was besieged and likely to go next, no matter how much of a fight they offered. So others figured the only safe place left was Jerusalem itself. Most believed God, despite all he'd made us suffer so far, would not desert the Holy City. The less faithful felt it was the one place in all of Outremer that still offered good walls and an army willing to fight. At least it wouldn't roll over as meekly as Acre, Joppa, Ramla, and the rest. Tyre was thirty or so miles away, Jerusalem a hundred through captured territory.

My companions waited for me to take the lead. Gerhardt stood silent and pillar-straight, holding the horses in a firm grip. Sister Marie-Pilar clung to the grey's mane with white knuckles, afraid the slightest motion might knock her off her seat. Nahida sat behind her, wide-eyed, one hand around Sister's waist, the other stroking the beast's haunches and singing that annoying Arabic song. It soothed her as much as the horse, I'm sure, but added to the nun's edginess.

People passed through the gate in bursts. They'd bunch up just inside the opening then wait , until a group was hustled through, spit out like melon seeds into the great dusty open space outside. As each new group passed through, the rest of us surged forward then stopped again.

I spotted the burly caravan leader from earlier. His bunch looked frightened but determined. I knew they were headed to Tyre, and it would make the most sense for us to travel with them. It would be slow, but better than traveling by ourselves.

I watched smaller groups and individuals struggle to escape. Some carried huge packs, some pushed wheelbarrows loaded with precious things from their homes. Women sobbed, men shouted orders to show how brave they were, and the animals pawed, stomped, and kicked up dust as if their protests would make anyone move quicker instead of adding to the general misery.

Through dust-clouded eyes, I saw the back of a very familiar head. It was Big Paolo with Eyebrows right at his elbow, head turning constantly to survey the crowd. The Armenian seemed calm enough, but in as much of a hurry as everyone else to be out of the city. As hard as I tried, I couldn't keep them in sight, so I pulled on Droopy's bridle to make up ground.

"Where are you going?" Gerhardt asked.

"We need to get a move on, don't we? Come on." The blond giant shrugged and shouldered two surprised and angry people out of the way. One of them, a fat woman with a load bigger than me on her back, nearly hauled off to punch him, then realized who bumped her and restrained herself.

From her perch high on the horse, Sister tisked at me. "Lucca, don't be rude. Everyone else is trying to leave too. Be patient."

Behind her, a nagging Arabic voice demanded, "What did she say? Can't we move any faster?" Sister turned suspiciously towards Nahida, not understanding a word the girl said. I said in French, "We have to get going." Then I repeated it in Arabic, which drew a lot of unwanted and hostile looks from people around me. It dawned on me then I'd have to repeat everything twice. That was going to get more than annoying over a long trip. I dropped my head, refusing to make eye contact with anybody, and tugged on Droopy's rope bridle again. My dumb pony picked up the pace. He nosed aside several merchants and a soldier, but the other two horses followed our lead.

I still couldn't see Paolo or Eyebrows anywhere. If I were them I'd have moved up with the larger caravan. Maybe we should try to join them?

Once spat out of the Gate of Flies into the vast caravan staging area, a traveler could see miles of flat road to the south and east. North lay the hills of the Lebanon and Tyre. The riptide of humanity carried us to the right, though,

117

which was the Jerusalem Road heading south and east. I took several steps in that direction before Gerhardt tapped me on the shoulder and pointed north.

I resented the deep chuckle that went along with the directions. "Okay, let's go this way," I said as if that was what I'd meant to do all along. This earned me a nod from the Hospitaller, a disgusted look from Nahida, and nothing at all from Sister Marie-Pilar, who was too occupied clinging to the grey mare's mane, her eyes wide and white above her dust-blackened veil.

Circling back so the sun was slightly over our right shoulders, I looked back—maybe for the last time—at Acre's drab brown walls. The sun beat down on the city, leaving sections of the walls in shadow. Except for the giant gates and some narrow archer's slits near the top, it appeared for all the world like my city had turned its back on us.

North. We were heading north. A long, snaking line of humans and animals slowly marched towards greenish hills in the distance. I knew the seacoast lay that way, as well as the mountains of the Lebanon—although, of course, I'd never been there. I had never been out of sight of the walls of Acre until a few days ago—and that hadn't been by choice.

Those mountains looked tall and green compared to the flat dryness of the drought-plagued plain. I thanked God we'd be taking the coast road along with the others choosing the relative safety of Tyre. All my life I'd heard stories about those mountains—of bandits and bears and the Lord alone knew what all. Only an idiot would travel through there. The road along the coast was narrow and slow, but there was safety in numbers, if only because the wolves would have to fight their way through a lot of sheep to find the four of us.

We fell into a frustrating shuffle as the big caravan organized itself and I led us to the outer ring. A priest held things up further by saying a long, rambling blessing over the group. Brother Gerhardt, Sister Marie-Pilar, and I all crossed ourselves, accepting whatever blessings we could get, even if they weren't meant for us. Nahida sat, comfortable on the horse but twitchy among so many Christians.

Finally, with a shout and the crack of a whip, the crowd ahead of us, perhaps fifty people strong, moved out. We were headed north to Tyre, Count Raymond, and who else knew what beyond that.

I was ten—silence and slowness were the two things I hated more than anything in the world. We moved like mute tortoises, and it left me plenty of time to make myself crazy playing "what if…"

What if Raymond isn't there when we get to Tyre?

What if nobody will accept Sister?

What if nobody accepts any of us?

What if Tyre has fallen by the time we get there?

I thought of Eyebrows and Paolo ahead of us somewhere on the road. *What if we're too late?*

All along the road were bands of Saracen soldiers. Salah-adin had promised safe passage to everyone who left, and these ragtag groups of six or eight soldiers every mile or so were posted to ensure that the refugees had no trouble—at least from his army. But just because they were there to keep us from harm, didn't mean they wished us well.

One group—mostly Egyptian Mamelukes from the looks of them—yelled obscenities at us from the moment they spotted us to the time we passed them, stiff-backed and mute. The curses stopped briefly when they saw Sister Marie-Pilar. Then they realized her veil didn't mean she was a good Mohammedan but a Christian, and the vile name-calling started again. I loved hearing people curse, and the more inventive the better, but this was too much even for me.

I whirled around with a really good insult loaded on my tongue (having never known my own mother, I had no qualms about insulting others'), but a huge hand gripped my shoulder. "Our Lord suffered worse abuse. Ignore them."

I wasn't Jesus. Still, shutting my infernal hole seemed the wisest course. It didn't mean my cheeks didn't burn with shame, and the flames grew hotter when Nahida yelled back something about one of their fathers and a donkey. That started another barrage of filthy insults. Hands moved to weapons and only the rough bark of a senior soldier—whatever they called their sergeants—restored order. That girl had more guts than I did. If less common sense.

We trudged a mile or more as the sun shuffled further west. I was surprised to learn that the Coast Road didn't just follow the seashore along the beach in a straight line but climbed slowly until it hugged a series of low hills. It hadn't occurred to me that we would have to walk uphill at all. I was pondering what that meant for my poor feet when we turned a bend and I saw a sight unlike anything I'd imagined.

The Middle Sea stretched out ahead and below us. There was just…so much of it. Growing up in a port city I'd been around water all my life but always saw it from its own level. When people talked about "over the sea" I had no idea how far that might be. Now I saw a huge silver mirror laid out with Acre behind us, but only a small piece of the coastline visible. On the clearest day from the highest roof, I could see quite some way out, but here it was just water, water, and still more water before it dissolved into a white line that formed a floor for the blue, cloudless sky that stretched even further.

Ahead of us and on the other side, hills loomed even larger than before, and even though we were up high, we still hadn't reached the base of some of them. The world was a much bigger—and emptier—place than I'd ever imagined.

Distracted by these thoughts, I forgot I was supposed to set the pace and moved too quickly. We gained on the slowest members of the caravan; whether we wanted to join them or not, it was happening. They were far too slow and too many; even at our snail's pace we were catching and passing some of them.

Maybe they wouldn't mind so much? After all, we were all in the same predicament, and we had our own supplies. They might even welcome us. Who wouldn't welcome a Hospitaller knight for physical protection, a nun for spiritual help, and me for…whatever they needed? I was willing to earn my keep. Nahida would be a problem, but she wasn't my problem.

Ahead of us, another road led off to the right, although I couldn't see where it led. It was just an empty grey scar leading north and east and skyward until it disappeared between two very large mountains. I tried to imagine what horrors lay that way, and how glad I was not to be going there. Then we came to a sharp turn in the road.

The caravan master and half a dozen even less reputable-looking men blocked the road. They held camel whips and had daggers or other blades on their belts. The black-bearded man held his hand out. "Stop right there, Sir Knight."

For a moment, I was relieved. He wasn't talking to us. Then I realized he meant Gerhardt. The giant took a calm step forward until he was even with me. "Is there a problem, sir? Ve're just trying to get to Tyre, same as everyone else."

The Master drew himself up as tall as he could. "Aye, the problem is that we can't share the road with you lot."

As the leader, I know I should have said something, but Brother Gerhardt seemed to have a better negotiating position, being both a knight and an adult, not to mention being the size of two normal men. I took a shy step backward, letting him handle things.

"Und vhy not?" he asked.

"We'd be glad of you, Brother. Even the boys." (He thought Nahida was a boy. Good thing she couldn't understand a word anyone said.) "The problem is *her*." A rough, sausage-sized finger pointed to Sister Marie-Pilar. "There's already talk of plague in Tyre, we don't need to bring pestilence with us. You think we don't know who she is? If you want to risk getting the rot, that's your business, but I'll not have it near me or my charges."

Nahida hissed in Arabic, "What's going on?"

I winced. Why couldn't she keep that mouth shut? The ruffians with the caravan master were probably under orders not to kill anyone so early in the journey. One, in particular, looked like he wasn't happy with that command. He grabbed a knife from his belt and brandished it in front of him. "A God-cursed heathen, too…" He squinted at me. "Maybe two of them. Plus, a leper bitch. That's some strange company you travel with, Sir Knight."

Nahida just couldn't let well enough alone. "What's their problem, why aren't we moving?"

I spoke out of the side of my mouth: "They won't let us travel with them because they think you're a Saracen. And because Sister Marie-Pilar has leprosy." Nahida did two things simultaneously. One, she shut up. Secondly, her arms flew open, and she jumped down from behind Sister to the ground, rubbing her sleeves as if scrubbing them, muttering a lot of unladylike things that only I understood. Sister lowered her head and worked her rosary, the beads clicking as she prayed under her breath.

My impatience got the better of me. I balled my fists and took a step ahead of Brother Gerhardt. "And what are we to do then? We must get to Tyre. It's a matter of great importance. I carry vital messages for Count Raymond."

That drew belly laughs from the men. The leader was not amused at my tone. "Watch your mouth, boy. Around this next bend there's another road. It leads through the mountains, but you can catch the other road to Tyre from there. It will take you longer, but you won't be a problem for anyone else."

He meant the scary, deserted road leading into the wilderness. I imagined us—me—on it. Sometimes cowardice requires a brave mask. I strode forward with my chin up, hoping to look authoritative, rather than ready to pee myself. "But we have important business. Honestly, sir, we won't be any trouble."

"No, you won't. Because you won't be anywhere near us." He gestured with his fur-covered chin to the left. "Take that road, go back to Acre, or go straight to hell, but it will go ill with you if we find you anywhere near us or those we're paid to protect. Understood?" He didn't say another word but motioned for the others to rejoin the crowd. His men backed up without turning their backs on us.

I gulped and asked Brother Gerhardt, "Do you know that road?"

He mopped his brow and nodded. "I know it, ja. It vill be very hard."

"But we can make it, can't we?"

The reply was longer coming than I'd have liked. "If God vills it, of course." *Inshallah* didn't sound any more comforting in French than in Arabic. "It's your decision, Lucca."

It might have been my decision, but it wasn't my choice. From behind me, I heard a sniff and a wavering voice. "Lucca, I'm so sorry. Leave me here and…"

"No, it's fine. We're not wanted, we'll take the long way. After all, God's on our side, right?" Sister smiled and wiped her eyes. She believed that more than me, but she had more sway with Him than I did.

The caravan master nodded. "God bless you. Good luck." Then he turned, hustling to catch up with his workmen. He let out a sharp whistle and waved his whip in the air. "What the hell are you waiting for? Go! Get!

The impatient throng behind us complained and pushed us further to the side of the road so they could pass. We gave them a moment, then fell in at a safe distance behind, keeping space between us and the folks ahead and behind. Nahida, avoiding eye contact with Sister, took the pack horse's reins from Gerhardt and walked beside us, rather than share a leper's mount. She patted and cooed to the horse, but she'd stopped singing.

Half a silent mile passed, and the road forked. I paused, but Gerhardt and Nahida kept to the right, heading north and east up the winding path, away from our destination. Since I was supposed to be in charge, I said a terrible word and dragged Droopy forward until I was back in the lead.

The trail got very steep very quickly. Our three-horse caravan continued, but much slower than before. At the top of the first crest, I could see for miles in all directions. The coastal road to Tyre was black with people who would make it to sanctuary long before us.

Among the throng were Eyebrows and Big Paolo. They'd get there long before we did. The scroll for Count Raymond burned like a hot coal inside my sleeve. Hopefully, we wouldn't be too late for Count Raymond.

Chapter 11

For the first few minutes, we trudged uphill in silence. Then I couldn't take it anymore. "Have you been through these mountains before?" I asked Brother Gerhardt. He nodded and wiped an arm across his forehead. His face was bright red, and I feared he'd burst into flame right there.

"Ja, I have. Once. It's farther but the road is passable and vide. Some small farms, but no real villages. Ve'll spend four, maybe five nights out here." That wasn't great news; we'd only packed supplies for three nights and three people.

"What about water?" After what happened at Hattin, I was painfully aware of what could happen if you didn't have enough on an expedition. Besides, it sounded like the kind of question a leader should ask, even if I didn't know what to do with the answer, which I didn't.

Brother Gerhardt smiled, "See? That's a good question. There's plenty of water. Don't worry." I tried to look reassured. It hadn't rained since before last Epiphany—nine months or more ago. The only time I had ever been outside Acre's walls was a straight trip across the plain to the Jordan River—as dusty and arid a place as I could imagine. Here in the hills above Acre, it was different though. The higher we climbed, the more remnants of life remained. Low brush sported grey-green leaves. Tall cedars loomed on either side of the road where they sometimes blocked out the sun, offering sweet-smelling shade and even a momentary cool breeze. As nervous as I was in such strange surroundings, this felt almost…not horrible. Of course, the last time I left Acre it wasn't under my own power, and that made a considerable difference.

Up ahead, a flock of sheep grazed on the steep hillside, and a toothless old man in a *keffiyeh* and Syrian robe squatted by the side of the road, singing to himself.

I heard rustling behind me. Nahida pulled a long piece of white cloth out of her tunic and placed it over her head in a simple hijab. It was just plain cotton, but suddenly she looked more like a girl than she ever had. And older. Sister Marie-Pilar looked askance at her, thinking she looked for all the world like an extremely sun-tanned novice.

"Why must she wear that…thing?" She asked quietly, as if she feared Nahida would turn and slit her throat.

It was a good question. In Arabic, I asked, "What are you doing? I thought you Druze weren't Muhammadans?"

In that tone girls use to make boys sound stupid, she said," We wear head coverings for modesty, but also to not draw attention to ourselves."

"So why put it on now?"

"Because out here, Christians aren't the ones I'm afraid of. Why does she," she said, meaning Sister, "wear a veil like a Believer?"

"That's to hide her…sickness. It's in her mouth and nose." I gestured and Nahida shivered. Sister sat taller and clung to the horse's mane with a little more dignity. Even though she couldn't understand a word, she had no doubt about the focus of the conversation.

"Is she your auntie? Is that why you're taking care of her?"

"No, she's a…a nun." I could tell by Nahida's eyebrows she didn't recognize the word. "She's *almar'at almuqadasa*—a holy woman." Then I remembered, "Actually, more like a *mumarada.*" Nurse was a better word.

In French, Sister was snippy, "It seems rude to talk about people when you know they can't understand you." I turned to Gerhardt.

"Do you speak Arabic?"

He chuckled and shook his head. "Not enough to save you from this. My job is to kill infidels, I've not had much chance to carry on a conversation." Terrific, not only did I get to hear my friends pick at each other, I got to say it all twice with absolutely no help.

We were close enough to the shepherd to hear what he was singing to his sheep. He stiffened a bit and squinted hard at Gerhardt but offered a friendly-enough salaam. The giant knight touched his fingers to his heart and attempted a polite greeting. He was right, he didn't speak Arabic.

The knight leaned in and whispered in my ear. "Ask him if the road ahead is safe."

I put on my most harmless street urchin face and showed way too many teeth. "*Salaam alaikum.* Good afternoon, Uncle."

He greeted me back. Then we stared at each other for a moment. I needed to say something. "Is the road ahead safe?"

He shook his head. "You have some interesting friends, my young friend. Where are you going?"

"Tyre."

"You should be going down, not up." I knew that, but adults always said obvious, unhelpful things so I didn't let it bother me.

"Please uncle, we're in a hurry. Is the road ahead safe?"

My heart dropped as his smile disappeared. "I'm afraid not."

"Are there a lot of soldiers, then?" I ignored Sister's demands for a translation.

"That's not the problem," the old man said. "There aren't enough of them. People would be safe if there were. Salah-adin, peace be upon him, is not yet the emir here. Not really."

That surprised me. We'd been led to believe Salah-adin had conquered everything from Egypt to Antioch. The old man continued, "And the Firangi haven't been any help like they used to be. Bandits run wild. Nobody's safe these days."

From behind me, Nahida squeaked, "Bandits? We can't go this way. We have to go back." I had seen her fight a fat Genoan with her bare fists and she'd never been so obviously frightened. Sister tried to shush her, but telling a girl to calm down seldom works, and doing it in a strange language is even less effective than usual.

"Hush up and let me ask him. Where are the bandits, sir?"

"Through the pass near Jebayyan. Maybe two days' walk. A good day's ride. One Firangi knight won't scare them off, boy—even one as big as a house." He shaded his eyes and squinted, attempting to make any sense of my traveling companions. "Especially with women along."

My brain was exploding with problems that had no solution.

We couldn't go back to Acre.

We had to get to Tyre.

We couldn't take the Coast Road.

We'd probably get killed—or worse—if we continued this way. And the trouble I was supposed to prevent would arrive days before we did.

With everyone staring, waiting for some kind of decision, the best I could do was "Uhhh…"

"We can't go that way. The bandits will kill us." Nahida was beyond terrified.

"We can't go back, Lucca. The infidels will kill us." Sister wasn't wrong.

"If God vants us in Tyre, ve'll get there, boy." I looked at the long sword strapped to the pony, and would have felt a lot better had it been strapped to Gerhardt's waist. "His vill be done."

God didn't indicate a preference but Droopy did. The big dummy nuzzled my shoulder and tried to take a small chunk of my flesh with his big square teeth. He did that whenever he was tired of my foolishness. Still, he hadn't steered me wrong yet. I thanked the old man. "*Shukraan jazilaan*—Peace be upon you, Uncle."

He nodded grimly. "And you. And your…family." Is that what we were?

Droopy almost pulled my arm out of its socket,

determined as he was to get moving. He seemed to believe forward was better than not moving at all. I knew how he felt.

Along the way, the world just continued to expand. Birds I'd never heard before sang wildly. Insects buzzed, clicked, and chased each other from one side of the narrow trail to the other.

At long last we stopped to eat and nap in a shady cedar glade. Sister immediately found a dark, covered space and knelt to pray. Her mumbles and clacking beads were quickly drowned out by the buzzing gossip of the insects and chattering birds. I'd never seen trees so tall or green, and their flat needles and tiny pine cones fascinated me, although they left my fingers sticky with resin when I picked them off the ground, and it tasted terrible when I tried to lick them clean. Nahida tried, unsuccessfully, to stifle a laugh.

"Don't eat it, you idiot. You'll make yourself sick."

I stuck my tongue out at her. "What are they?"

"The cedars of Lebanon. Aren't they beautiful?"

"They're so big. I've never seen trees so tall." I took a lick of the spiny brown cones that littered the ground. "But this fruit is awful."

Nahida waved me over to where she stood, a pace and a half from a steep drop. "They grow even bigger near Beirut. Come here."

I took a few tentative steps closer to her, but my heart pounded in my ears and breath caught in my lungs. The last time I'd been on the edge of a cliff this high, someone died. To be sure, he was an evil man, but I couldn't shake the image of that fat body falling, and the black, shapeless spot in the sand where he landed. I inched as close as I dared and followed her hand with my eyes.

From up here we could see for miles. Behind us lay the way we'd come, a grey-brown line, thinning and tapering to a point where it disappeared into the green rolling hills. Ahead were more mountaintops than I could count. One after the other, each appeared taller and more intimidating than the next.

To the east, a steeply slanting grey wall of stone and brush reached to the blue sky, blocking any hint of what lay beyond. The really impressive vista was to the west. From our height, the hills rolled out and down—an undulating carpet of green ending in a pewter expanse that faded into the white-blue of the sky. I stretched my arms out, but my fingertips couldn't encompass all that water. It went on and on for miles. A silvery line of what might be grey clouds lay inconceivably far off to the west.

"It's so big."

I didn't think I'd spoken out loud, but Brother Gerhardt loomed over my shoulder, "Ja, the world is a big place, Lucca. Bigger than Acre, isn't it?"

It was too big. There was just…so much of it. I looked to the left, but couldn't see any sign of the city we'd left. Up the coast, there was nothing that looked like Tyre. After all that walking today, we were precisely nowhere, with four days or so of more nothing before we reached our destination.

"Where is your village from here?" I asked Nahida.

She pointed up the coast. "Beirut is five or six days travel past Tyre by caravan up the Coast Road. We're close by, but in Tripoli. That's how my father knows *Effendi* Raymo." Ten days? Could you even walk that far and not fall off the edge of the world?

I tried to imagine how much further Rome, the home of the Pope, must be but couldn't begin to imagine it. "Where is your home, Brother? Can you see it from here?"

"I'm a brother of the Hospital, my home is everywhere people travel to Jerusalem and need protection. But where I was born? If you walked that way long enough," he pointed a little more west than Nahida had, "you might get there. In a year or more."

A year? Impossible. "What's it called, where you're from?"

After ensuring the horses were secure near a patch of tall green weeds, the big man plunked himself down and took a long drink of water from a skin. "Swabia. A little village called Albstedt. The mountains are even bigger than this." I'd heard of Swabia, but only because many of the Teutonic Knights came from there.

"Why did you join the Hospital, instead of the German Knights?"

He smiled. "Ever hear any stories of Our Lord walking the streets of Livonia or Sudovia?" I shook my head. "Neither had I, but that's where most of the Sword Brothers are fighting. I wanted to see Jerusalem and help others do the same. Plus, it's far too cold there. A man can't fight in the snow." His face was sunburnt, and his blond hair was matted to his cheeks and neck. The bald skin of his tonsure was even redder than his face. If he worried about the cold, the heat wasn't doing him any good either.

"Anjou." Sister Marie-Pilar's voice piped up from behind us. She came closer as she spoke. "I was born in Anjou." She put pointed north but further west than Gerhardt. "Only I came by boat, not on foot. Still, it took weeks across stormy seas. I feared I'd fall overboard and drown." The little nun sat beside me and offered a bag of dates and dried fruit. "Don't eat too much, now."

Nahida had been sitting off by herself, nibbling on some of the dried food crumbs in her pocket. Sister waved her over. "Come here, child. Would you like some?" She held the bag out and Nahida shook her head timidly.

In Arabic, I told her "It's good, and you'll have to share our food sometime. It's safe. Look." I grabbed a plump raisin and shoved it in my mouth. Nahida scrunched her eyes at me like I was crazy, but eventually came toward us, like a street cur that had been kicked too often. She kept Gerhardt between herself and Sister, stretching out a long, bony hand. Sister Marie-Pilar dumped some dried fruit slices in her palm without touching the food or Nahida herself.

"Mair-see," Nahida said, in a comical attempt at French.

"Lucca, how do you say *you're welcome* in her tongue?" I told her, and she mangled "*Ahlan wa sahlan.*" Nahida looked confused until I repeated it. Then she smiled and nodded. This was a promising start, at least.

Gerhardt stood and dusted himself off. "Ve'd better get going. Night comes early up in these mountains. Ve'll need a place to sleep."

I didn't have any idea how nightfall could come earlier in one place than another, but I nodded anyway. "Let's go then." I walked over to Droopy, who somehow had unwrapped his reins from around the bush and wandered over to the greenest, choicest grass. "Come on, you silly thing." He nuzzled me in the chest until I petted his soft, fuzzy nose. He gave me a happy little *chuff.* "Nahida, why don't you ride Droopy? He likes you. Better than he likes me, even." She didn't even hesitate or offer to let me ride before settling comfortably aboard the pony.

A metallic jangling from up the road drew our attention. There were four Saracen soldiers in light mail and pointy helmets riding light-colored ponies. They shouted a warning when they saw Gerhardt, and stopped, lances pointed at us. Then their leader looked at me, and at Nahida. He and Brother Gerhardt glared at each other for a moment. If I'd stepped between their eyes, I might have burst into flame, but neither said a word for several long moments. Then the leader nodded. "You're lucky, Christian. The Emir is a man of his word. No one will harm you."

I translated for Gerhardt, who nodded and offered a polite salaam. "Go vith God, sir." Then he gestured for me to pass the message on, which I did with as big and innocent a smile as I could manage through chattering teeth. I added a quick "thank you," just for good measure.

The greeting accepted, their leader gestured the soldiers forward with his head and not so much as a look back. As they trotted away, I heard several words over the sounds of hooves on dirt, including "idiots," "damned infidels" and "dead, anyway."

That confrontation may not have been friendly, but it wasn't overtly hostile, and set the tone for the rest of the afternoon. Chilly politeness from the few soldiers we met—which meant they would not be a problem—and stunned silence from the few farmers, children, and women we passed.

Brother Gerhardt was right about one thing. The shadows quickly lengthened, and the breeze grew cooler. We found a slowly trickling stream, only the second running water I'd ever seen in my life, besides the river Jordan. Even in the midst of a drought, there was still water in this land. The stream ran beside the long-cold ashes of a shepherd's fire heaped in a circle of stones. Gerhardt bent over and cupped his hand in the water, lifting it to his lips and smacking them contentedly. He filled his water skin and gestured for us to do the same, which we did. Squinting at me he asked, "How does this look for a place to sleep tonight?"

Like a sure place to get killed or eaten by bears or carried off by ghosts or even demons. I nodded wearily and said, "Good. It looks good." He agreed with my sage assessment.

Just as I plunked down on the ground, thinking that cedar needles would make a fine bed, he shook his head. "Ve'll need firewood."

It took me a moment to realize he was talking to me. What did I know about making a fire, or what wood was right? I picked up a dead tree branch, holding it out to him. The branch turned out to be full of ants, who immediately left their home to run up and down my arm. I screamed like a girl and slapped myself silly trying to get rid of them.

This made the only girl in the group laugh hysterically at my plight until she snorted. She bent and gathered up twigs and small, dry limbs, cradling them in her elbow. "You need dry wood and little branches to start a fire. Don't you know anything?"

I bit my tongue and followed her cue to gather a pathetic bundle of my own. We presented them to Gerhardt, who took a firebox from his bag and with two strikes of flint against steel started a small, smoky excuse for a fire. Once more, I targeted a nice soft piece of ground, and again he stopped me.

"I'm going to do guard duty tonight, but I'll need a nap first. You have first vatch, Lucca. Let me know if anyone comes near, or you hear anything out of the ordinary. Ja?"

I nodded bravely, but what was I watching for? Normal was a city's walls and people crowded together on top of each other. Normal was the bellowing of animals and the shouts of angry merchants. There was nothing routine about quiet, gigantic clouds of insects, and too much sky.

The doubts caroming around in my head were quickly drowned out by the loud, droning snore of the Hospitaller. Brother Gerhardt had thrown himself down in the very spot I'd chosen for myself and was already dead asleep.

I took a few tentative marching steps one way, then back the other, trying to look like a guardsman. I didn't realize how exhausted I was, nor how hungry. I didn't know exactly what I was on guard against, but I did know one thing—I needed to pee.

I turned away, preparing to do what God made it so easy for young boys to do, then realized I was in full view of Sister and Nahida. "I'll walk around a bit and check things out," I said importantly. Sister nodded, while Nahida just giggled.

"Don't pee in the stream. People drink that water."

"I know that. What do you think I am?" A little annoyed that she'd spoiled my plans, I pushed past a bush and disappeared from their view long enough to do what I needed to do. I wreaked havoc on some ants by knocking them off a branch with my stream, which was fun. Relieved, I squatted on top of a tall rock, where I could see the campsite, the road, and nothing else but trees and rocks. I slipped the knife from my sleeve and clutched it in my hand, blade pointed sensibly towards the road and any possible danger.

It was my first sentry duty, and I was determined to take it seriously. "I'm on guard, like a real soldier. I'm in charge". The late afternoon sun was still warm and pleasant, and the tight feeling in my stomach and neck began to ease. My eyes got heavy, and there didn't seem to be anyone or anything other than us in the world.

The next thing I knew, Gerhardt was roughly shaking me awake. "Vat are you doing? You're supposed to be keeping vatch?"

I tried to babble a lame excuse, but his eyes blazed with righteous anger. He bent to the ground, picked up the dagger that had fallen from my grip, and held it out to me accusingly.

"Do you know vat happens ven soldiers fall asleep on

vatch? They are executed for neglecting their duty. Especially ven they lose their veapon. Every man in your troop depends on you to keep him alive. You cannot fail your fellows. Never fall asleep on duty, boy."

I tried to babble an excuse. "I wasn't sleeping, honest. I listen better when my eyes are closed." My defense sounded stupid and shameful to my own ears.

"In that case, you also listen better ven you drool. Vipe your mouth and go to bed."

I slunk back to the fire and passed out, too tired even for nightmares.

Chapter 12

I woke up shivering. In part it was the mountain air, much colder than in the city. The other problem was my dreams had found me, even in the wilderness. Again, Brother Idoneus and Al Sameen popped out of the darkness, accusing me of murder and betrayal. They added deserting my duty and probably getting everyone killed on my watch to their list of my crimes. One, then the other, then both together. I finally woke when the fat spy asked how long it would be before my companions joined them in the dark. Oh, and he wanted his horse back. I wondered if Droopy dreamed about his former master.

It was still dark, although the eastern mountains showed the slightest hemline of light blue, and the stars shone brightest over the sea to the west. Sister Marie-Pilar was a blanket-covered ball snuggled next to the smoking embers of our campfire. Nahida had found warmth snuggled next to my pony. I wished I'd thought of that. Instead, I stood rubbing my arms for heat and jogging in place.

After a mouthful of water, I walked up the trail to the rock where I'd sat watch—or should have. My heart sped up when I didn't see Brother Gerhardt. He should have been standing guard, and I felt the panic swell. If he wasn't watching over us, who was? What if something had happened to him. It would be up to me, and I was obviously useless.

"Come to relieve me, boy?" I hadn't heard him approach and I let out a little shriek. The giant chuckled. "Everyone falls asleep on guard duty sometime. Most don't do it on their first night, and seldom as quickly. Ve can forgive the first offense, but no more, ja? They hang sentries who don't do their job." He looked fresh and alert, although the slightest yawn escaped the corner of his mouth.

"I'll take over. You should get some more sleep." I hoped I sounded like a soldier. He nodded at my new-found sense of duty.

"It's about another hour until dawn. Ven you see about half the sun over those hills, come get me. Not a minute earlier."

"Yes, Brother." Between the cold and my shame, there was no danger of going back to sleep. I perched on the rock with my knees pulled up to my chin. Brother Gerhardt walked down the road to the camp, and I heard him long after I couldn't see him anymore. The few sounds I could detect hung and resonated in the predawn stillness—Droopy puffing, a lone bird in a cedar. My own breath was the loudest thing out there. That was no comfort because we couldn't possibly be alone in the world.

After who knows how long squinting one direction, then another, and seeing nothing, I heard the skitter of pebbles and the shuffling of bare feet on the dirt trail. I jumped to my feet, knife in hand, but it was only Nahida approaching, scratching her armpit and yawning so her whole face almost disappeared.

"You couldn't sleep either?" I asked. She shook her head.

"My stomach hurts too much." She ran a hand over her tummy. "How long have you been out here?"

"A while, now. I let Brother Gerhardt get some sleep." It was true enough.

Nahida climbed on the rock next to me. She smelt like Droopy and smoke. She and I said nothing together for a long time. We sat listening to the birds and insects compete to see who could be the first to wake the rest of the world.

"Don't you love the mountains?" she finally asked me, more out of boredom than for my opinion.

"They're awfully big, and there are no people." I'd lived all my life within (sometimes literal) spitting distance of twenty thousand people. I knew the rhythms of the city, its smells, and noises. I knew nothing here, except that it was cold, and we were all alone at the mercy of bandits and bears and God alone could imagine what else.

"That's what I like about them. Cities stink, and there are too many people."

"What was your home like?" I asked.

"We live on a horse farm in the mountains of Tripoli just beyond Beirut. I could go out all day and not see anyone until dinner time."

I couldn't imagine anything more opposite to my own experience. I hated horses and craved the company of people. "But you must have lived with someone. Do you have brothers or sisters?"

"No, it was just my parents and me. I had a whole pack of cousins down the road—six or seven of them. They were horrid. Most of them are boys and not very educated. They couldn't even write their own names."

It was still dark enough that she couldn't see me blush. "Can you? I thought …girls weren't educated."

She sat up proudly. "We *Druzeh* believe everyone should better themselves. Many of our women can read and write. My mother even has her own property. That's why I'm going back. If I don't claim what's mine, my aunt and uncle and all those cousins will."

I knew the next question to ask. Some people loved to tell the tale, others would refuse to say anything at all. As an orphan myself, I never minded talking about my parents, not that there was much to say. I always made up half the story anyway. "What happened—to your parents?"

She took a ragged breath. "We were on our way to Metula with four prize horses. Normally, Mother and I stayed home, but Father wanted to visit his brother in Al Zabadani afterward, and asked us to join him."

"Why would he take women with him on such a dangerous trip?" I was having a hard time believing anyone—especially a girl—would want to leave home voluntarily. And wasn't it a man's job to protect his women?

"We weren't worried. Count Raymond and Salah-adin had declared a truce. He treated us well. Christian solders kept the roads in Tripoli safe. Once out of his territory, we should have been protected by the Saracens, even though they hate us. They are counting on us siding with them against the Firangi. But there were bandits…"

For a moment, I thought that was as far as she'd go. I almost hoped it was; I'd reached my limit on bloody adventure stories. But she took a deep breath, nodded to herself, and told me the rest.

"We should have taken the Coast Road, but it was very crowded and so hot. It was cooler in the mountains, and we could make better time traveling with a few others families in a caravan, Father said. We didn't know the bandits were waiting. They attacked in the middle of the night." Nahida's eyes focused far ahead of her. Although it was becoming light, it wasn't this mountain trail she saw.

"At first, it was just screaming, and nobody knew what was happening. Father and the other men ran out to see and…they died. I heard them. It was awful… Mother and the other women…" She hugged herself tightly, rocking as she told her story. "The other women tried to fight them off. Mother and I ran as fast as we could. We hid behind some rocks. I couldn't see what was happening, but we heard…everything. The bandits were laughing, and the horses were screaming and carrying on. I knew they were stealing them. Then the women started screaming, and those men were laughing even more. I wanted to help them, but mother said it was too late, and that the bandits would do the same to us if they found us. She told me they wouldn't treat us as believers. The animals believed Allah would smile on them for raping and killing heretics."

As she told her tale, Nahida ran bony fingers through her hair. "Momma said I should try to look like a boy. That they wouldn't…touch me…if I was a boy. They'd just capture me and make me a slave. So she took a knife and cut my hair off." She sniffed loudly and wiped her nose. Again she played with her spiky hair, running her fingers through it faster now, and scratching at her scalp. "They all used to make fun of me because I was so skinny and looked like a boy anyway. I'm older than I told you—a bit, anyway. I look… I used to have such…long…pretty hair." She looked at me and her eyes brimmed with tears. "I used to be pretty when I had my beautiful long hair…" She began sobbing, her whole body shaking as she hid her face in her hands. She stopped crying only long enough to take desperate gulps of air.

I squirmed, useless and uncomfortable. I understood crying for her parents, but I'd never seen anyone cry like that over hair. I wondered again how I could ever make sense of women. Watching her, I almost started crying myself, which wouldn't do. Yet as incomprehensible as she was to me, she was in pain and I should do something. I offered a tentative hug, which she rebuffed, pushing me away and jumping to her feet.

She shook her head, clenched her fists and shouted, more at her own feet than at me. "No, I'm strong. I'm going to get home, and I will take over my father's farm, and my cousins are going to work for me, and I'll never have to go to a city again. Not with Christians or Muslims or…anybody."

It wasn't me she was trying to convince, but I believed her. At least a little. I tried to imagine what she'd gone through—that she had to hide who she was, and what she was, just to stay alive.

I knew another thing, but I didn't tell her. Being a boy might not have saved her from…that. Unbidden, Brother Idoneus' angry, red, scarred face flashed across my mind.

"Get me as far as Tyre, Lucca. I'll get home on my own after that."

"I will, I promise." What else could I say? I noticed she still rubbed her stomach. "Let's get you something to eat. You'll feel better." Nothing made me feel better than a full stomach. It was worth a try.

The sun was long past Gerhardt's marker, and long morning shadows stretched downhill towards the distant sea. As we trudged back to our poor excuse for a camp, I caught the slightest glint of the sea between cedar branches. Far away the grey line of clouds was the only limit to the world and the only change in a hot blue sky that stretched forever in all directions.

It was all too big. Or I was too small.

Back at the camp, Sister Marie-Pilar knelt in a corner, working her rosary and muttering to herself—and God and His Mother, I supposed. I crossed myself out of habit and just in case. Gerhardt was awake, of course, since the sun was long up. He looked at me, then glanced at the sun, then back at me with one eyebrow raised. He didn't say a word. I was making a terrible mess of the whole guard duty thing. Utterly useless as a soldier.

Droopy had wandered to the far edge of the camp and tugged on tufts of dried grass. Gerhard's grey warhorse was already loaded and looking bored, while the black pack pony raked the dusty ground with one hoof, snorting unhappily.

I wouldn't have gone near a cranky horse for all the gold in Jerusalem, but Nahida walked over, shoosh-shooshing her and holding out her hand. Slowly, she bent down and lifted the front right hoof, taking a firm grip as the horse tried to pull away. She rubbed the hoof, sending up a cloud of dust and dried clay until she could see what lay underneath all the caked-on mud and horse poop and filth.

Brother Gerhardt and Sister watched her as well. The girl picked at something with her thumb, then asked, "Do you have a knife?" Before I could pull mine, Gerhardt handed her a beautiful dagger, worn with use but razor sharp, with a Hospital cross etched into the hilt. Nahida hesitated just a moment before taking it. She used the tip to pry a small pebble out of a crack in the horse's cracked hoof. The animal tried to pull away; but she held tightly, and continued making soothing noises until the animal stopped squirming. Then she allowed the hoof to drop and waited while the animal took a few tentative steps.

"Her hooves are in terrible shape," Nahida told me out of the corner of her mouth, smiling at Brother Gerhardt all the while.

"Vat did she say?" Gerhardt asked.

"She says the horse's hooves don't look good. She's trying to be polite."

Brother Gerhardt nodded. "Ja, you didn't think they'd let me take one of the healthy horses, did you? Ve need to make do. But she knows vat she's doing. Thank her for me. And tell her good job."

While I pretended to understand the details of what the

young girl and the knight were talking about, Sister Marie-Pilar brought over some dried meat and fruit. I eagerly grabbed a handful, for which I got a smack on the hands, so I offered some to Nahida. She shook her head, gesturing that her stomach still wasn't right. Sister knitted her eyebrows together over her veil. She gestured that the girl should eat anyway, and Nahida took a reluctant, dutiful bite. At least everyone was getting along this morning.

We set out again, climbing until the back of my legs ached. To our right, the sun struggled to climb over the mountains, but the sky behind it was blue and clear. As my eyes followed our shadows to the left, the western sky was mostly clear, with just a thin line of grey marking the horizon. The breeze was cooler than yesterday, which did wonders for everyone's mood, especially the horses'.

We made good time without seeing anyone else on the road, which was either good or bad news. I wasn't sure which. We passed the occasional hovel, usually with a few scraggly fruit trees around it and a yard full of chickens. We even passed a five- or six-hut hamlet just before noon, but it was deserted.

After our lunch rest, we descended into a valley, and I saw the most tantalizing sight. Off to the right was an orchard with oranges dangling from branches. Despite the drought, a man-made ditch sparkled, winding its way between more trees than I'd ever seen. In Acre, rich people might have a tree in their courtyard or garden, but so many in one place was more than my eyes could absorb. All those oranges just dangled there, practically begging for someone to pick them.

I grinned at Nahida.

"Want some oranges?"

She shook her head. "No, Lucca. That's stealing." Well, yes, it was. But there were so many trees, and while the oranges were a little shriveled and sad-looking, I'd never seen anything in my life so tempting.

"It's also fun. Come on, don't you want an orange? It might help settle your stomach." I ran off the trail into the orchard and looked around, overcome by so much bounty just sitting in the open.

Sister shouted over, "Lucca, that's not right. Those don't belong to you." True enough, but I couldn't see whoever they belonged to, and there were so many. Surely they wouldn't miss only a couple.

Examining the tree in front of me, I saw a couple of relatively healthy-looking orange treasures hanging about the height of a rooftop in Acre. The tree's bark looked rough and it left a nasty scrape mark when I brushed against it, but that wasn't going slow me any. I was good at two things in life: stealing and climbing. This allowed me to do both, and I wasn't about to be deterred.

I grabbed a thick branch and pulled myself up so I hung over it, the top half of my body on one side of the limb, my legs hanging over the other. I positioned myself so I stood on the branch and took a tentative sliding step forward. The branch swayed a little but held. Straight ahead of me were the two prizes, perfect—well, slightly spotty but oh-so tempting—globes capped by dark leaves like a little hat

It took a stronger tug than I expected to pull the fruit free, and I nearly lost my balance. That brought a gasp from Sister and a loud laugh from Nahida. I caught my balance in time, dropped the orange to the ground, and grabbed the next one.

It was warm, even with a breeze making the leaves shake all around me, and my cheeks burned pleasantly. I also felt a tingle through my feet and legs running up my spine. It occurred to me I was having fun. When was the last time I really enjoyed myself? I let the feeling take control and indulged myself. Grabbing a branch above me, I swung up to where three or four relatively healthy oranges hung. I shouted at the top of my lungs. "Nahida, come on. Help me."

The girl hesitated, as they always do when there's fun to be had, then ran over to the base of the tree and shouted up, "Throw them down, I'll get them."

"No, come on up. It's fun. See?" I demonstrated the bounciness of a limb by jumping up and down. I could tell by the size her eyes got she didn't find it as amusing as I did. I shook a fragile-looking branch, and two oranges almost brained her.

"Hey, watch it," she shouted, but her smile was louder than her complaining. I continued clambering around the branches, knocking fruit loose when I could. Sure, some dried or rotten oranges fell, but we also got an armful of healthy ones. We gathered enough to have one a day for the rest of our trip. Nahida picked each of them off the ground and made a basket out of her tunic.

"Enough, ve have to keep moving," Gerhardt shouted from the trail. I waved to him and looked down, momentarily worried I may have climbed too high. As I bent down to plot the best path to the ground, something whizzed over my head and tore leaves off the tree behind me. I hesitated, trying to figure out what it was, when a second stone just missed my skull. I looked behind me. Maybe a hundred yards away, and closing fast, were two local boys about my size. They charged at us, whirling slingshots over their heads.

Nahida ran for it, as fast as she could without dropping our treasure. I scampered down, scraping my shins and elbows raw, but my instincts found me the quickest route to the ground. I landed in the dried grass and dust, dropping to a squat. My legs pumped immediately. I heard the boys shouting and cursing, but I was faster than them and far more motivated to get out of there.

They stopped short of the trail, probably because I ran behind Brother Gerhardt, who stood with his hands on his hips, glaring at the slingshot-carrying lads. Sensibly, they halted at the sight of a giant Christian knight glowering at them. They must have been unfamiliar with David and Goliath because they turned tail and ran away.

I had to admit the big man looked awfully terrifying, except for the fact that he bit his cheek to keep from laughing. Adults did that a lot when trying not to look as amused as they really were.

Determined to show I could defend my people, I picked up a stone about the size of a pigeon's egg and chucked with all my might. It flew true and struck the oldest boy in the back. It didn't knock him over, but certainly made him increase speed.

Gerhardt grunted. "You've a fair arm and eye, boy. Ever shot a bow?" I shook my head. The very idea struck me as odd. As if someone like me could afford a bow or even know how to find one.

"No, Brother. Why?"

"Someone your size should know how to fight from a distance." I wasn't sure what he meant but stood beside him as we watched the boys retreat back into the orchard. Gerhardt made sure they were gone for good, then turned and unhobbled his horse. Without another word, he helped Sister up onto the animal's back.

She sat silent for the longest time, then she giggled. "Aren't you going to share those oranges? Greed is a terrible sin, you know." I gladly passed everyone an orange, put the rest in a sack on the pack pony, and off we went, headed north.

The breeze from the west picked up, making travel pleasant. The rest of the day passed and we made better time than expected. Nahida and I jabbered away like birds in a nest, but the adults stayed mostly silent.

Gerhardt and I took turns walking ahead of everyone else. As dinner time drew near, he was in the lead. We rounded a bend to find him standing on a rock, staring out west towards the sea. From over his shoulder, I saw the sky wasn't its usual blue but white with thin clouds. Further off to the horizon the grey line was now black and threatening.

"Ve need to find shelter for the night." He said. "Quickly."

He wasn't fooling.

The drought that had gone on for almost a year, and brought disaster to the Kingdom of Jerusalem, ended that night with a vengeance.

Chapter 13

From atop Droopy, Nahida spotted it first. "There's a shepherd's hut. Up on the hill." Calling it a hut was generous; it was a slanted thatched roof supported by two tree trunk beams and open in the front, sloping back towards the mountainside. If we squeezed, the four of us might stay out of the storm, but right now it looked like a palace.

In a civilized city like Acre, you could dash from doorway to doorway and not have to just stand there drowning while God poured bucket after bucket of cold water over your head. The ground—hard after months of baking in the sun—didn't soak up any of the flood and acted like a gutter. A growing river of water rushed over the horse's hooves, Gerhardt's boots, and my toes.

We moved as swiftly as we could. I got there first, so I dropped Droopy's reins and ducked under the roof, wiping my face and hair while Sister and Nahida were right on my tail. Brother Gerhardt stood outside, looking at me like I'd pooped on the dinner table.

I'd made some kind of mistake, but for the life of me couldn't see what I'd done wrong. "What?" I whined.

The Hospitaller shook his head. "Ve've got plenty of vork to do. Let the vimmen get dry. You and me—ve need to take care of the horses and the gear. Come on, boy." I rolled my eyes at the word "boy," then realized that's how I was acting. Being a man was more work, and a lot less fun, than I expected.

As I stepped once more into the downpour, Gerhardt handed me Droopy's reins and turned with the other two mounts towards a big cedar a few yards away. He hobbled his grey and unbuckled the pack on the pony, reaching down to check her hoof. He grunted, patting her neck and murmuring in that language I didn't understand at all but sounded like he was clearing his throat.

I tried to follow his lead, and patted Droopy, more out of duty than affection. Mimicking Brother Gerhardt's actions, I stacked my few belongings alongside the rest. Then we stretched a waxed sheet over top of the packs and tied it down with hemp cord, using two pegs and the cedar's roots.

"Keep them as comfortable as you can. You can't forget your horses—ever. It can mean the difference between life and death. And you alvays—*alvays* manage your camp before you take shelter. Understand? A man has his duty. Alvays your duty, ja?"

I made understanding-like motions with my head. "Yes, Brother. Can we go get dry now?"

"Ve? No. Me? Yes. Someone needs to stand guard, no?" My disappointment must have been scrawled all over my face because he chuckled. "Now, if it vere me, I'd find a nice branch in that tree over there, under all those leaves vhere it's dry as a house. Of course, it's not me, I'm too big…"

All that staying dry stuff was bold talk for someone

wearing a cloak, a cuirass, and a coif on his head, not to mention taking up most of the dry space under the cedar. But I got the point. He handed me a blanket and told me to make a run for it.

Gerhardt's suggestion was a good one. It was an easy climb to a comfy spot where two thick branches met to form a perfect bum-shaped saddle. Between the thick leaves and the blanket, I could stay dry and warm, or warmish. I could also see a long way in all directions, although the dense brush on the downhill side meant I only needed to watch the road. I could do that by swinging my head side to side. There'd be no falling asleep this time.

A high shriek from the hut caught me looking the wrong way, and in my shock, I tried standing up to see what the cause was, which is a bad idea when you're ten feet off the ground. I caught my balance and saw Sister screaming outside the lean-to, pointing, shrieking, and doing a crazed dance. I squinted and noticed a bunch of black dots darting everywhere. It seemed a nest of mice had claimed the hut and took it upon themselves to evict the unwanted visitors.

I laughed to see how upset the nun was by a few little rodents. They were creepy, to be sure, but almost adorable compared to the vicious rats that lurked in the corners of Acre I did. How did women ever survive without us men to eliminate life's annoyances?

I nestled back into my seat, feeling brave and manly and proud of myself for not falling asleep on duty. I scratched my nose. Then I rubbed my arm. Then I rubbed my other arm, and the first arm again. Confused, I looked down to see a solid line of black ants running up and down my arms and legs. I gasped and slapped at myself until I had to climb down so I could dance around and dislodge the unimaginable numbers of bugs using me as a ladder. I managed not to scream, although the gulping sobs of horror that escaped my mouth didn't do me any credit. At least no one was around to hear.

When I'd slapped myself black and blue and was sure there weren't more of the little monsters on me, I realized I was standing in the downpour. While my little nest was dry and comfortable, it had lost its appeal if I needed to cohabitate with all those crawly-things. People who complained about cities and praised living out in the country clearly had no idea what they were talking about.

Tempting as it was to return to the hut, it wasn't time for me to ask Brother Gerhardt to take over guard duty. Determined to do my part like a man, I wrapped the blanket around myself and set out to explore further up the trail.

Trudging head-down, dodging rivers of muddy water, my eyes were focused on my sandaled feet. My toes tingled as I sloshed through muddy puddles that were deeper than they looked Ahead of me, the road disappeared around a turn but reappeared a way down as the mountainside curved back towards the sea. I figured I'd just explore what was in that missing bend, then head back towards the others. Looking over my shoulder, I made out a thick, sad, grey smudge of smoke. Gerhardt had somehow started a fire, pathetic as it would be in this rain. It had to be outside the hut, or he'd smoke everyone out or maybe even burn the lean-to down.

Still, a little warmth would be a blessing. How could it be so cold in the mountains? It was still summertime.

Pulling the wet blanket tighter around me, I walked maybe a quarter of a mile, then stopped to look around. I knew I had to keep my eyes open but didn't know what for. Trees dripped with huge drops of rain. The birds and bugs were silent now, trying to stay warm and dry—which made them smarter than me. Somewhere ahead, I heard the faint swishing sound of running water—there was a creek ahead. I noted it, thinking that's the kind of thing a scout should notice and Gerhardt would want to know about. I heard, or at least sensed, something else as well. I managed to detect the deep bass of men in whispered conversation.

Heart pounding, my eyes sought the source of the sound. I ducked low to the side of the road and into the brush, checking first for ants. I tried to still my breathing so I could hear over the noise that filled my ears—my heart pounding. Eventually, my ears located them.

They were uphill a little bit, to the north. It sounded like two voices, but I needed to see how many, and what manner of men they were. I dropped the blanket in a soggy pile under the bush, then stuck my head out and swiveled it in every direction. I couldn't see much, so I sneaked up the road in a low crouch, sticking close to the brush in case I needed to dive for cover. For a few yards, it was just frustrating and scary, but at last I could make out men's rough laughter and snatches of conversation.

"No. Why bother?" The voices spoke Syrian Arabic. *Maybe they were soldiers.*

"Your mother didn't think it was a bother," then even more laughter. *Definitely soldiers. But how many?*

I reached a fast-running stream about five feet wide and maybe eight inches deep where it ran across the trail and down the mountainside. The voices seemed to drift downhill, following the current. Whoever it was, their camp lay up the hill, where they would have a good view of the road. If they saw me coming, it didn't concern them much. The laughter got louder the closer I got. *Or maybe I was just lucky.*

With some work, I made out three voices. I squatted low behind some underbrush, parting the leaves to see a filthy, saggy tent in a clearing. Four horses whickered nearby, hobbled and tied to trees. *Why were there more horses than men?* That made no sense.

Then I heard the angry crash of someone stomping towards the camp and dove into the brush. I tried not to make a sound, despite receiving a nasty scratch down my arm from a thorn. The man stomped past me and didn't care much who heard him coming. Before he even got past my hiding spot, one of the men in the tent yelled out, "Well?"

"I didn't go all the way, but it's not much of a fire. There can't be many of them." He was a tall man, with a dagger in his belt and a battered sword hanging from one hip. On his head was a sad-looking black turban that matched his thick and ratty beard. If he was a soldier, he wasn't a good one, and certainly not one of Salah-adin's men. That meant he— and the other three—had to be bandits.

"How do you know, if you didn't check?" That voice had

the tone of put-upon authority to it. That would be the leader.

The mopey-looking bandit outside the tent didn't care for the man's tone but wasn't about to do anything about it. He took a deep breath before answering, this time in a far more respectful tone. "Forgive me. But with that pathetic excuse for a fire, they don't seem to know what they're doing—it's not big enough to keep them warm, but it would still draw attention. Plus, I didn't see a watch." He stood outside the tent, deciding he was safer out in the elements than within smacking distance of the leader.

A younger voice asked, "Should we go get them?" This was met by chuckles inside the tent, and another sucking, bubbling pull on the hookah.

"Why bother? Whoever it is, they didn't come from the north, which means they'll come to us in good time. And if they don't, we'll pay them a visit once this cursed rain stops. Only an idiot would volunteer to go out in weather like this."

The leader laughed when he said that, and it made me feel a little bad for the soldier standing outside the tent. The poor man raised his head in frustrated supplication to Allah, then plunked onto the ground between two of the horses to finish his watch, his heart not in the job of watching out for people like me.

I looked around, seeking a way out. I had to warn the others, but nothing good would happen if I was caught spying. Sad-Face wasn't looking my way, but the slightest noise would change that. I wasn't sure my fast, shallow breathing wouldn't betray me. It sounded loud and echoey in my head.

I have no idea how long we sat there with me staring at him, him staring into space, and occasionally casting a lazy eye around the camp. The dampness and the gurgle of the creek caused a different problem. I had to pee badly. When people tell adventure stories, nobody ever talks about the fact that waiting and watching are boring and uncomfortable, and there's no glory in trying not to go in your pants.

Sad-Face shifted position a couple of times, and I realized I wasn't the only one suffering. Unable to hold it, he got up and took a few steps uphill and across the stream. That was my chance. I slithered out from the thorn bush and backed down the hill to the trail, watching the guard's back until my sandals hit the hard-packed road. I ducked low and squat-walked along the bushes until the road bent to the north and I figured I was out of sight. Then I ran as fast as I could, with one short unavoidable stop, to our camp.

I saw the pathetic spiral of black smoke above the trees and took the shortest route, off the trail, up the hill, and through the brush until I came barreling into the clearing near the hut. "Brother," I panted. "Bandits."

Brother Gerhardt was squatting near the fire, poking it with a long stick, more out of boredom than anything. He stood up, immediately alert and caught me by the arms as I stumbled into him. "Vat bandits?"

Nahida demanded to know what I was so upset about. I held up a hand pleading with her to stop asking questions until I caught my breath.

Brother Gerhardt wasn't in a waiting mood. "How

many?"

"Three or four…"

"Vich? Three? Or four?" he demanded.

I knew how to deliver a report, and it helped me focus. "Four. There were four horses. I only heard three men but I think there's another one."

"Vell then, it's four. Vhere are they?"

I pointed up the road. "Close, just around that next big turn."

"How far away, boy?"

How in hell's name would I know? How could a person measure distance when everything was so big and far away? "Maybe eight or ten streets?" That felt about how far I'd run.

He looked at me like I was crazy, but then he grunted at me. "They saw our smoke." Brother Gerhardt grimaced and cursed himself under his breath. Over my shoulder, Sister and Nahida huddled under the shelter, looking a lot warmer and drier than I was. It had been a calculated risk to attempt a fire, and the knight regretted his decision, but there was nothing for it now.

"You couldn't know. And we'd have walked right into them. They're sitting there waiting for the rain to stop…"

The knight paced back and forth, talking to himself in his own language before stopping dead in his tracks. Taking a deep breath, he closed his eyes in prayer, then crossed himself. My hands flew up and across out of solidarity.

Sister's voice trembled. "Maybe we should go back the way we came." That seemed like an awfully good idea. Gerhardt showed no emotion. I glanced at Nahida, whose eyes were wide, and she shivered even though she was way warmer and drier than I was.

The scroll inside my shirt weighed a ton.

"No," I heard myself squeak. "We have to get to Tyre." It was the right decision, but a damned fool thing to do. There was no way around them on the narrow road; our only choices were to attack or wait. Even I knew attacking was ridiculous. Waiting for them to come to us wasn't much smarter, given we were a sick woman, a tough but skinny girl, a nearly useless boy, and one lone knight, even if he was big as two of the bandits put together.

Gerhardt looked up at the sky to confirm my answer and nodded. "Gut, ve'll set a trap for them."

The plan was as simple as it was ludicrous. Sister would hide up the hill and away from the camp since there wasn't much she could offer in the way of protection. I insisted she stay as far away as possible, and she was the only one who didn't agree. Nahida's job was to hide up the road and let us know when they were close. Brother Gerhardt and I would fight them—or Gerhardt would fight them while I tried really hard not to die. Not a brilliant strategy, but it was the closest thing to a plan we had.

As if God Himself tired of waiting and just wanted it over with, the rain tapered off. A lone ray of sunlight penetrated the clouds, striking the ground right in front of me. Over my shoulder, Nahida pointed to a rainbow.

"Look at that, it's a sign from God." Everyone but the girl crossed themselves in agreement. I chose not to mention that the four bandits had the rainbow as well and were thinking the exact same thing about their prospects. In my limited experience, God wasn't very specific with his omens.

It only took a few minutes to get things arranged. Sister took the bags of food with her, and walked up the muddy hill and deep into the brush, not to return until events shook themselves out. Nahida would let us know when the bandits passed her by using the bird whistle she'd shown off earlier—one tweet per rider so we'd know whether it was three or four potential murderers we faced. In a moment, Gerhardt and I stood face to face in a damp, empty camp.

I watched in just my sandals and tunic as the knight pulled his helmet over his coif and tugged his thick leather gloves on. He reached for his longsword, then withdrew his shaking hands to grab his oak quarterstaff. He pulled a short sword from the pack on the pony and dropped it at my feet. Droopy snorted and shook his head in dismay.

"I don't…"

"No, you don't," he agreed. "Just keep them busy until I can get to them one by one. Don't do more than you can." He added, "Try not to kill anyone and don't die. I couldn't stand that."

Four sharp bird calls echoed through the trees. They were all coming. They'd likely all got bored sitting in the tent for so long and decided it was time for some fun. Four killers against one knight. And whatever I was.

I stood as tall as I could, holding the sword two-handed in front of me for a second, then it clunked point-first to the ground. Those things were heavy. Gerhardt put his gauntleted hand on my shoulder like Brother Marco always did, and I felt a wave of nausea-flavored fear roil in my guts. He muttered something, and I realized it was a prayer so I ducked my head out of respect. At long last came the "amen." Our eyes met.

"*Beau-Jean!*" That was the Hospitaller war cry, although it was more of a whisper than a cry. The clop of hooves made my heart race, and Gerhardt gave a final wink and ducked behind the cedar tree and under the leaves of a bush.

Moments later, the four bandits found me standing like an idiot in the entry to the little hut, arms crossed, hoping it would stop me from shaking. They halted, shocked to see me. Sad-Face was at the rear. The meanest looking one—he must have been the leader—rode at the front of the line. The other two maneuvered their horses past him to see if anyone was coming from the north or south. Since I was incapable of speaking, nobody said anything for the longest time.

I managed to croak out in Arabic, "Nice day, isn't it?"

The leader, a scary looking Turk with charcoal eyes and a mangy beard, barked out a laugh. "Yes, Allah sent us just enough rain to make everything green again. Where is everyone else?"

I looked around bewildered. "Oh, there's no one else. Just me."

He gave me an exasperated look and placed his hand not very subtly at his sword hilt. "Is that so? All alone with three horses loaded with gear? That's a lot for a young man to handle. Even one as obviously brave as yourself." His eyes grew blacker the longer he glared at me.

"I don't see anyone else around," offered Sad-Face. That

earned him a smack on the back of his head from the nearest bandit. "What? I don't see anyone. Do you?"

Rolling his eyes, the leader waved to the other two thieves, who dismounted and walked towards the pack horses. "Don't make a fuss, boy, and we'll leave you one of your horses." One thief grabbed the reins of Gerhardt's mount, the other the limping pack pony. It seemed even these men weren't desperate enough to choose Droopy.

"You can't," I stammered, running over to the animals. "I'm watching them for someone."

"That's better," the chief said with a smug grin. "Now, who are you watching them for?"

"Him." I pointed to where Brother Gerhardt had emerged from the brush behind them. Quick as a beggar at a food stall, the knight grabbed poor Sad-Face by the robe. He ripped him off his mount to the ground, banging the poor fool's head on the hard ground twice, leaving him unconscious.

The leader yelled to the others, "There must be more. Watch the little one!" He pointed with his already drawn sword and whirled around to face Brother Gerhardt. If he was surprised to find a fully-armed Hospitaller knight in this place, it didn't slow him down or even give him pause. He charged at Gerhardt, sword raised high for a killing blow. The blonde giant stood rooted to the spot, holding his quarterstaff across his body, carefully balanced in both hands.

Transfixed as I was by the duel, I ignored the tallest and youngest of the bandits until he grabbed me, pinning my arms painfully behind my back. I squirmed and kicked backward towards his balls, but he cursed and squeezed even harder. Shooting pain in my shoulders halted any further escape attempts. The second bandit circled, sword drawn, watching for any other surprise visitors.

In the middle of the road, the chief gave his horse a kick and charged Gerhardt, shrieking "*Allahu akbar*". His sword scythed downwards, but the knight took a single step out of the way, and the horse carried the bandit past him and almost off the road.

Gerhardt bent his knees a tiny bit but otherwise never moved. He shouted, "Come on then, you motherless dog." I don't know if the man spoke French or not, but he took great offense and lifted his sword higher, squeezing with his knees so he rose higher in the saddle as he bore down on my friend. He leaned forward, swinging the curved blade with all his strength.

Again, Gerhardt didn't move his feet, but ducked low and swung his oak staff straight out, catching the horse between its front legs, right at the knee. The animal screamed so loudly it echoed off the hills as he and his rider hit the ground. The chief rolled three times but leaped immediately to his feet. Meanwhile, the poor animal lay on its side, writhing, screaming, and kicking three of its legs while its front right leg flailed limply.

Now the bandit swung his curved sword in menacing great circles, grabbing the hilt with two hands. Slowly he shuffled to his left in a wide circle, forcing Gerhardt to move as well, with his back towards the big cedar where our ponies stood. His two compatriots shouted encouragement to their leader and terrible curses at Gerhardt. The giant knight never so much as blinked. He kept shuffling in an ever-widening circle, until he was within arm's reach of his grey horse. He dropped his staff and quick as an adder's strike, his left hand flew out. He snatched up the lance strapped to the horse's flank.

With a lion's roar, he hurled the spear directly at the leader's chest. The bandit's face expressed more shock than pain as the point caught him square in the ribs, knocking him backward. The tip stuck out of his back and several inches into the ground as the bandit chief fell, staring blindly at the sky. He made awful, gurgling sounds and waved his hands feebly. My captor and I watched in horror as he took far too long to die.

One man was dead. Sad-Face still lay unconscious on the ground. That left two more. The bandit holding my arms jerked me to one side as his companion drew his own sword and took two awkward, terrified steps towards Brother Gerhardt. He knew he was outmatched, but pride and a burning desire to survive dictated he try anyway. The man huffed and puffed, waving the cheap blade menacingly, but not too convincingly.

The thief holding me had more sense and shouted, "Stop. Hold it." His partner froze in place. "Drop your weapon, or the boy dies." When Gerhardt didn't respond, he shouted louder. "I mean it. I'll slit his throat." The threat needed no translation. We all believed him. Gerhardt and the other bandit turned to stone. Even I stopped wriggling.

Time stood still as we took turns staring at each other, waiting for someone to make a move. We could hear the pitiful cries of the wounded horse and the wind through the leaves. My captor push-dragged me closer to his partner, never loosening his grip for even a second. Gerhardt held his empty hands up, but not all the way, and he was far too close to the pack for the bandit's liking.

The silence was broken by a girl's shout. "Hee-ya." I looked to my right in time to see Nahida jump out of the bushes and take a running leap onto the back of one of the bandit's ponies. The shocked animal danced maniacally, but she held on until he settled, then grabbed the reins of both the other horses.

"That's my horse you little brat," the man holding me shouted. Nahida didn't care. She kicked the black beast in the flanks and led the others by the reins, and took them down the road.

Now the remaining bandits didn't know what to do. Three of their mounts were gone and one was crippled. They stood in the middle of nowhere, faced with a giant Christian knight and an annoying, wiggling boy. My opponent decided to eliminate at least one of the obstacles and reached for his dagger. He had to loosen his grip on me a bit, though, and it was all I needed to shimmy free. I took three fleeing steps but tripped backward into the mud. My attacker shifted the blade in his palm for a back-handed, throat-slashing stroke. Gerhardt shouted a useless warning, and the second bandit's eyes widened in confusion.

I heard a high-pitched shriek and saw a blur of white as

Sister Marie-Pilar ran past me, waving a tree branch over her head. "Aieeeee. Leave him alone you animals!" Brandishing the thick branch like a club, she charged, taking wild swings at the knife-wielding killer. It took a moment to size up his opponent and realize it was a tiny veiled woman. He struck her with the back of his hand, knocking her to the ground and laughing with relief.

I looked on, horrified that anyone would strike a woman—especially a nun. Especially the most wonderful nun there ever was. "Sister!" I shouted. I ran at the man who'd struck her, fists windmilling, sure I would die but past caring. He sidestepped my attack and pushed at the back of my head, driving me face-first to the ground. He stood over me, his knife in his hands. I looked up from the mud as a piercing scream came out of his mouth.

Over my shoulder, I saw Sister take a second run at him. This time was different from her last attempt. Her veil had fallen away and flapped, useless, from one corner of her wimple, leaving her face fully exposed. Instead of her kind eyes, there were bloodshot pinpoints blazing out of a pale background. Worse, the leprous right side of her mouth was exposed. Hellish cries came out of what looked like half a mouth. Where the right half of her mouth should have been was a scabby, skinless mess exposing white teeth in rotting gums. I'd never seen behind that veil and had only imagined what she might really look like. This was worse than I ever thought.

My attacker froze for a moment, then screamed to his partner. "It's a djinn… A demon. Run…" He took off on foot screaming, without waiting for his accomplice. I guess he thought if the demon was going to drag one of them to hell, it wouldn't be him. The second bandit followed right on his heels. The two of them stopped for just a panicky second when they realized their horses were missing and they were leaving Sad-Face unconscious with us. Then they ran off down the road, praying for Allah's protection against the monster who fought for the Firangi.

Chapter 14

I gave a loud, laughing victory whoop. I watched the men flee up the road and looked around at my compatriots, a big stupid grin on my face. "Did you see that? That was great. You were…" I was the only one smiling.

Sister Marie-Pilar was on her knees in the mud, sobbing wildly and frantically trying to reattach her veil over her damaged mouth. She held up a hand, averting her eyes in shame. I took another step, but she let out a small, strangled "no," and I stopped.

I looked over toward Brother Gerhardt; surely he understood what a great victory we'd achieved. But he took no notice of me. The giant knight stood over the impaled body of the bandit, head bowed. He frantically crossed himself over and over with shaking hands, repeating prayers in a quavering voice that sounded as if he'd been the victim of the slaughter, instead of the clear winner.

The wounded horse continued shrieking, although not as loudly, and the screams were interspersed with heavy, groaning breaths and the sound of its hooves striking muddy ground. Brother Gerhardt stood over it for a moment, then walked slowly to his pack and pulled the long sword off the palfrey's back, running an experienced hand over the blade.

Nahida sat quietly on one of the horses, a big black mare, holding the reins of the others. Unable to speak to Gerhardt directly, she looked from him to me. Her dark eyes shone with tears, although she somehow stifled them for the moment. She held one hand across her lower stomach, looking a little ill.

Gerhardt shook his head and bit his lip as he told me quietly, "He's too far gone. It's a mercy to let him go." I looked back at my friend, prepared to translate, but being raised around horses, she recognized the tone in his voice and knew what it meant. She just sniffed and blinked back more tears, nodded once, and turned the horse she was on towards the line of trees so neither of them would have to look.

Gerhardt took the huge sword in his hands, and, muttering what might have been a prayer, although in his language everything sounded angry, he carefully placed the point right behind the pony's ear, lifted his eyes heavenward, and with a grunt, drove the point into the creature's brain. There was a sudden groan, then the animal went silent. So did everything around us. No birds, no insects. The only sound was a lone, wet, sniff from Nahida that we all pretended not to hear.

Finally the insects and birds realized that the madness had passed and went back about their business. Sister Marie-Pilar rose and tried to slap the filth from her robes. Nahida brought the black mare's head around to face me, and Gerhardt leaned on the hilt of his sword, which was point-down in the dirt. He let the sword fall to the ground and managed to pull his eyes from the dead robber long enough to look at me. I gawked back, until I realized he was awaiting orders. From me.

What would Brother Marco do? I know he wouldn't ask the question I did. "Do you think they'll be back?" *You already know the answer to that one, you idiot.*

"They'll come back to kill us." Nahida's voice was quiet and flat.

Gerhardt nodded. "Ja, ve'll have to get moving as qvickly as ve can." He looked at me for approval. Not having any better idea, I just nodded as if I'd made an actual choice.

There was one more decision to be made. The old, beat-up black pony that had carried our materials had a bad hoof, and we had two new horses, fresh and healthy. "Maybe we should use the other horses?" It came out more a timid suggestion than an order, but the knight and the girl nodded with more enthusiasm than I felt and got to work.

Nahida had evidently claimed the young bandit's black mare for herself, so she and Gerhardt began transferring the bags from the pack horse to Sad-Face's chestnut gelding. The poor, wounded horse had no idea what was happening, but was relieved to be rid of the weight, and stood quietly whickering, lifting and lowering its injured foot.

While they worked, I turned back to Sister Marie-Pilar, who hadn't said a word. She quietly went about her own work, gathering the few bits of food and equipment we'd used and stashing them in another bag. I stood at the opening to the lean-to. I searched desperately for the words to say, but as usual when I needed to talk, I couldn't, just like when I needed to shut up, my mouth wouldn't stop working. She caught me looking, and her small hand flew up to where her veil hid her scarred, scabby mouth.

I couldn't help myself. I ran to her and wrapped my arms around her waist, nearly crushing her. She looked away and patted my arm gently. "Lucca," she said. "Enough."

I tried to find words that would help. "It's really not so bad…" That certainly wasn't the balm I was looking for, but it was the best I could do. "You don't have to hide from us… It's okay." Everyone else at St Lazar went around uncovered. We were all used to the stumps, scars, and scabs.

Sister Marie-Pilar sucked a wet breath through the gauzy material. "It's not for anyone else. I pretend it is, but it's not. It's for me. It's pure vanity…and sinful, I know…but…" She pulled her arm away from me and wiped her sleeve across her eyes. "I used to be quite pretty, you know." Nahida had said the same thing. I guess that mattered to women. "When I was a girl. The other girls used to be so jealous and mean about it. Mother Superior used to tell me it was sinful to be so proud."

She stopped, looking the line of hills in front of us, but her eyes focused far away and long ago. "I'm being punished for my vanity. God's will be done." God's will. *Inshallah*. It seemed cruel and stupid to make someone a certain way and then punish them for enjoying it, but God, or Allah, or whoever Nahida believed in made no sense to me, and made me angry more often than not.

"We need to get moving," I said, when the words finally formed.

Her watery eyes crinkled in a smile above her veil and she nodded. "Yes, sir." We gathered our bags and walked over to where the others had the horses ready. Gerhardt took the burden from Sister, being careful not to touch her at all, and threw them up on the brown horse.

Sister stood silently watching the rest of us load up. When we were ready, I motioned her over to get up on the horse, but she just stood, her eyes cloudy.

"I'm so useless to you all. I shouldn't have come. I'm only a burden"

I ran over to her, shaking my head. "No, I—we need you."

She gave a most un-nunlike "harrumph."

"No, really. You saved me back there."

"Because I'm so hideous."

Despite her obvious misery, I couldn't help giggling a bit. "They thought you were a djinn." She looked confused. "A demon... They thought you came from the devil and were going to kill them and drag them to hell. You scared them more than Brother Gerhardt did." She looked unconvinced, and I remembered the look on their faces as they fled. I couldn't help laughing.

Sister let out a little giggle. "Yes, I am fairly scary."

"Terrifying." I threw my hands in the air and acted like a monster. "They thought you were six feet tall."

Sister laughed and raised her hands threateningly over her head and pretended to be a demon. "Watch it, or I'll take YOU to hell," she cackled. I laughed and ran away, and for a few seconds we chased each other around the camp playing the strangest game of tag the world had ever seen.

We were interrupted by Brother Gerhardt's deep voice. "Ve need to get moving. If you're done there, of course."

Sister's head dropped in a meek gesture of compliance. Gerhardt helped her onto the pony. Because we'd moved so much baggage to the new, healthier horse, there was now room on Droopy for me. I climbed up, a head shorter than everyone else because my mount was so small and pathetic.

The lame pony watched us, then turned away to pull at some low-hanging leaves. It didn't care if we left him or not, which was just as well for everyone. We left her. She was just a horse, plus we had two better ones now. And we were all alive. That seemed like a good trade to me.

Nobody said a word as we passed the bandits' camp. It was abandoned; only broken branches, an empty tea kettle and smoldering embers showed where they'd camped. The duo fled on foot, but we'd still have to be on our guard.

Gerhardt rode ahead, holding the reins for Sister's pony. Nahida and I rode two abreast right behind. I watched Nahida's eyebrows scrunch up, like they did when she was thinking. Then she leaned over and whispered, "The nun…" She checked with me that she had the right word, and I nodded. "She's very nice. Odd, but nice." I couldn't disagree, so I just nodded and concentrated on not falling from Droopy's swayed back.

After a while, Brother Gerhardt did something nobody could have expected. He broke into song. The big, frightening killer had a very pleasant voice, and he led us in singing a battle hymn. First he sang it, then looked around surprised that we weren't joining in.

"Come on," he boomed. "Everyone knows this song." We all just looked at each other. Encouraging us, he sang the first line of the old Hospitaller song and motioned for us to repeat it. I joined in, just to make some noise after having held still for so long. Then Sister piped up. Her bird-like voice seemed out of place singing songs about smiting enemies.

Nahida, not understanding any of the words, and her stomach still bothering her, just sat moping on her horse until the chorus—a bunch of tra-la-las—and then she joined in, too. Unfortunately, she sang like she laughed—loud and like a wounded goose—but we all enjoyed ourselves for the moment. It was probably not great military strategy, especially with bandits in the area, but for the first time we actually enjoyed ourselves.

This went on for a few miles, until we heard running water. Gerhardt sent me ahead to see if there was a place to rest and if it was safe. He never told me what to do if it wasn't, but Droopy and I trotted—or as close to a trot as the lazy beast could manage—ahead.

A wide stream formed a pool before continuing on and dropping down the hill in a pretty cascade. I rode back and we made plans to rest the animals. I jumped off Droopy, giving my bum a quick rub, and helped Sister down, who did the same, although a bit more subtly. Gerhardt dismounted and led three of the animals to the stream.

Nahida sat very still on her black mare, neither moving nor saying anything. She slowly lifted her hand, and it was covered in blood. She stared at it, looked down, and let out a terrified scream.

Gerhardt and I both ran to her but I pulled up short, absolutely horrified. Just above the saddle, there was a fist-sized blood spot on her dress. She stared stupidly down at it, not able to do anything but scream, whimper until she gained enough strength, and scream again.

As quickly as I'd ever seen a man move, Gerhardt put his huge hands under her armpits and lifted her off, then laid her gently on the ground. "Are you all right, *Schatz*? What happened?" Nahida just shook her head. I couldn't tell if she didn't understand the question, or couldn't answer it.

Brother Gerhardt began checking her for obvious wounds, but not finding signs of a knife, sword, or lance wound, his medical knowledge was exhausted. He furrowed his brow in confusion. As usual, I was no use to anyone and just stood there asking "Are you all right?" until Nahida called me a terrible name in Arabic and I shut my mouth.

Sister pushed me aside and bent over the girl. Nahida at first pulled back and tried to push the nun away. Sister just slapped her hand away. "Tsk, stop that. Let me see if you're hurt." The Syrian girl didn't know the words, but that tone of voice is understood by everyone, man, woman or child, and she obeyed, laying back with a whimper.

The older woman ran her hand over Nahida's waist and stomach, poking and checking for pain. Finally, she moved between us men and the girl, blocking our view. Uttering "shh, shh, shh," she ran her hand under the hem of Nahida's gown. After a moment she looked over her shoulder at me.

"How old is she?"

That seemed an odd question, but her tone didn't leave much room for argument. "She said she was eleven...no twelve."

Sister snorted derisively. "Twelve at least." She turned back to Nahida, and even though she knew the girl couldn't understand her, smiled and said, "You'll be fine. You're fine."

She didn't look fine to me. "What is it? Will she live?" Even though my friend couldn't understand the words, I could see she had the same questions.

Sister sat back into a squat and wiped her hands on the ground. "She's fine. She just has her curse."

At the word "curse," Gerhardt crossed himself. I did the same just to be safe and asked. "She's been cursed?"

Sister laughed. "No more than any other woman. She's got her monthly flow, that's all."

"What's going on? What's happening?" a plaintive voice called in Arabic.

"She says you have your...curse? Flow?" My Arabic was pretty good, but I didn't know the word for whatever this was. "She says it's a woman thing." Nahida seemed to understand. I certainly didn't. I'd never seen anyone lose so much blood and live before and was genuinely concerned. I turned to Sister and demanded, "But she'll live?"

The nun nodded and laughed. "Yes, once a month she may feel like dying, but she'll be fine. It just means she's becoming a woman."

"You mean this will happen every month? That's

terrible." I had never heard of such a thing, and the idea that my friend might suffer like that seemed awfully unfair.

"It's the plight of every woman since Eve," Sister said and crossed herself.

"But not to you, right?" I asked, and you'd think I'd said something hysterically funny the way she howled.

"Yes, even me."

"But you're not a woman, you're a…" Even I knew how stupid that sounded.

Gerhardt had taken the horses upstream for water, purposely not paying us any attention. I quickly translated for Nahida as best I could and once she was assured she'd live, she began to cry.

"Does it hurt?" I ran to her side, bending down as if there was anything I could actually do. She just shook her head.

"No, it means I'm not safe any longer… If I'm a woman, that means I can have children and that means they can…" The rest made no sense. What this blood and chaos had to do with children, or who "they" were, or anything else was beyond me.

Sister had me help get Nahida to her feet. My friend reluctantly obeyed and took the older woman's arm. They began to walk slowly to the stream, and I fell in behind them.

Sister snapped at me. "Go help Brother Gerhardt with the horses. This is women's work." I stood there like an idiot, then went to make myself as useful as I could. I walked over to the knight.

He must have seen the confusion on my face and chuckled. "I don't miss living vith vimmen." Having never lived with one, I had no way to compare.

"Is it always like this?"

He threw his head back and laughed. "Thankfully no, and there are other things that make it all worthwhile, lad. Someday you'll find out, unless you take vows like me and Brother Marco."

I'd never seriously thought of becoming a monk. But if it meant you didn't have to deal with girls and curses and a thousand other inconveniences, it might be worth it. I couldn't imagine anything making *that* worthwhile, but there was way too much I didn't know these days.

We had about two more days to Tyre. They couldn't go by fast enough.

Chapter 15

While the women—it was the first time I'd thought of Nahida that way—were away, I helped Brother Gerhardt with the animals. Sister's new brownish-red pack horse didn't care much for that role and hated being touched on the right flank so, of course, I got stuck dealing with her. Nahida's new black prize wanted nothing to do with me, so I left it for her to take care of when she got back. Brother dealt with his skinny grey, then watched in amusement as Droopy nipped at me while I tried to pull a thousand burrs from his mane. Stupid animals, horses. I couldn't wait to be back in a city where I didn't have to deal with them.

It was the first time we'd been alone since leaving Acre and there was a question that nagged me like a fishwife. It was rude, but I needed to know, regardless. I guess there should have been some polite conversation first, but I couldn't help myself. Out of a clear blue sky, I asked him, "Why can't you use your sword?"

The smile faded into his beard and his lower lip disappeared into his mouth. He said nothing and I feared I'd angered him, but he nodded thoughtfully. "You vaited a long time to ask that, ja?" He sat on the ground and pulled his knees up close to him then patted the dirt and I squatted beside him.

"All my life, boy, I've been bigger than most people. Ven I vas a child, that meant people always vanted to fight me, and I vas a fantastic fighter. I didn't vant to—but I didn't seem to have much choice. God fashioned me like this, and he had his reasons. I thought, 'If he vants me to fight, I'll fight for Him.' For a good reason, a holy cause. Does that make sense?"

I realized he was awaiting a response, so I gave a quick nod. "Yes, sir."

"I joined the Order of St John and the Hospital. I'd get to see Jerusalem for myself, and serve God and others by protecting people who vanted nothing more than to visit the Holy Sites. Sometimes that meant taking up a sword, but in…service to God and others…not because I liked it, you understand. I never vanted to take another's life—not even an infidel's. But it vas the task before me, and I did it. For Him, you understand."

I'd seen what he did to those bandits, and had no trouble accepting his expertise. But while his story had interesting parts, it didn't answer my question, and I was in no mood for subtleties. "But didn't you have to use a sword?"

"Every day. Ven I fight, Lucca, I lose myself in the battle. I don't see or hear anything except my enemy. I don't stop until he's dead and the danger's passed. It's vat warriors do. They don't think, they fight. And my sword—do you know vat Marco used to call it? Skull Crusher."

A piece of the puzzle fell into place. Brother Marco had been a Knight of the Hospital before becoming ill. That's where he knew Brother Gerhardt from, and why he had such faith in his abilities.

If the giant was reluctant to speak before, the words gushed out of him now. "Everything around me vould disappear, and my only goal was to kill the enemy. Many times I'd take on two or three to my brothers' one and win— every time. I killed a lot of men, but felt nothing for them. They were Unbelievers, so it didn't matter, you see? When the battle was over I'd come back to myself, sometimes not knowing where I was or how I'd gotten there. Frightening, but it was what God asked me to do, and I did it."

He rocked back and forth the slightest bit as his story went on, but his eyes never left mine. "One day, we came across a caravan—Damascene soldiers, sure, but also families and regular folk. We were escorting pilgrims from Jaffa and I would have gladly let them go. We would…should have, but some of their young soldiers and ours…who knows who started it…but the battle began. And I did my duty." His eyes became redder and waterier and his focus shifted to somewhere over my shoulder. "They tell me I fought well, not that I remember. Vhen my senses returned I was covered in blood and bodies lay around me as a hundred times before. But some of the…they were not soldiers. A mother with a babe in her arms was lying at my feet. They'd both been hacked to death by some kind of butcher, a madman. Not a soldier's death, mind you. It was pure bloody murder."

I know he heard me gasp. Holy knights didn't hurt regular folk. Stories of Salah-adin's hordes murdering and pillaging were rampant, of course, but our people didn't do that kind of thing, or at least none of the poets mentioned it if they did.

"I sent them to hell, Lucca, and didn't even know I was doing it. Do you think God wanted me to do something like that? In His name?" Brother Gerhardt was asking the wrong person to be God's advocate.

I tried to help. "But they were infidels, so weren't they going to hell anyway?" I tried not to think of Nahida.

"And now they'll never have the chance to repent and learn the True Way. He sent me here to protect innocents, not slaughter them."

Something still nibbled at me. "What about the sword? Why can you use a staff, and a spear, like on that bandit?"

He shook his head. "I don't know. Perhaps because I still have a job to do, and the Lord's not done with me yet. I can still fight, but I can no longer draw a sword against another man. My hand shakes, and my guts boil like I'm about to…I'm useless as a fighter."

I could see why Brother Samuel was so angry with him. A soldier who couldn't wield a sword—or wouldn't, which was the same thing—was useless. So was a bodyguard, come to think of it, yet here we were. He stood up to his full height, put his hands to the small of his back and stretched until I heard a "crack."

"Come," he said. "You have more burrs to get rid of before the women come back. We have miles to make up." He walked over to the stream so he could splash water on his face while I picked the sticky brown balls out of Droopy's mane and tried to avoid his big square teeth.

Sister Marie-Pilar and Nahida returned from whatever they were doing downstream. They both had several inches torn off the bottom of their dresses, leaving ragged hems a little higher than either of them found acceptable. Nahida's knobby knees showed immodestly, bare and caked with mud. The girl held on to the nun with one arm and rubbed her stomach with the other.

"Are you all right?" I asked. Neither of them spoke, but made it clear it was an idiotic question.

I ran over to help Nahida aboard her black mount and got waved aside for my trouble. Confused, I looked at the other man in the group. He shrugged in that universal symbol for "Women. What are you going to do?" that all men instinctively know. If this was what living with them was like, joining an Order didn't seem like such a bad idea—except for the whole God, and not having any money, parts.

We headed out with the sun lower in the afternoon sky than we'd have liked. It was midsummer, so there was still plenty of daylight, although the clouds threatened more rain. The women rode close together, silent and lost in their own thoughts. The urge to sing had passed, and Brother Gerhardt was his usual quiet self. I wanted to talk to someone, about anything, and thought my head might explode if I didn't talk to another person soon.

I twitched and fidgeted, making several attempts to ask questions or get someone to say anything at all, but every attempt met with either a shake of the head or a one-word answer, so I gave up. The birds weren't shy, though, and the squawks and whistles and trills had me wondering. Just how many kinds of birds there were, anyway, and why did we need so many?

As often happened, thinking of birds led me to ponder seagulls, which reminded me of the sea, and ports, then Acre, then home, and finally Brother Marco. I tried to imagine what it would be like giving him my report on this trip. He'd be most disappointed in my performance so far. We were days behind in getting to Tyre and Count Raymond. We'd been refused protection from a caravan, attacked by bandits, and escaped with our lives through luck more than wisdom. And what had I learned, besides things about women's lives I'd have been happier not knowing?? Marco's deep, sad voice echoed in my head. *It's not just what's there that shouldn't be. It's what's not there that should be.*

So, what was here to see? I looked around with more purpose. There was a lot and nothing at all. The mountains loomed over us, covered in trees and rocks as far as the eye could see. The sky went on for miles, starting in the east above the hilltops and then stretching forever to the west. There was a lot of world out here, that was for sure. And it was full of too many birds, God knows how many insects, and not enough people.

That was it. Where were all the people? Since we'd passed the bandits' camp, we'd seen shepherd's huts and small orchards, but all the houses stood abandoned—or seemed to. I remembered when Ali took me to Salah-adin's camp people would hide at our approach and try to make their homes seem unoccupied. It made sense to fear soldiers, but we were hardly the scariest of war parties—one soldier, one sick nun, a frightened girl and…whatever I was supposed to be.

"Brother…" I drew up enough nerve to ask a question I didn't really want the answer to. "Where are all the people?"

The older man looked over his shoulder at the women, then kicked his horse forward to catch up to me. He said nothing until our mounts were shoulder to shoulder—well, leg to shoulder since Droopy was so much smaller than his grey mare. "I don't like it, either, lad. But ve should find out, don't you think?"

I knew that tone of voice. "Ve" meant "You, Lucca." My thoughts, as usual, were visible on my brown face, and Gerhardt chuckled. "Ve should come to a village soon. At least ve'll find answers. Vhy don't you ride on ahead a little bit and see? I'll stay and protect de vimmen."

"Yes, I'll go scout." It came out far squeakier than it was supposed to.

"Lucca, listen." He towered over me, and I know his words and gestures were meant kindly, but the shadow he cast felt ominous. "Ride slowly and take notice of everything. I know Brother Marco has taught you to do that, yes?" It wasn't a question. "Don't go into the village. Ride on ahead and look for trouble. If you can find a place for us to camp, it vouldn't hurt. Schatzie will have to get some rest. "

"Me too," I admitted.

"Then the sooner ve find a place, the better, ja?"

I nodded glumly. He reined his horse in, slowing to a stop. That allowed Nahida and Sister to catch up to him.

I patted Droopy's neck and gave his reins a shake. He chuffed, turned his head to me as if to argue, then decided I wasn't worth the trouble and picked up the pace only the tiniest bit. "Oh, come on. Please?" I felt rather than heard Brother Gerhardt laughing behind me, and my cheeks burned. The stupid animal gave his mane a shake and broke into the slowest, saddest trot in the history of horses. At last, we pulled away from the others.

To be honest, I was in no hurry to be separated from the others, but I knew I was being childish and cowardly. Like a good scout, I kept my eyes sweeping left and right, rather than up and down with the bouncing of my bum on the pony's back.

The countryside was hilly and the trail rose and fell, putting more hills than actual distance between me and my friends. Thick groves of cedar trees closed in on either side, while only a dusty thin line marked our path. But the partial sun was comforting, the birdsong amusing, and the breeze so gentle I could breathe and relax again.

Climbing yet another steep grade, I saw half a dozen large, black birds circling above. One, then another, dropped straight down to a spot somewhere ahead until the whole flock had gone to ground. My stomach tightened like a fist. I'd seen flocks like that on the way back from Hattin.

Over the next hill, a dry plain stretched out. Generations of farmers had cleared the land of trees, and dried grasses and tall weeds spread out for about a city block. Further ahead, I saw the birds hopping and picking at something. Those had to be vultures, which meant something up there had died. And lots of birds meant plenty to eat.

I examined the field from the safety of Droopy's back. I begged him to stop, and he obliged, but not without giving his shaggy head a shake, making horse snot and sweat fly everywhere. There were no sounds of humans, but a low buzzing drew my attention.

My eyes traveled across the field, east to west. Small clouds of black flies had formed in several places. The grasses were trampled flat, although some shoots had tried to right themselves. It had been hours at least since whatever had happened, and I felt pride in figuring that out.

A glint of metal caught my eye. I squinted and made out a broken lance on the bare ground. The brave, responsible part of me wanted to investigate, while most of me wanted to stay right where I was. But that wouldn't do; I was a scout. Taking a deep breath, I kicked Droopy forward half a dozen steps—as slowly as he could manage. Neither of us was in a hurry to learn what had happened.

Clods of dark earth had been kicked up and hoof prints were evident in the dusty ground. With each step, I saw arrow tips, shattered lances, and broken leather straps. An enormous cloud of flies not too far off the left side of the trail drew my attention. Holding my breath, I willed Droopy closer. I closed my eyes and prepared for the worst, fully expecting to see a dead body when they opened.

I was wrong. The flies feasted, but only on dark, dried patches of blood and gore. Whatever—whoever—was wounded here had been moved. Bandits have no honor; soldiers care for their own. They never leave a man behind.

So whoever had fought and died here had been soldiers. But whose? Franks? Saracens?

Both would be bad news, although Salah-adin's troops would be worse for Brother Gerhardt and Sister Marie-Pilar. I knew this was no place for me—us—to be. I had to tell Brother Gerhardt. But tell him what? *You don't know anything, yet.*

I couldn't go back to him without knowing for sure what had happened, and there was nobody to ask. The gut-ripping squawk of the vultures brought me out of my daze. Maybe there was someone who could tell me. Odds were there was a body over there if I got to it before the birds ate it all. I'd be able to tell who'd fought here. On one side, at least.

I crossed myself and nudged Droopy towards where the birds cawed and battled each other over scraps of…someone. The stubborn horse refused to go any further. Despite my heels on his rear, he dug his hooves into the roadway and whinnied.

"I don't want to go either, but we have to." Droopy's eyes were wild, and he sniffed and blew snot everywhere. I was in no mood for the animal's silliness. I slid off his back and tugged on the reins. "Come on."

My supposedly brave, trusty steed snorted and bared his teeth. He backed up and yanked the reins from my hands so that the dry leather burned my hands and I let out a terrible word. Two raw stripes ran up the middle of my stinging hands. "What's wrong with you? Why can't you just do what you're told? You think I want to go up there?" We stood and glared at each other, one of us much calmer than the other.

I made one last desperate grab for the reins but Droopy was too smart and fast for me.

"Fine. Be like that, you stupid donkey." He didn't like that one bit, which was fine with me. I turned my back to him and steeled myself for the walk through the field to where those evil-looking birds were. I took a determined step off the trail into the knee-high grass, ignoring Droopy's shrill warnings.

With each step, I drew closer to the flock of ugly birds. One turned to look at me. It was about knee height, with wild white feathers on its chest and wing-tips and an ugly, bare face made of orange skin like badly tanned leather. It opened its sickle-sharp hooked beak and shouted at me to mind my business, but I balled my fists and stalked towards it anyway.

The sun was lower in the west now, and behind me, so my shadow must have appeared enormous to them. I lifted my hands, making myself as big and scary as I could. A couple of the more timid scavengers hopped a few steps away, far enough to let me pass, then went back to what they were doing.

With ever-slower steps, I craned my neck to see how much I could see without having to get too close to the corpse. I'd seen a few dead bodies and had no desire to see one that had been picked over by these ugly, disgusting and, I realized with a sniff, foul-smelling birds. I waved away a swarm of fat flies seeking their dinner and froze. The corpse was dressed in filthy black robes. In his dead, gnarled hand was a simple but vicious-looking knife. I knew that blade, and the man who held it. It was the young bandit who'd threatened to slit my throat. The bloody hack marks on the body told me his opponents had been much better equipped.

A rag of cloth was visible, flapping in the slight, warm wind. It was a heavy weave, dark blue with yellow running across it. Probably French. He'd been killed by Christian soldiers. I crossed myself and spit out a prayer, unsure of an answer but not knowing what else to do.

All right, you know there's a Christian army nearby. That's something at least. But where are they? What would Brother Marco want to know?

A few steps from the body was a jagged grey boulder that might give me a better a line of sight. I chased a few of the vultures out of the way, more to make myself feel big than because I needed to. Behind me, Droopy let out a bellowing whinny but I called him a blasphemous name and made my way to the rock.

While I attempted to puzzle out what had happened, my stupid horse wouldn't stop screaming and carrying on. Before climbing onto the rock, I turned to yell, "Shut up. Stop it," but the words stuck in my throat. Something rustled through the tall grass, and another sound—a low grunt, like someone getting punched in the stomach—came from just out of sight. I shaded my eyes from the afternoon sun to see what—or who—it was.

At first, it was a grey form, about belly-button height, lurking in a tall clump of grass. Another series of grunts revealed it was the biggest boar I'd ever seen, and the only one not hanging from a meat hook. It was a dusty grey, with spiky hairs all over it, but the scariest things were the two big tusks sticking out of its lower jaw like curved ivory knife blades. I suddenly recalled every fateful story I'd ever heard of people being attacked and maimed by these beasts, but couldn't remember one thing about how to fight them, especially without a weapon.

I looked for an escape route. There was no doubt the animal was heavier than me, and a whole lot faster. The boar took another step towards me, its front hoof pawing at the ground.

Maybe I could reason with it. "Nice piggy…" But the animal's only response was another step forward and a grunt that meant "Don't even try it." I tried shuffling to my left, but his black eyes followed. The body kept shifting to stay head-on with me, and he let out another series of grunts, each lower and more menacing than the one before it.

A lifetime of being chased taught me when to make a break for it, and as the big beast lowered his head and rushed, I dashed for the boulder. I grabbed ahold of the rock and hoisted myself up just as a rush of wind told me my opponent had missed. A frustrated squeal from the boar was met by a shout of "Missed me, you ugly bastard."

Frustrated, the killer pig squealed and pawed at the ground. He jumped at me, jaws snapping and head flailing, hoping to catch me on the end of those tusks, but he missed again. I huddled at the top of the rock, making myself as small a target as I could and held my breath. For a few seconds, all I heard was squealing and puffing from the boar and the sound of my own panicky sniffling. Then I heard something else.

What sounded like drumbeats were horse's hooves. A brown flash came from nowhere, and the boar turned at the same time I did. Droopy reared up on his back legs and brought a hoof crashing down where only a second ago my attacker had been. With a furious scream, the pig ran far enough away to avoid getting its skull crushed, but now it turned and faced my pony.

"Droopy, get out of there," I shouted. The stupid animal had never listened to me before and had no intention of starting now. He turned and kicked with his hind legs, this time at the boar, who feinted a charge but stood digging up the earth in frustration. Droopy whinnied a warning and reared up again. This time the charge was real.

The boar lowered his head and ran at the pony, faster and faster like a rock rolling downhill. Droopy lifted his front legs to kick out, but the boar dodged, lowered his head and then, when he was under the flailing hooves, raised his head and squealed.

My ears filled with the terrible shrieks of horse, boar, and boy. Under all that dreadful din, I could discern a terrible sound, like ripping leather. Something hit my face, and I knew without a doubt it was blood. Droopy cried out and dropped to the ground.

The boar's tusks had struck my horse right in the gut and torn him open. Poor Droopy collapsed on his side, legs kicking feebly in what looked like signs of life, but his red, blue, and white entrails were already falling out of him onto the ground. The boar ripped at the wound again. Then again, huffing and squealing in triumph.

My own screams added to the chaos. The pony lifted his head and looked at me accusingly. Those big brown eyes locked on me, and I watched as the candle that lit them went out and his stupid, ugly, shaggy head hit the ground.

"God damn you. Go away," I shouted, my eyes burning with tears.

The boar stopped his victory dance, spinning and tearing up the earth, and looked at me with one last satisfied "huff." As he lowered his head again, I thought for sure he would charge the rock and try once more to get at me, but we stared each other down.

Then I heard a different noise. This time it was the "thwack" of an arrow hitting its target. The boar shrieked in anger as a thick black shaft buried itself in his neck. He spun to face his attacker, and another "thwack-thwack" and two more struck home. The boar leapt in the air and crashed down, still and dead in the dirt.

I didn't see who'd rescued me. I didn't check to find out if they were a friend or yet another enemy. Without thinking, I leaped down from the rock and ran to Droopy, wrapping my arms around the lifeless neck and squeezing as hard as I could. I know I yelled something useless like, "No... No...," but he was dead and past caring what I said.

I dropped my head to his and buried my face in that sweaty, smelly fur. My eyes bulged, then exploded with tears, crying like I'd never cried before. Not for my dead parents, not for Gilbert or the other victims of this stupid war, and not even for myself. Not ever. I sobbed and shook and carried on in pure, soul-deep grief. Over a stupid horse I didn't even really like.

I didn't care who saw, and couldn't have stopped myself if I did.

Lost in my weeping and attempting to shake Droopy awake, I didn't hear or see the men approach. I opened my salt-scalded eyes to see a pair of boots, and then another. Soldiers. Three big, blurry-looking men in armor stood over me.

I blinked tears away and said stupidly, "He killed my horse."

One of the men knelt down beside me. In Arabic he asked, "Are you hurt?" His accent was terrible.

I sniffed and wiped my arm on my sleeve. In French, I offered a squeaky, "I'm fine." That's when one of the other soldiers pushed forward. His body was between me and the sun, so he was just a vague, shadowy black blob. That blob asked, "Lucca, is that you?"

Chapter 16

I tried blinking away the tears, but the mention of my name made me cry even harder, and then I was crying about crying, and the whole thing started over. My eyes were so clouded there was no way to make out the form of the man who spoke as if he knew me. I rubbed my arms across my sleeve and squinted again, trying to make out my rescuer's face and how I knew him.

A kind, young, albeit haggard-looking face peered down at me. "Lucca, it's me. Pierre." A rough hand took my chin and tilted my head upwards. I recognized the face before the name came back to me—it was the young trooper from Count Raymond's entourage. He was a brave young soldier who acted like it was my purpose on earth to torture him when I'd stayed in Tripoli's camp.

"Pierre?" I said, first as a question, but then realizing who he was. I tried to stand, look around, and wipe my nose all at the same time. All I did was fall back on my bum. He offered a hand, and the second time I managed to get to my feet. "W-what are you doing here? Is Count Raymond here, too?" My eyes darted around for a glimpse of the Count, but all I saw were two older, tired-looking knights. One of them stared at me like a simple-minded camel, the other ignored me and bent over the boar to retrieve his arrow. The arrow that saved my life. *How far away had he been from us when he took that shot?*

Pierre shook me until my teeth rattled. "Lucca, what are you doing out here by yourself?"

"I'm not by myself." *Where were the others? Were they safe?* "There are other people...with me...back on the road." The stupid-looking knight shouted an order to find my companions, and an unarmored man on a grey horse gave a quick nod and a whistle, leading two men down the road.

"What. Are. You. Doing. Here?" Pierre repeated, shaking me with every word. His body stooped so we were at even eye level. He looked like Brother Marco did when he wanted me to stop being an idiot and report out. I knew how to do that, at least, so I straightened up and took a deep, snot-blocked breath.

"I have a message for Count Raymond. From Brother Marco." Pierre ignored the disbelieving snort from the stupid knight and straightened up.

"From Acre? When did he send it? Where is it?" He held out his hand and I grinned, reaching up my sleeve.

My eyes widened and my face fell as the only thing I found up my sleeve was my bare arm. I looked around my feet. Had it fallen out? Where was it? *I had one task.* One *simple task.* "It's here. I swear it. Somewhere..." I looked from Pierre's perplexed face to the rock on which I'd taken shelter, to Droopy's lifeless corpse, to the tall grass around us, without seeing my scroll.

I glimpsed a bit of blue and green among the drier, darker-brown grasses between the boar's feet. How close had it come to being ground to powder under those hooves? I pointed. "There…"

The grizzled archer who'd killed the boar picked it up and showed it to Pierre. The younger soldier snatched it from him, examining it like a snake that may or may not be poisonous. "Do you know what's in it?"

Before I could help myself, I puked up the whole story. I started with Salah-adin's threat to the city, and how we had only a few days—fewer now—before it was lost forever. Then about the mysterious Armenian and what people were saying about Raymond of Tripoli. "But I told them it wasn't true. He's not a coward. Or a traitor." I had no idea if that part was true. I'd seen the Count and his army escape unmolested from Hattin with my own eyes. Had that been Divine intervention or a deal he'd cut with the Saracens? Pierre bit his bottom lip and said nothing. His eyes kept drifting to the parchment in his hands as I spoke.

"Why didn't Marco deliver this himself?" he demanded. Over my protests, he slid the ribbons off and unscrolled the letter.

I didn't tell him it was because Brother Marco was sick again. Sick and trapped in a dying city along with Fadhil and Sergeant Jacques and Gilbert and every friend I ever had. Or that he'd sent me more to save my sorry life than because he believed I was of any real use. "He thought I'd have a better chance of getting to Tyre without him." That was more or less true, but my face burned and my guts churned with shame anyways. A horrible thought crossed my overloaded mind. "Count Raymond is still there, isn't he?"

Stupid Soldier mumbled, "Oh, he's there, sure enough." Pierre shot him a dirty look and went back to reading. "You can read?" the fool asked, amazed.

Pierre ignored him. It was obvious he could read. Equally plain, though, was he couldn't read very well. His lips moved, and his eyebrows came together then parted then came together again as he struggled to make out what was in that precious parchment that was worth risking a life—even mine—for. Not being able to read even my own name, but having seen plenty of people do it, I shut up long enough for him to finish.

When he was done, he raised his eyes and studied me for a minute. Finally, he asked, "Do you really know everything that's in this?" I nodded, although I had no clue other than what Marco told me. "Fine, you're coming with us, then."

"What about this bunch?" another voice called from the trail. The scout sat mounted, and with him were Brother Gerhardt, Nahida, and Sister Marie-Pilar, atop their horses. Sister looked relieved. Nahida was frightened, and had removed her head covering again in the presence of Christian soldiers. She clutched the cloth in her hand.

Pierre ran a hand through his hair and looked back at me. "Who are that lot?"

"My friends. Marco sent them with me."

"Even the women?"

"Yes." Mostly true kept my conscience clear.

"Why?"

I ignored him and asked a question of my own. "What are

you doing out here? If the Count is at Tyre, shouldn't you be with him?" I'd never seen Pierre out of Raymond's eyeshot. It turned out, what little army remained at Tyre sent out sorties from time to time to shepherd refugees back to the city and protect them from marauders and Salah-adin's men.

"We were clearing the country of bandits when we heard someone scream for help." I wouldn't have called it screaming, but this wasn't the time to be proud.

"Were you looking for four men?" I asked.

He gave me an odd look. "We only found two. How did you know?"

"That's one of them. They attacked us a while ago. That's why I was out here. I was...the scout." *The scout who'd gotten his horse killed and nearly lost the only reason we were out here in the first place.*

"Four of them attacked you? Where are the rest? How did you get away?"

"Ve fought them off. The boy is a lion," came a loud, deep voice. Brother Gerhardt had dismounted and lumbered towards us. The others looked stunned to see a fully-armed Hospitaller knight traveling with such a strange party, but it wasn't the oddest thing any of us had seen. He placed a huge hand on my shoulder.

"Are you all right, Lucca?" Brother Gerhardt squinted, surveying the battleground. First, he made note of the dead boar. Then he saw Droopy's brown, disemboweled carcass. "I'm sorry, boy. Are you hurt?" That almost started me crying again, but I blinked the tears back into my head and told him I was unhurt.

After brief introductions, everyone agreed we needed to get moving. If we camped at nightfall, we could reach Tyre before noon tomorrow, and none of us wanted to delay that possibility. Gerhardt bent down and stripped Droopy of the saddlebags.

"Lucca, you ride with me," Pierre said, assuming command. He placed my letter inside his jacket, but I grabbed his arm.

"No, I'm supposed to give this to Count Raymond with my own hand. Marco said so." I held my hand out, and my friend nodded, handing me the parchment.

"Lose it and I'll kill you myself."

I tucked it into the belt of my tunic. There was no need to hide it now—I only had to ensure it reached its destination.

"I want to ride with my friends." Pierre made an exasperated-grown-up noise but agreed. He shouted orders to the others, insisting Stupid take the lead; he'd ride with us.

The other soldiers packed up the boar's carcass—there was no reason to let good food go to waste. Gerhardt and I returned to the women.

"Who in God's name are these?" Pierre asked in exasperation. I was a little surprised at his tone. A veiled Christian nun and an uncovered Syrian girl didn't even strike me as odd any more. Instead of answering, Sister jumped off her pony and ran, clutching me to her chest, offering prayers of thanksgiving for my safety and cursing me for being so reckless. I barely heard her, snuggled into her chest as I was. Hugging her close was something I was getting used to. She stroked my head with those delicate but filthy hands.

Poor Pierre watched, looking up, around, down at his boots, and then at me to please, for the love of Christ, say something. I reluctantly pushed away and introduced them. "This is Sister Marie-Pilar of the House of St Lazar. Sister, this is Sergeant Pierre of…"

"Captain," he said and offered a polite bow to the nun. If he was a captain, he'd been promoted since I'd met him only two or three weeks before. Twice. I knew he was a good man, but his promotion spoke more to the desperate straits of the Crusader forces than the young man's skills. "Marie-Pilar? You're Brother Marco's…"

"Friend." She completed the sentence for him.

He made no comment. Then his eyes fell on Nahida. "And her?"

"That's Nahida. She's coming to Tyre with us." I explained.

"Like hell she is." He spit on the ground. "They'll never let her into the city."

Nahida wriggled uncomfortably on her black horse. She couldn't understand the conversation, but the disapproving scowl on the soldier's face and shaking of his head didn't bode well. I tried to smooth things over.

"She's accompanying us to Tyre. Her family will meet her there. It's fine; she's Druze, not Saracen," I added cheerily. Pierre didn't care what flavor of unbeliever she was. "She's not bloody coming to Tyre with us. Neither is the…Sister. They'll never get through the gates." The little nun said nothing; her eyes dropped to her pony's neck and her fingers picked at its mane.

"But Brother Marco said…"

"I don't care what that leprous…what he said. He's not here, is he?" No, he wasn't. I was, and I had the responsibility for my friends—all of them. I heard my voice get shriller and didn't care.

"They have to come with me. She's got nowhere else to go. I promised her I'd get her to her family. And…I'm in charge. He said so."

Nahida's voice honked even louder and squeakier than mine, but with far more bravado. "My father is the personal provider of horseflesh to *Effendi* Raymo, and a close personal friend." Both Pierre and I stood open-mouthed. He, because he hadn't the faintest idea what she was yelling at him in Arabic about. I, because I couldn't believe her gall. Still, we could make it work. Ganging up on adults had worked before.

"That's Nahida. She's the daughter of Count Raymond's personal horse breeder, Jaffar Azzam. Her father and the Count are good friends, and he'll be very angry if anything happens to her. She's like a…a niece to him"—that sounded important, if ridiculous—"and he'll be furious if any harm befalls her."

She continued lying at the top of her lungs, and I abetted her. She shared in great detail how her father would meet her there, and was bringing many fine horses for the *Firangi*, and the Count's wrath would fall on anyone who interfered. It sounded even more ominous—and convincing—in Arabic, which I knew Pierre didn't speak. I translated, adding appropriate flourishes, taking special care to explain the punishments awaiting anyone who dared get in the way.

"They can't come with us…either of them," Pierre said weakly.

"Vell, ve can't stay here, either," Gerhardt interjected. It was more a command than a stated fact, I suppose. He reached down, grabbing me under the arms, and plopped me like so much baggage behind Nahida atop her black horse. The big beast danced unhappily but didn't throw me into the dirt at least.

Pierre shook his head and whistled to his own mount—the same color as Droopy, and much prettier, but not as strong or smart, I couldn't help noticing. The other soldiers were a good ways ahead of us, and we trotted after them. Sister was first, riding head down, Nahida and I followed, with Pierre riding at our shoulder, and Brother Gerhardt kept a keen watch at the rear.

It was one more night and most of the morning to Tyre. We'd figure something out by then.

Chapter 17

Never mind how blue the sky was or how brightly the sun shone down on the small troop of soldiers leading us to Tyre. A thick, black cloud hung over those of us at the end of the sad, bedraggled caravan, and it threatened more than just more rain.

Brother Gerhardt rode stoically at the end of our little troop. Gone was the singing, happy man he'd been earlier. He was once again the watchful, dour, frightening warrior we needed—despite what I *wanted*—him to be. Sister kept a one-handed death grip on her pony's mane, looking neither where she was going nor at anyone else. She stared down, muttering to herself, in prayer I suppose, and worked her rosary beads over and over. Nahida rode her black horse (and Lord help anyone who tried to tell her it wasn't her property), head held high trying to look every inch the daughter of Count Raymond's best friend. When anyone looked back, or Pierre tried to make sense of her, she'd sit straighter and look even haughtier

I had my hands around her waist, horseless and sad and bored. When Ali kidnapped me and took me to Salah-adin's camp, I rode on the front of the horse. It was bumpier, but the view was way better. This time we were traveling along a

211

high mountain road. Some would call it beautiful, but to me, it was too big, too wide, and too full of things that could kill you and seemed determined to do so. At least in the city, I knew what to expect.

The city. Acre. My mind drifted two days back to my home, and the people in it. Poor Gilbert, shifting back and forth between stone silence and muttering gibberish. Fadhil and Firan and their family. Sister Fleure. And Agnes. And Sergeant Jacques, Vardan, and the others. Brother Marco, too, sick but still trying to save the city. To save me, if you can call being cast out into the wilderness safe. It wasn't bad enough they visited and blamed me in my sleep; now my nocturnal visitors wouldn't leave me alone in the daytime.

The only way to keep them at bay was running my mouth. I turned to Pierre and blurted, "How did you…" *How could I ask this so it didn't sound like an accusation?* "…get to Tyre?"

Pierre avoided my gaze, pretending to study the hills for danger. "When it was certain there was no hope, and we'd taken terrible losses, a messenger came for Count Raymond from Salah-adin. He would give us safe passage back to Tripoli if we ceased fighting. Raymond could save all his men except the Hospitallers and Templars who fought with us."

I mumbled, "People in Acre—not me but, you know, people…like the man with the eyebrows—they're saying he was a coward." That brought Pierre's dark eyes level with mine.

"No. He had a terrible choice to make. We could fight and die, and I think part of him wanted to, but they had his wife—and all those people—hostage in Tiberias. They'd be spared too. They still have his wife and lands, but they're safe for the moment. As is the County of Tripoli, as am I and most of his men. He did what he had to do. A lot of people owe their lives to him."

I thought of all Nahida had been through, and our own battle with the bandits. "But they're not safe. The bandits that attacked us are from Tripoli."

Pierre nodded. "The dogs were under control when we were home and taking care of our business." I understood why a Mussulman robber wouldn't accept the rule of a Christian nobleman. This new state of affairs was confusing.

"But wouldn't the bandits be subject to Salah-adin now?" I asked. I felt Nahida tense up, straining to understand what we were talking about. Her frustration took the form of tight muscles up and down her back.

"Now it's Salah-adin's job to protect the people. The Caliph of the Devil commands the area, true enough. But that doesn't mean he has control of it." Ali had told me the same thing. "Some are taking the opportunity to stake out their own territories. A few of these bandits would like to be Emir themselves."

"Where's King Guy? Isn't he in charge?"

"Has he ever been?" Pierre shook his head to rid himself of such treasonous thoughts. "Captured. They're all captured. Balian d'Ibelin sits in Jerusalem with the Queen, and they're holding out for now. He's a good man but has no real army left. The infidel bastards have taken the rest of the Kingdom. Tripoli still holds out—and Tyre—although God alone knows for how long. Salah-adin is quite content to let us stew in our own broth until he's captured the real prize. Then he can pick at whatever bones remain."

I worked through what he'd told me, then brightened a bit. "So, Count Raymond is in command of Tyre?"

Another sad shake of the head. "You'll see, soon enough." And that was the last thing he said for a while, leaving me bumping along and bored.

To my left, Sister rode and worked her beads. Her lips moved, but the only sound was an occasional teary sniff. Behind me, Gerhardt sat straight up in his saddle, eyes drifting left and right. One hand clutched his lance, his sword packed behind him out of reach. He whistled between his teeth, sounding almost happy, but stopped when he caught me looking at him.

The toothy smile and straw-blonde hair made him appear almost childlike, although he'd have to have been the biggest toddler ever. I tried to imagine what he'd been like at my age and whether he knew what it was to feel small, vulnerable, and insignificant. Probably not. He had his own troubles, though. Each person had battles to fight, and they never seemed to win no matter how powerful they appeared to be.

Pierre rode up ahead to talk to his compatriots, then waited for us to catch up. That left Nahida to talk to, although she'd been awfully stiff and quiet since we'd set off.

"What are you going to do when we get there?"

"Ask for Raymo's protection, like I said." She seemed so sure this would work.

"Do you think he'll grant it to you?"

"He swore an oath to us. To protect us from Salah-

214

adin…and the Franks…and everyone else. He's already failed us once, he won't let it happen again."

"But what if they don't let you past the gates?"

"They will."

"Why would they? You're Syrian…"

She spun around to glare at me. "I'm Lebanese. And *Druzeh*. Your precious Count Raymo swore to protect us. Didn't you say yourself he's a man of honor?" *Was he? Is that what making a deal with the enemy makes you?*

"They won't let *her* in, though," Nahida added.

"Who?"

Nahida gestured with her chin towards Sister. "She's sick. They won't let her inside the walls." When Pierre said it, I shrugged it off. The simple, plain truth spoken like that, though…

"What's she…what are we…going to do? I am supposed to protect her. Marco told me to."

"She has the *jadham*—they'll never allow it. And they shouldn't. I wouldn't." She must have felt my anger burn the back of her neck. "She knows it, too. No matter how kind she is, Lucca, or how many friends she has, she's still sick. Not just her—a lot of people will be denied. There won't be enough food or room even for healthy people. Her only hope is her God. *Inshallah*."

At that moment I hated that word more than I ever had. "What will happen to her?" I knew the answer, but that didn't mean I wanted to hear it.

"She'll probably die. A lot of people will, of disease, or bandits, or hunger. But not you. And not me." She said it like she was telling me it was raining. A simple fact, neither good news nor bad.

I didn't want to ride behind her, anymore. I wanted another horse. My horse. But he was dead, too.

"Are you crying?" She asked.

"No." We rode on in silence, my friend pretending to believe me.

Occasionally, on a ridge high above us, we'd see a banner flapping in the breeze and men in Saracen armor on horseback. Salah-adin's troops watched but made no threatening moves. Our soldiers seemed to accept their audience, except for Brother Gerhardt, conspicuous in his Hospital garb and all too aware of what awaited any knights of the Christian orders.

After another hour we stopped for the night at an abandoned farm. The soldiers searched every building, haystack, and well for signs of bandits or Salah-adin's soldiers. When they found nothing suspicious, they gathered everyone around. Nahida and I got the glamorous task of gathering firewood. Gerhardt joined the other soldiers in setting pickets, deciding who would keep what watch. Sister Marie-Pilar wandered alone to a log bench beside the stone well, accepting the role of outcast with as much grace as she did anything else that came her way.

When Nahida and I returned with our arms full of wood, I checked with Pierre, who found some other insignificant chores for me to do. I combed the new packhorse. In reality, I did three-quarters of it, as she wouldn't let me touch her right rear flank at all and it wasn't worth losing a hand over.

My friend did her usual two or three horses in the same amount of time. She earned some pleased nods from the soldiers, who paid her a coin or two to tend their horses as well. She set to the task, humming to herself. If anyone found it odd to have a Syrian, female groom, they kept it to themselves.

That left me with nothing to do. After confirming my uselessness with everyone, I sat on the bench with Sister. I sat a respectful distance away, but the little nun lifted her left arm in invitation, and I snuggled against her. She laid a protective wing over my shoulders.

"Thank you for bringing me with you, Lucca." My confusion must have been obvious. "I haven't been out of that cursed city since before I took sick. A ride in the mountains has done me a world of good."

"I like the city better."

"But why? You have clean air, and sunshine, and trees, and birdsong…"

"And bugs, and boars, and bandits, and there's so much… Too much. Too much of everything."

She chuckled and squeezed me against her. "The world is a big place for us small people. But it is also wonderful and exciting, and there's so much to learn."

"I don't think I'm ready for the world." That was the fact of the matter.

"The world certainly isn't ready for the likes of you. But it had better be. You are going to do great things, Lucca. God has great plans for you, I think."

I didn't agree. And I wasn't sure I wanted Him making

plans for me without asking. "What about you? What has he got in mind for you?" This drew as sad, soft sigh.

"I've been asking Him that same question all afternoon. I haven't yet received an answer." She braced herself to tell me the next part. "But what I do know is that we'll be parted when we get to Tyre."

"No. I told Brother Marco that I'd get you to Tyre safe..."

"And you have, my darling boy. You brought me there safe and sound—or will tomorrow. But you know they won't let me into the city. Not as I am."

I looked up into her eyes. So kind, and such a counterpoint to God's cruel joke that lay under the gauze veil. "But it's not fair. And why did Marco send you if he knew you couldn't..."

"Because I asked him to. I was afraid, Lucca. So afraid of dying in that stinking, awful midden heap of a city. Afraid of what would happen to me and the other women if we stayed, afraid of watching him die and being left alone. I had to leave. It was cowardly and shameful, and most likely a terrible sin, but there you have it. I was a frightened, stupid girl and he took pity on me. Again." She looked up, her blue eyes bulging with tears that refused to fall. Her gaze drifted off to the west, over the tree lines to where the sinking sun was painting the first lines of orange and purple on the deep blue backdrop of the sky over the sea.

"I think that's why Marco sent me, too. To get me away from the city and keep me safe." Sister's small but strong hands gripped my shoulders and shook me.

"Lucca, don't you believe that. You're delivering an important message to Count Raymond, one that might save many lives. You matter. More than you know. And when you've delivered your message, you'll return to Acre and help many more people. You'll do great things, my beautiful one. May I show you something?" She pulled her beloved silver cross from around her neck. She caressed one of the arms with a grimy thumbnail. "Do you see this?"

Where she stroked, I made out the faintest line in the metal. It looked like it had been broken and then mended by a smith. "Uh huh."

"Well, I'll let you in on a little secret about metal. Where it's been broken and forged again, it will never break. It's stronger after it was damaged than before. This cross may snap again someday, somewhere else, but not where it was once broken. Isn't that interesting?"

"I guess so." Politeness seemed the best way out this conversation, which had become very confusing.

"I think you're like this cross, Lucca. You've been so hurt in so many ways, but you keep coming back, and each time stronger than before. You are a wonder to me."

"It's a wonder I'm still alive, you mean."

"Tsk, don't be foolish. The Lord looks after sparrows, but drunkards and fools as well. You don't have to be the smartest or the best, although you might well be. This is only the beginning. After you've done what you are meant to do in Tyre, you'll move on to your next grand adventure."

The notion of what I'd do after I delivered my message hadn't occurred to me. Everything and everyone I knew was back in the city I left behind. Of course I had to go back. That had to be what Marco's message to Count Raymond was: my next set of orders. And I'd gotten Nahida and Sister Marie-Pilar out safely. Maybe I could do the same for Firan and Fadhil, and Gilbert, and maybe Brother Marco and the others as well.

And I did get everyone this far. Unless you count getting my horse killed. And failing to warn everyone about the bandits. And nearly losing my life to a stupid pig. Suddenly I felt less sure I was much help to anyone, but I let Sister go on about how brave I was, and how smart, and how bright my future was. It seemed to make her feel better. Who was I to deny her such pleasure? I laid my head on her shoulder and let her prattle on.

The soldiers didn't share the nun's faith in my abilities. Once dinner was over I got conscripted to clean up and tend the fire. Nahida was making herself truly useful combing manes and picking hooves. The men all either dozed off or took up their assigned watches. I didn't get an assignment, so I took a blanket from one of the animals and snuggled next to Sister Marie-Pilar.

The little sleep I got that night was interrupted by wave after wave of nightmares. The cold damp dawn came as a relief.

After a quick breakfast, we began the last leg of our journey. Again, Sister, Nahida, Brother Gerhardt, and I brought up the rear. After that terrible night, I was pouty and sullen. The rest of the party seemed in no better mood, so we rode along keeping our thoughts to ourselves.

I noticed that for the first time in days, the road sloped downwards. It was gentle at first, the east side of the trail rising higher and higher over the track bed. Then the soldiers grouped closer and closer together as the trail became steeper. I felt, rather than saw, Gerhardt stiffen and arrange himself for battle. I peeked around Nahida's back to see what the trouble was.

Some distance ahead—how did people tell distance out here without buildings and streets to gauge by?—the road took a sharp turn left and downwards. At the far side of that bend, a ragged troop of perhaps ten or fifteen Saracens, dressed in dust-caked Turkish armor, watched our approach. They muttered amongst themselves, but nobody moved anything more threatening than their eyebrows as our small band approached. The Christian soldiers and their counterparts locked eyes, but otherwise nobody spoke. As Gerhardt approached, a murmur like the buzz of a beehive went through the sentries. Salah-adin's edict applied to civilians. Knights of the Orders were not guaranteed safe passage.

One of the Saracen sergeants—broader than he was tall—stepped forward and banged his sword on his shield. Brother Gerhardt gripped his lance tighter but said nothing through his gritted teeth. I felt the heat, like a lit fuse, between the two huge men and caught myself holding my breath. A commanding officer muttered something out of the corner of his mouth, and the Turkish fighter rolled his eyes, spit on the ground, and backed away.

Pierre's troop felt the tension. While they'd passed

unmolested, they now slowed and held their hands close to their weapons just in case. A few voices drifted towards us from the enemy side. "What kind of women are these? Is that the best you have?" and "Keep walking, Christian dogs. When we meet next we'll finish the job."

Pierre and the officers kept a close eye on their troops. One soldier with a pockmarked face turned around as if he wanted to shout something back, but an officer's gloved hand smacked against the back of his head and he reconsidered. Pierre fell back to ride with us, his mount between the women's horses and the Turks. He and the enemy commander nodded to each other. No words passed, but an entire conversation about honor, truces, and the futility of fighting was transmitted in those glances. As when I was with Ali in the desert, it occurred to me that common soldiers were more alike than different, no matter what side they were on. We passed without further incident.

The trail took a sharp bend left again, now south. We were greeted by the vista we'd sought for four days. I took in both the sight and the welcome cool breeze wafting up the hillside from the water. Ahead, the mountainside dropped into the sea. The wide expanse of water and sky was no longer broken by hilltops or trees. Blue met blue at the horizon, broken only by tiny whitecaps on the water, and perhaps half a dozen sails. My eyes dropped to the bottom of the mountain and got my first glimpse of the city of Tyre.

It was smaller than Acre and looked different. Tyre was comprised of an island, with ports at the north and south end. It had not one wall, but three, each taller than the next.

The only approach, other than by sea, was a strange road, like a very long bridge that stretched from the island to the mainland. At the landward end was another wall and a gatehouse. I could make out the shore road, the one we should have been on all along. It led from the south to a smaller town, swollen with tents and figures too small to make out, that spread over every inch of flat land as far as the eye could see. The road then continued further north into the Lebanon towards Beirut and Antioch. I tried to take it all in, planning my report to Brother Marco.

I turned to Pierre. "They can't attack a city like that, can they?"

He hesitated, then asked a question of his own. "Why not?"

"Wouldn't they have to come down that narrow road-thing? It would be impossible to keep up an attack, wouldn't it?"

"You've a good eye. They could do it. They even made a halfhearted try last week, but it will be bloody and ugly. Worse without archers, although they're an odd lot." He looked at the old archer riding ahead of him. "Besides, they don't have to attack us if they want to win." He pointed to the mass of humanity gathered on the shore. "See that? The city can't feed them all. If there's a siege, we can't hold out for long unless we are provisioned by sea. And there are too many people—the sick, the injured, the poor—they can't all get in even if we wanted them to. And there are a lot we're turning away."

He didn't need to tell me why. As in any city, it wouldn't

take much for a plague to descend. The sick couldn't be allowed admission—and even then, there was no guarantee the water wouldn't sour or hunger set in.

My heart sank as I thought of Sister Marie-Pilar and looked to her. The strengthening breeze blew her veil against her face, and I imagined I saw the outline of her scarred mouth through the cloth.

Nahida sat and cast her eyes over the mass of people hoping to gain entry. I leaned forward and said, "Maybe your uncle is down there waiting for you."

She nodded and played along with my fanciful idea. "I'm sure he is. The Christian army will need horses, won't they?"

"A lot of them." I slapped at a mosquito. Then another one.

"And then I can go home." She smiled for the first time since working the soldiers' horses last night, and looked almost pretty, despite the dust covering every inch of her except that nose. I swatted another mosquito. Then a big horsefly that tried to take a chunk out of my arm.

My hand touched the parchment in my belt. All I wanted was to reach Count Raymond, deliver my news, and get back. I wanted to see my friends; and when I was awake, rather than in nightmares. I'd had my fill of mountains and insects and wondering what was around every bend and hiding in every tree. What I yearned for was my city and a world I knew, even if it was dangerous. Outside could be deadly, too.

"Ve're almost there. Ve should go." Brother Gerhardt's deep voice rumbled next to me. I nodded, and we carefully made our way down the steep trail, switching back three or four times before reaching the flat land at the bottom of the hill.

At first, the salt air smelled wonderful and fresh, but only briefly. Before long, the smell of animals—horses, camels, donkeys—wafted toward us on the ocean breeze. As we got lower, and closer to the crowd, the sour stink of unwashed people seeped into our noses. Our ears filled with a thousand sounds, none of them happy. The horses picked up on it as well and shuffled in place with their ears at attention. The buzzing and twittering that had so annoyed me the entire trip were now replaced with moans of pain, and angry shouts of "Thief!" and "Let me through!" Curses rang out, and the clang of metal on metal. The mood was ugly and impatient, and it reeked of potential violence.

Within minutes, our progress came to a complete halt. Pierre and his men huddled in the middle of the trail— widened now to a full-blown road, not that we were making any progress. They were arguing with some other soldiers, who gestured and yelled at our soldiers, then pushed and barked at the crowd pressing around them.

People swarmed the guards and soldiers. Some demanded entrance to the city right away, being important people and all. Others wanted help for the wounded, or food for their children. One woman, in rags barely stitched together, plucked at a guardsman's sleeve over and over. "Please, sir, won't you help me? She's just a little girl." The shove she received was gentler than it normally would have been but was a firm rebuff just the same.

When the raggedy woman hit the ground, I heard Sister

gasp. Without another word, she slipped off her horse and marched forward. She held her hand out to the woman on the ground.

"What's wrong with your little girl?"

The woman looked up gratefully, reaching out for Sister's hand. Then fear crossed her face at the sight of the masked nun, and she pulled her hand back as though she'd scalded it on a pot. Sister took her by the arm and insisted, "Your daughter. What's wrong with her?"

The woman paused, then accepted the offered lifeline. "She's sick…I think."

"Show me."

The woman scrambled to her feet. The soldiers parted and allowed the two women past. I jumped down to follow, gesturing for Nahida to do the same.

From behind me, I heard Gerhardt's voice, "Lucca, vhere are you going?" I ignored him, desperately looking for Sister's tiny form among all those bodies.

Nahida pulled away from me and shouted, "Hey, that's my horse you son of a motherless dog!" Whether it was her tone, or the Arabic voice cutting through all the French, everyone froze. She ran back and shoved a teenage boy who'd grabbed the black horse's bridle. He backed off, hands up to ward off the crazy young woman. She looked over at me and waved me on. She wasn't going to go anywhere and leave her prize unguarded. I ran after Sister by myself.

The nun and the mother arrived at their resting place near a boulder. A younger woman, maybe a year or two older than Nahida, bent over something on the ground. The woman practically tossed her out of the way. On the ground was a tiny child. It wasn't a baby, but couldn't have been more than three or four years old. A shock of dark hair was the only thing visible above the shabby blanket.

Sister knelt beside the child. The other woman did too, but Sister gestured for her to stand a few steps away. The poor mother meekly backed up, her eyes never leaving her child. Sister Marie-Pilar bent over the child and ran a gentle hand over her forehead. After a moment, she gave her head a frustrated shake. She continued running fingers over the puny body, poking and listening for changes in breathing or the tiny, kittenish mewling that came out from under the blanket.

"What's wrong with her?" the mother demanded.

"The fever isn't the problem. Her belly is too hard." Her experienced fingers caressed the poor thing, trying to feel around without causing any more pain than she had to. Sister turned to the girl and simply said, "Water."

The flustered girl handed over a flask, making sure that their fingers didn't touch. Sister snatched it, offered it to the baby, then stopped and lifted it to her nose. Her eyes shut and she groaned. "Ugh. This is foul. Don't you have any clean water?" The girl looked at her mother, panic-stricken. That was their full stash, it seemed.

Sister lifted her head and shouted, "We need clean water here. Who has some?" Her eyes lit on a young family a few blankets away. "You, give me that water skin." Then she added, "Please. The child needs it."

"So do we," the father countered. I could see he was

protecting their precious supply and was prepared to fight bandits, soldiers, or other refugees to keep it. But he couldn't do battle with both a determined nun and his own wife, who grabbed the leather sack from his hand and passed it over.

"Please, it's all we have," the pretty but filthy woman whispered.

Sister nodded. She splashed a few drops into her hand and cupped it over the baby's face.

The mother pressed close. "May I hold her?"

"It won't hurt her, go ahead." Sister touched the child's forehead, making a quick sign of the cross and crossing herself, then stood up. Her place on the blanket was quickly taken by the panicky woman, who clutched the baby hard enough to make it mewl miserably again. Sister stood up and backed away. I tugged on her skirt.

"Will the child live?"

She breathed a ragged sigh. "Not without clean water and some luck. A few hours at most."

"But you said it would help."

"No, Lucca. I said it couldn't hurt. And it might make them both feel better for a time. Sometimes that's the best we can do. Offer a little hope or at least some peace of mind." She looked around at the throng of frightened people.

From a few yards away, a voice called out, "Please, can you look at my son's arm?"

Sister hitched up her skirt and marched over. No one dared touch or stop her, but they all made way. Desperate people were prepared to have even a leper save their children. She bent over the boy and tugged at the bandage around his forearm. "What idiot tied this? It's too tight. Do you want him to lose the arm?" Her fingers plucked at the ragged tourniquet. The sad, quiet woman I'd traveled with the last few days was gone. This was the experienced nurse who ran the leper ward with an iron fist. I smiled to see it.

Sister looked up and caught my look. Her eyes crinkled above the veil, then she turned her attention back to the boy. After issuing directions on how to properly secure a sling, she stroked the hair from the lad's face and stood up. Then she motioned me towards her.

"Where are we going?" I asked.

"To unpack my horse. I'm staying here where I can do some good." I froze in place, and she turned back and barked, "Don't stand there gawking, boy. These people need me."

I needed her too, but how to tell her that? And what good would it do? I knew that look on her face, and I hoped this was truly God's plan, because even He wouldn't be able to talk her out of something once she'd made her mind up. Certainly I couldn't. She took my hand and led me through the crowd back to where our party waited.

Without another word, she approached her pony and pulled her bag down. I reached up to pull the blanket off as well, but she stopped me. "You're going to want that blanket. Now you don't have to ride behind Nahida. Besides, I'm not going anywhere. Take her."

I watched, mute, as she gathered her few things. Nahida walked her big black horse over to watch. She said nothing and didn't grasp the conversation, but she could see what was happening.

Taking up her bag, Sister looked around and spotted the boar's carcass hanging over the back of the soldier's horse. "We'll be taking that. These people need food." It wasn't a request, even though the soldier tried to respond as if it was. Gerhardt's presence and the fact he was already cutting it free from the ropes ended any opposition. The big knight flung it over his shoulder, awaiting further orders.

Sister Marie-Pilar reached out a hand and cupped my chin, tilting my face up to her. "Thank you, Lucca. You did what you said you'd do for me. You gave your word you'd bring me to Tyre, and here I stand. Brother Marco would be proud of you."

No, he wouldn't. He would be furious at me for leaving you here. He'd think I ran away. He'd think I did all this for nothing. How was I so sure? Because that's what I thought about myself. But she would have none of that.

Sister bent low. "This is God's plan, Lucca. This is what I am here to do, and we can't argue with that. My job is to help the sick and those who need God's love. Your job is to deliver your message to Count Raymond and then help your friends escape Satan's grasp. We all have our jobs to do. Do you understand?"

I did something I had never done—lied to Sister Marie-Pilar. I looked her in the eye and said, "Yes, Sister." Then I buried my face in her bosom, nearly crushing the wind from lungs.

"Lord bless you, Lucca. You're a good man. You really are." She reached into her robe and pulled her cross—the one with the reforged arm—out from around her neck. She pulled it over her head and slipped it over mine.

"No, Sister. I can't..."

"I want you to have it, my boy. Now, off with you."

"What will you use? Who ever heard of a nun without a crucifix?"

She looked around her. "I'll find another, soon enough."

"Lucca, it's time. Ve must go." I tried ignoring Brother Gerhardt.

"Yes, Lucca. It's time." Sister pulled away from me and smoothed out her habit. "Hey, you!" she shouted at a young man carrying the boar's carcass. "Over there. Please." He looked surprised, but nodded and followed her directions, like any sane person would.

"But... What..." I couldn't even form the question. There was nothing more to ask. Or say. Nahida led the confused chestnut packhorse by the reins and helped me climb aboard. From my perch, I saw her march into the sea of people. Some shrank back, avoiding her. The desperate called for her help, and I had no doubt they'd receive it.

Pierre shouted, "Enough. Let's go." Gerhardt, Nahida, and I followed, pushing our way through the crowd. With a little conversation, we passed the pickets and through the gate at the landward end of the causeway. My eyes nearly popped out of my head as we rode towards the walled island of Tyre.

Only three of us who'd left Acre entered Tyre, though we'd started as four. Five if you counted Droopy, which I did.

Chapter 18

Even though I'd never been to Tyre before, I felt at home. The cool breeze on the causeway vanished as soon as we entered the walled city. The clean, fresh sea air gave way to the dank, sweaty smell of people and animals crowded too close together. I relaxed for the first time since leaving Acre, days that felt like weeks ago. I knew this world.

From atop the reddish-brown mare, I saw scenes identical to the ones I'd left behind. Fishmongers here looked like fishmongers in Acre. The brutish, toothless men struggling to control their animals would have been at home in Firan's corrals and pens. City guards had the same overwhelmed, frightened, and ready-to-hit-someone-for-no-reason look I knew so well.

The tension, at least most of it, left me. I grinned, taking in the view—not to mention the chaotic, familiar sounds and nose-assaulting smell—of a port city. Nahida had a different reaction. She shrank down, bent low over her horse, hoping to avoid the hateful stares and hand-covered whispers. The people wondered why a young Syrian girl was riding such a fine warhorse, surrounded by soldiers, and going around uncovered. I gave her the best comforting smile I could muster.

"Isn't this great? Safe and sound. I told you," I shouted, ignoring how close we'd come to not arriving at all. Nahida just cowered lower, looking far less impressed. Since she was no fun, I asked our escort, "Pierre, is Count Raymond in there?"

I pointed to a great fortification in the dead center of town, rising far above the high city walls. A ratty-looking, smoke-fouled banner of Tripoli hung limply alongside several others. Only a single pennant, one I didn't recognize, was clean and stood out from the others. The rest no doubt reflected the state of the few surviving nobles in the building. Badly outfitted guards in moods ranging from bored to surly to murderous surrounded the keep. The crowd went about its business. They all kept a safe distance from the armed men.

Pierre never looked at me. "He should be. First, we need to get the horses stabled."

Yes, a man had to look after his horse—even if it wasn't *his* horse. I patted the mare's neck. The boring old nag placidly followed the other horses to the stone-walled stable.

Pierre held up a gloved hand and we halted. Several young stable boys ran over, bowing and scraping. They grabbed the soldiers' reins, holding the skittish horses as they dismounted. Once on the ground, they stretched, groaned and complained—which meant everything was fine. Then it was our turn. A boy about my age looked up, a little confused at what someone like him was doing among these soldiers. I shrugged down at him and slid off the mare.

"Take good care of her. She's a good horse." She was.

Good enough, at any rate. Nahida was having no part of anyone taking care of her animal, though. She leaped to the ground and seized the reins from one of the grooms, giving the black monster a loving and very possessive neck rub and a nose-nuzzle.

"Which stall's mine?" she asked, the challenge clear in her voice.

The poor boy's mouth just moved up and down on its hinges. He shot a panicky look over to the senior groom, who was about eighteen or so. He was tall and fair-haired. Good-looking except for a missing eye tooth.

"You have to let us stable him…" He paused, flummoxed by how to address her.

Mademoiselle? Madame? Nahida glared at him, the reins gripped in white knuckles, dark eyes daring anyone to take her prize. Brother Gerhardt slipped off his mount and turned his grey over to the care of a filthy-looking lad about my size. He walked up behind Nahida, put a gloved hand on her shoulder, and smiled at the groom. The younger man got even twitchier, since it was now two to one. Not sure who else to appeal to, he turned to Pierre for help. "No one is allowed in the barns… sir." The young man took another, longer look at the foreign woman, then the giant Hospitaller, then back at the soldier. "Is it really hers?"

Nahida frowned, not following the French words but knowing her honor, and her horse, were at stake.

Pierre nodded. "It is. For now."

I tried not to betray my panic at the notion that someone might try and claim the beast. God help them if they did. I gave Nahida my most reassuring smile. "They'll take good care of him." That seemed to make her feel better, at least enough to hand over the reins.

She muttered, "I'll check up on him later. He needs a good combing." The groom nodded, despite having no idea what she said. The fact that it was in another language was frightening enough, he didn't need to know the specifics.

Pierre and another trooper whispered to each other. My friend nodded toward the keep, and the soldier took off at a run. I stretched my legs and rubbed my sore bum. "Can we see Count Raymond now?" The note tucked in my belt seemed to scorch me through my clothes and I wanted to be rid of it for good.

Pierre shook his head. "Not yet. Let's get some food into us. Count Raymond will see us when he's ready.

"Dat's a good idea." Brother Gerhardt clapped me on the back and steered us towards the guardsman's barracks. Pierre led the way and the quiet giant followed, staring down anyone who grumbled too loudly or eyed us a moment longer than necessary.

I didn't really notice the whispers and dirty looks, but we must have been some sight. A brother of Christ and one of Count Raymond's most trusted soldiers marched us past the exhausted, dispirited, and grumbling men. Nahida shuffled closer to me. I was stunned when she grabbed my hand and clasped it tightly. She held her head high and clenched her teeth. The way she crushed my fingers was the only outward sign that she was struggling to keep her composure.

"It will be fine, it's almost over." I hoped it sounded more convincing in her ears than my own.

We found a table in the farthest, darkest corner of the barracks. Pierre shouted orders at a young foot soldier, and soon we were offered half-full bowls of lukewarm stew that may or may not have contained something that once may or may not have been meat. I dug in and moaned my gratitude. Nahida stared at it with suspicion, poking at it with her spoon, hoping there was nothing in it that would damn her soul. Hunger won out, and she, too, began to eat, slowly at first, then sopping up every drop with the slightly moldy bread on offer.

For a moment the only sounds were spoons scraping bowls, and Brother Gerhard slurping broth out of his beard. Pierre ate slowly, his eyes watching the door for signs of deliverance. At last, a young page in Raymond's livery appeared.

"It's time, Lucca." Nahida, Gerhardt, and I stood as one. Pierre shook his head. "Only Lucca and the knight. You stay here."

Before Nahida could complain, I said, "No, she has to come with me."

Pierre was about to argue when a weary voice added, "That's a good idea. Ve can't leave her here." Gerhardt gestured with his chin at the soldiers frowning at the brown-skinned girl and muttering amongst themselves.

"Fine. Let's go." Pierre led us out of the dark room into the bright afternoon sun, then back into the shadows of the keep.

My heart pounded. When I first met Count Raymond, I

thought he was the stuff of legend. He seemed to be taller than he actually was, lean as a whippet with straight dark hair. From that sun-blasted face, his eyes burned into your soul and brooked no foolishness. He was the only adult I'd ever met who always seemed to know what he was about to say every time he opened his mouth. He would pause, then speak without an *um* or an *er* or a stammer. I had never been so in awe of anyone before, not even Brother Marco.

He'd been kind to me then. I hoped he'd be glad to see me, although even Pierre, whom the Count liked and trusted, was sometimes the victim of his sharp tongue and dark moods. Still, I was bringing him valuable information, and I had saved his life once. In point of fact, I'd tripped over his assassin and kept him occupied until Raymond could kill the attacker himself. But I was there, and he wouldn't have known about the killer if I hadn't screamed so loudly. That had to count for something, if he remembered.

The ground floor of the keep contained a gigantic, echoing entryway that opened into another brightly lit room. Through the open doors, I saw it set for an audience. Banners hung on the wall behind an enormous oak table and benches. I hesitated, thinking we were going in there—but Pierre just walked right past the doors, towards a well-worn staircase. Nahida and I didn't want to be too far away, so up the steps we went, right on his heels.

With each flight of stairs, the walls loomed closer and the keep got darker, despite the bright sunshine that sent dusty streamers against the wall. On the fourth floor, at the very top of the keep, Pierre pounded on a brown, ironbound door, and a weak voice bid us enter.

I took a moment to collect myself. Standing as tall and straight as I could, I prepared to meet the man who some said should have been our king. Depending on how things turned out, he still could be. I took Nahida's arm. "Stand tall and don't speak until spoken to, understand?" She swallowed hard. Then we stepped into the room.

I squinted against the candlelight. Even though it was still daylight, the windows were shuttered, and a dim flickering light was the only illumination. The room contained a table, two uncomfortable stools, and one thin, sad-looking man. I had to look twice to confirm the figure was, indeed, the mighty Count of Tripoli and former Regent of Jerusalem.

Raymond was dressed in uncomfortable-looking French court clothes. Normally, he wore local robes to accommodate the damp heat. He slumped in a wooden chair, rather than squatting on the soft, colorful cushions that I knew furnished his traveling pavilion. One arm—his left, I noted for when I'd have to report back to Brother Marco— was wrapped in a filthy sling high on his chest.

I immediately dropped to one knee and tugged on Nahida's dress, so she'd do the same. I looked up after a second, to see if he'd motioned me to rise as he usually did. She kept her head down but looked out of the corner of her eye for her cue. The Count sat there a moment, blinking at me, so I stayed kneeling and bowing. He gripped the table and pulled himself to his feet.

"Up, lad. It's good to see you well, my little louse." Nahida's eyes begged for a translation. "Stand, boy. Stand."

That little speech seemed to exhaust him. The Count coughed wetly, grimacing against the pain in his arm.

I stood, tugging Nahida to her feet. I heard Marco's no-nonsense voice in my head as I managed a weak "I'm glad you're well, My Lord."

The Count had no time for pleasantries. "I hear you bear news." I stiffened, looking him in the eye, more or less. I tried to gather the million stray thoughts in my mind to make a decent report.

"I do, Your Grace. Brother…" I was reluctant to use his name, even though we were among friends. "Your friend sent me with a message."

Count Raymond nodded. "And some company, I see. Who is your companion?" I'd been preparing this introduction all the way up the stairs. First, I'd introduce her as one of Raymond's loyal vassals. Then I'd tell him who her father was, and how he'd bought horses from them, and now she sought his protection. The words were only halfway up my throat when Nahida stepped forward unbidden.

"*Effendi*, I am Nahida, daughter of your trusted servant Jaffar Azzam. You promised him your protection, always. Now he's dead, as is my mother. I seek the protection you promised them and failed to give." The Arabic hung in the air like an old man's fart. Pierre, Gerhardt, and I gasped. No doubt she'd been planning her opening statement for a while but now second-guessed herself. Count Raymond's eyes flashed for just a moment and then his shoulders sagged. He looked up at the ceiling and expelled a sad, tired, ragged sigh.

Between clenched teeth, he answered her in her own

tongue. "Many people are dead, little one. And more to come. Still, he was a good man and a friend. And you've suffered greatly…" Nahida and I both dared to breathe again, but if we thought she'd be forgiven her effrontery, we were wrong. Raymond turned away, his good hand balling into a fist that crashed onto the table. The sound echoed through the room. He spun back on us: "But I am the Count of Tripoli, and I have greater concerns than one *Druzeh* brat. You demand protection? What makes you so special? My wife deserved my protection, and she's in Salah-adin's hands. Jerusalem deserved my protection, and it is about to fall. My men deserved my protection and I have failed them. All of them." He shook, spit flying as he raged. After a moment, he ran his good hand through his hair, puffing and panting in an attempt to regain control. He looked at us, then away in shame.

Nahida flinched as if the words left bruises. Her head dropped and tears welled up, although she managed to hold them back. With a loud sniff, she looked up. "I'm sorry for offending, *Effendi*."

Of all the things she could have said, that struck home. Raymond ran his palm over his face as if washing it. "No, I beg your forgiveness. We are all of us tired and on edge. Pierre, give this young lady over to Miriam until we figure out what to do with her. Get her a bath and a bed."

Pierre touched Nahida's arm, gesturing to the door. "It's fine," I told her, "Go with him. He's taking you somewhere safe." Not having any other choice, the girl shuffled towards the door, looking back at me for assurance.

"Really," I smiled, hoping it looked sincere. "It will be fine."

"But my horse…" she whined.

"They'll take good care of him. Honest."

Pierre gave her over to a guardsman with instructions to take her to Miriam, whoever that was. She was to have the girl washed, fed, and offered a bed, and to await further instructions. It was pretty much the same thing they'd said about our horses, but she'd be safe. For now.

When Nahida and the guardsman left, Pierre again closed the door and joined the rest of us. Raymond resumed his seat in that horrible chair. "Now, Lucca, Report."

I pulled the sweat-stained, filthy parchment from my sleeve and handed it to him. I willed my hand to be steady, but it ignored me. "It's all here, Your Grace."

He took the document and put it on the table without as much as a glance. "Just tell me. What does our friend have to say?"

Ignoring my shaking knees, I straightened my back and held my head high. I imagined it was Brother Marco I spoke to. The story spilled out of me.

I told him of Acre's fall to Salah-adin. There were a few questions, but he seemed to already know most of my answers.

Then he asked about the mood of the people. I told him as best I could—about the riots and the forty days' grace. Fewer now, I realized.

"And what do they say of me?" I hesitated. What was I supposed to tell him? That those who didn't think him a coward were certain he was a traitor?

"They don't know what to think, Your Grace."

"Bollocks. Tell me. It can't be worse than anything I've heard here."

Still, I hesitated before an answer suggested itself. "There's someone trying to turn the people against you, my lord. An Armenian... I don't know his name."

"What in Christ's name does an Armenian care about me?"

"I don't know for certain," I said, knowing he'd smell a lie. "But he's working for someone he calls 'The Lady.'" That didn't seem to help at all, so I told him about the man with the bushy eyebrows, and how he seemed intent on stirring up the crowd, and that he also knew Taqi-adin, and that he was on his way to Tyre when we set out. "I don't know if he's here yet or not."

I expected a grilling. My report had been as thorough as my panicky brain allowed, but I knew Brother Marco wouldn't be satisfied with it. I was a little surprised to see the Count take it at face value. He picked up the scroll from the table. As best he could with only one good hand, he tore off the twine and spread it out to study it.

After a moment, he asked, "Did you read this?"

"No sir. Although I know what's in it."

"Are you sure?" The way he asked it wasn't casual. He rerolled the scroll against the table. "He mentions a Sister of St Lazar. Where is she?"

I looked down at my feet. "Outside sir, in the camp with the...sick people and the ones who can't come in."

"What in hell's name was he thinking?" Raymond asked, more of the air than me.

"She wanted to leave…" I then told him about the journey over the hills and the bandit attack, and the men thinking she was a djinn. It made me feel better to tell the story. And sadder at the same time.

After that, I related Nahida's story. "Do you think she can work in the stables?" I asked, already knowing the answer.

Pierre chimed in. "No, boy. She's good with them, I grant you. Better than most of the scatterbrains we have working for us, but we can't leave a girl…like her…down there." He didn't have to finish; I could only imagine what a barn full of ignorant, hateful, frightened peasants might do. I also knew she'd be heartbroken.

Then it was Gerhardt's turn. The Count asked him to confirm my story, and he did, playing up my efforts and skipping over the unpleasant bits. He mentioned Droopy dying without making it seem like my fault, for which I was grateful. He added a lot more useful information, like the number of Saracen troops we'd passed, and that they were mostly Seljuk Turks. If a healthy Hospitaller accompanying such a bizarre caravan surprised the nobleman, it didn't show. Maybe it was explained in the letter. At any rate, we both reported all we knew.

I wanted nothing more than a bed and could feel myself wobbling from exhaustion.

The Count noticed. "You've had quite a journey, my little louse. I'd love to get you a bed. And a bath, for all our sakes. But you have to tell your story one more time, I'm afraid."

I can only blame exhaustion for my whining. "To who?"

"To a puffed up Greek cockerel who thinks he's running this cesspool of a city. There are a handful of us left, none with a rightful claim. And then there's Montferrat." I didn't know who or what a Montferrat was, but the look Pierre and Count Raymond exchanged told me I wouldn't like the answer.

A knock at the door interrupted us. A page, perhaps a year older than me, poked his blond head in. "They're ready for you, Your Grace." Raymond gathered Marcos' note in his fist, nodded, and led us down the stairs to the big reception room we'd passed on our way in.

The four of us entered the sun-drenched room. At the wooden table sat five men. Half a dozen knights of Outremer were there, including Count Reginald of Tyre, whose insignia I recognized. One of the nobles was a tall, sunburnt man with perfectly trimmed hair and beard. He was meticulously dressed in spotless armor and had that "just arrived" look about him. That had to be Montferrat, and it was likely his banner displayed on the wall outside.

Next to the newcomer was another man, dressed in courtly robes, and looking very official. I'd have never recognized him if it weren't for those mysterious, bushy eyebrows.

Chapter 19

Around the table sat some of the most powerful men in the Kingdom, or what was left of it, and what was left of them. With one exception, they were tired, haggard, and slumped in their chairs. Besides the noblemen, there were a Templar and a Hospitaller knight, looking more worn out than the others but twice as angry. A tall, skinny cleric in full vestments stood in a corner, biting his fingernails. I'd seen someone dressed like that in Acre, and guessed him to be the bishop of Tyre or at least a fancy priest.

At first, there was too much arguing, table-banging, and wine-swilling going on for anyone to pay us much mind. At last, the well-dressed nobleman looked up. His dark beard was trimmed in a Greek style, and he'd taken the time to oil it, creating an even sharper contrast to the others. He was taller than the others at the table, even sitting. His dark eyes blazed but there was ice in his voice. "Ah my Lord Tripoli, I see you've deigned to join us."

The rest of the room hushed. The other men dropped their eyes and I could tell this would not go well for Count Raymond. Their tired faces said they didn't envy him but were glad it was someone else's turn to take the heat. I knew that look all too well, and out of habit I took a step back and to the side, behind the Count.

Raymond's shoulders slumped but he raised his head and locked eyes with the other man. A lot of adults were doing their best to stay calm, and I wondered how long that would last. "Forgive me my lord…lords. I have received a messenger from Acre and wanted to learn what I could before reporting to you all. My apologies for being tardy, but I thought it wise to hear him out."

The well-dressed knight tore a piece of bread off the loaf in front of him and popped it in his mouth, feigning disinterest. As if he didn't care about anything my protector had to say, he brushed crumbs from his beard and his tunic. "And have you learned anything we didn't already know? I arrived in that city three days ago only to find they had surrendered the most important port in all of Outremer without a sword being drawn. They laid down like dogs, rather than trust in their God and fight the Infidel like good Christians, as they were sworn to do. We know all that already."

The most beaten-looking of the nobles offered a weak, "My lord, surely…"

The angry one—there was no doubt he was Conrad de Montferrat—turned and pointed a perfectly manicured finger at him. "My Lord Tyre, if I had not arrived when I did you'd have surrendered already. I practically had to wrestle Salah-adin's banner from your hands so you didn't place it on the battlements yourself."

The Templar and the churchman nodded in agreement, along with Eyebrows, who chuckled and took a big swig of wine. "Quite right, my lord. Who knows what would have become of this city without God sending you as he did." The Armenian grinned as the warrior priests banged on the table and the Lord of Tyre sank lower in his seat. He was enjoying the back-and-forth far more than was polite. The look he gave Count Raymond was the same expression I'd seen on the face of butchers sizing up which goose was the next to go. He paid no attention to me at all, for which I was very grateful.

De Montferrat held up his hand and the noise ceased. "And this oh-so-important messenger. What did you learn from him?"

Raymond stiffened his spine and lifted his head like I did when reporting out. He related everything I told him, adding things I didn't know myself. Sidon, Beirut, and other cities had already fallen in far bloodier fashion than Acre had. All those lives hadn't delayed their falls by even a day.

Conrad de Montferrat did not have Brother Marco's patience, and cut Raymond off. "So, for the next thirty days, we'll have more useless, hungry mouths arriving. Is that the only news you have?"

Count Raymond hesitated, then added, "Only that it would seem there are those who would sow discontent among the Christian lords and prevent a united front. Rumors of betrayal, and false accusations of collaboration with the Saracens."

De Montferrat let out a sarcastic laugh. "You mean you're worried they might think the nobles of Outremer failed them? What would ever give them that idea? They need no one whispering in their ears. Their own eyes would suffice well enough. I heard of your failures in Constantinople. If only the Holy Father knew what a mess you've made of things here…"

Count Raymond was trying to remain polite, but not doing a very good job of it. "My lord, if the Holy Father and the Emperor and the kings of France and England had sent the aid we requested when we pleaded…"

Montferrat slammed his fist on the table, nearly spilling Eyebrows' wine. "My cousin, the Emperor of the Holy Roman Empire himself, is preparing to send men and treasure. Surely, if we'd known how Guy and you lot would fail we might have spared everyone the trouble. Now my own father is prisoner, along with what's left of the army. That upstart d'Ibelin is going to surrender Jerusalem, and the True Cross is halfway to Damascus in the filthy hands of unbelievers. Please, stop me when I say something false."

I felt the heat radiating off Count Raymond. His voice grew quieter and lower, like a cur's growl. "King Guy listened to those newly arrived, not those of us who knew the real danger we faced. My own lands are threatened, my wife held hostage, not to mention the Holy City herself is under siege. With all due respect, my Lord de Montferrat, you have been in Constantinople listening to women's gossip. You don't understand the situation."

Montferrat stood up, both hands on the table as he leaned forward. "What I understand, my Lord Tripoli, is that over the years the people entrusted with the Holy Land have grown rich and fat—dressing like Moors, behaving like heathens and forgetting the true reason they are here. Your sacred duty was to protect the Holy City and the kingdom from the Infidel. Instead, you made deals, and treaties, and hoped he'd just go away. The dog grew stronger and stronger and you did nothing about it. Now I have arrived, prepared to follow my oath, only to find my father a prisoner, your lawful king captured, and not one of you prepared to fight for your God or what's left of your honor. Isn't that so?"

A shiver scrambled up my back as he berated Count Raymond. *It's true, everyone's given up. How are we supposed to rescue Acre and the others if we don't fight? Raymond looks beaten, but this man—my God he looks like he could beat Salah-adin single-handed.* I hated the disloyal thought, but as the local nobles hung their heads, the Templar, the Hospitaller, and the churchman nodded in rapturous agreement. Perhaps I wasn't the only one inspired by the newcomer. I nearly cheered when he added, "As for the city of Tyre, we will hold out until every drop of blood is spilled or we can once again claim what God has demanded of us."

"Your grace, I must go home and protect my people from what is coming." I couldn't help looking up at Count Raymond when he said those words. Was he, too, going to abandon the cities when they needed him most?

"Go ahead, slink home while the City of Christ falls into heathen hands. While Christian men and families fall under the Saracen yoke."

"I am no coward. But there is no one else…"

De Montferrat snorted. "Can't your heirs manage affairs while you do your sworn duty to God and your useless king?"

At this point, Eyebrows gently placed his cup on the table and leaned forward to hear the answer. I swear he licked his lips.

The air left Count Raymond's body, and he answered in a voice just above a whisper. It was hard to hear him through the cloud of shame. "There is no one, my Lord. I have no natural heirs. My family in Toulouse is caught up in affairs in France, and there's no clear successor... Yet I...we always assumed there would be time..."

"If I may, your Grace?" Eyebrows focused directly on Count Raymond, although he addressed de Montferrat with a title usually reserved for princes. "As the sworn representative of King Bohemond, it's vital that Antioch understand events in the surrounding counties. To be blunt, my Lord de Montferrat, in the event Toulouse proves too cowardly or negligent to do his duty and designate an heir, the regency of Tripoli falls to my King Bohemond of Antioch, per a long-standing treaty. He has two sons prepared to step in, although that may cause problems with their own succession. We've seen this coming for some time and have been preparing...contingencies."

"Thank you, Ambassador Barseghyan. Is that true, my lord Tripoli?"

Raymond nodded. "My dear friend the King and I have that agreement. But..."

Eyebrows—*so his name is Barseghyan?*—seemed to be enjoying himself. He topped off his wine and continued. "There's another solution—only as a placeholder until

Tripoli has fulfilled his greater duty, of course." He took a sip and sat back, making sure every eye was on him. "My King's new wife, Queen Sybilla of Antioch, has a son of the appropriate age and education…"

He never finished the sentence. The room exploded in shouts and protests. The men at the table, even the churchman, kept saying, "No" and "Never," except for the Templar and the Hospitaller, who crossed their arms across their chests and remained mute.

Raymond's hand flew to his sword and I jumped two steps back in case he decided to draw his blade. "That treacherous slut's bastard will never…"

Eyebrows patted Conrad's arm. "If I may, my lord. You are newly arrived and may be unaware of the situation in Antioch. Our king's lawfully wedded wife, Queen Sybilla…"

"…Is an Armenian whore who seduced my friend Bohemond into putting aside his true wife and marrying her. Everyone knows she and her family are in league with Salah-adin." Raymond was almost whining. To my ears, it sounded childish and unbecoming of the great man I knew. "No son of hers will ever sit in Tripoli."

"As the Queen's cousin, I take offense at that, your Grace. We Armenians have always behaved honorably with Tripoli and the Christian counties. And surely, even for a Christian nation, it's no sin to have previous good relations with Salah-adin. Isn't your past friendship with Salah-adin the reason you're standing here today, Lord Raymond? No one questions your loyalty to Christendom or to Jerusalem. Do they?" It was obvious, even to a fool like me, that plenty of people did exactly that. Eyebrows—Barseghyan, I corrected myself—was doing all he could to ensure it.

"Count Raymond, since I've arrived in this flea-bitten midden heap, King Bohemond's ambassador Barseghyan here is the only man among you who's behaved as if the survival of Outremer and the Holy Sites is more important than your own lands. Need I remind you that you—all of you—are here at the sufferance of the Holy Father and the Christian sovereigns of Europe." Eyebrows took a satisfied sip of his wine and leaned back in his chair as de Montferrat continued slapping Raymond senseless with his harsh words. "Now, you say there are mysterious agents afoot trying to shatter what little unity is left among the lords of Outremer? What proof have you?"

Oh no. No please…

Count Raymond put a finger to his nose and blew a snot-rock to the floor. It gave him time to steel his nerves and made him look less frightened than I knew he was. "Indeed, my lord. My sources assure me it's true."

Please God, don't do it. If you've ever loved me…

"And may we question this agent ourselves?" That wasn't really a question and everyone in the room knew it. I didn't know what authority de Montferrat really possessed, but everyone had ceded the power to him. Maybe it was out of pure exhaustion, but Conrad accepted it as if it were his by right.

No… Just… No.

"Is the written report or our spy not enough?" Count Raymond held the rolled parchment in his fist.

Thank you, Jesus.

"Is there some reason we can't question this informant ourselves?"

Yes, I might pee myself. Is that reason enough?

"No, my Lord." The Count stepped aside and took me by the elbow. He brought me in front of him. Now nothing stood between me and the nobility at the table but air. He leaned down and whispered, "Stand straight and tell the truth. Just as you were taught." Introducing me to the others, he said, "My contacts in Acre have sent Lucca, here, with the news."

Most of the men around the table chuckled at such a ludicrous messenger, Barseghyan among them. De Montferrat, though, steepled his fingers, and those eyes bored into mine. "What's your name, lad?"

My mouth formed the words twice before any sound came out. "Lucca, your grace. Le Pou," I added, feeling foolish. Nobody laughed, though.

"When did you leave Acre, boy?"

Determined not to shame Raymond, or Marco, or myself, I began. "Four days ago, my Lord. I think." Many of the others ignored me as I spoke. To my dismay, Barseghyan was not one of them. He had gone still, except for his eyebrows, which tried to join each other just over his nose.

"And what exactly did you see—with your own eyes, mind you?"

I gave the report as best I could, exactly as Marco had trained me. Just the details. A few times Lord Conrad asked me to clarify something, as Brother would have.

Once he asked a question of the rest of the table. "This toady, Peter Brice. Who is he?" Nobody at the table could answer the question, but I offered what little I knew.

"A merchant, my lord. From England, we believe. He was—is—one of Count Joscelin's men." This was news to everyone in the room, and eyes began shifting my way. They seemed to think I was worth listening to, which I wasn't sure I wanted. Count Raymond put an encouraging hand on my shoulder.

If de Montfort was testing me, I must have passed, because his tone became friendlier as we spoke. He even demanded one of the serving girls get me a drink of water, which I accepted, without slopping too much of it with my shaking hands.

"And this agent, this *provocateur*, you say you saw him speak directly to Taqi-adin?" Barseghyan leaned forward to hear the answer.

"No, my lord. To his…" *What in blazes was the word?* "… his uh, do they call it a lieutenant? General Taqi never spoke to any Christian other than Peter Brice, that I saw."

The ambassador relaxed and placed his wine cup on the table in front of him but kept those beady eyes on me. I held my breath. Lord Conrad paused, then mercifully broke his silence. "These charges are serious, lad. Did you have any idea who this mysterious agent was?"

I had a lot of experience lying to adults and found it was easier when your story was *mostly* the truth. *Had I seen him before that day, and did I know his name or rank? Not then. I sure as hell had seen him since, but that's not what the man asked me. I* bowed politely, my eyes drawn to the Ambassador "Once, on the street. But before that, no, my lord. I know that he wasn't from Acre, that's all I know for certain." Eyebrows took another, longer drink as he studied me back. I tried not to let him see me squirm and prayed he believed me.

Count Raymond patted my shoulder. "Well done, lad. My lords, will there be anything else? This young man has traveled a long way and has earned his bed. We all need rest and time to consider what we're to do next."

Conrad sniffed. "Some of us know what is next. We do our damned duty. Perhaps you should consider the same." He waved us away without another word, although I'm not sure it was his job to dismiss us. Count Raymond looked as if he might say something else but thought better of it. With a quick spin on his heels, he herded me, Pierre, and Brother Gerhardt from the room. The doors slammed behind us.

Count Raymond stopped in the anteroom and bent forward, struggling to control himself. He cursed through his teeth. "That arrogant whoreson. Married a queen meant for his brother and still thinks he's the cursed Emperor. Who does he think he is? And that Armenian lick-spittle, what's his name, Barseghysomething?"

I tugged on the Count's sleeve. "My Lord, there's…"

The Count jerked his sleeve away from me without a word. Pierre talked right over me. "What are you going to do, my lord?" His voice shook. He was as unnerved at seeing Raymond this way, as I was.

"My duty. I'm going to do my sworn duty, by God." I smiled. So we were going to fight after all. We'd rescue Acre and I could help free my friends. I decided I would tell him about Barseghyan later, when he was in a better mood and we wouldn't be overheard.

Then he continued, "My duty is to Tripoli and my people. We're going home just as fast as we can."

My mouth betrayed me yet again. "But, what about Brother Marco, and…and…" I was using my little boy voice but couldn't help myself. "And that man, Barseghyan, he's…"

"Don't argue with me, you little brat. We're going home, and you're coming with me as promised. Are you happy now?"

I wasn't. Not even a little bit. "But what about the Kingdom? What about Acre? We can't just leave them. Can we?"

"Shut up, you ungrateful little… I'm only taking you with me because I owe a debt. To you and…him. Now come along." With that, Raymond strode off. The way he marched left no doubt he expected us to follow. I trotted beside Pierre.

Breathlessly, I asked, "What's he talking about? What promise?"

Pierre kept walking, shortening his strides to match mine. "That letter from your leper friend. He asked Count Raymond to keep you safe and take you in. You knew that."

I stopped and looked up. My confusion had to be obvious. "So we're not going back to Acre?"

"It doesn't look like it, boy."

"But what about my friends? What about the people back

home?" He shrugged at me. "What about Jerusalem? Aren't we going to fight?"

Pierre stopped and watched the Count storming off ahead of us. "I think our fight is over for now. At least his is. And you go where he goes from now on. You said you knew what was in that letter." Pierre gave me a shove and we walked quicker to catch up "He's probably less happy about it than you are."

I very much doubted that. I grabbed the young soldier's arm, and he spun around to shout at me, but the look on my face brought him up short. "Pierre, about the Ambassador. There's something Count Raymond needs to know."

Chapter 20

My unhappiness and confusion were nothing compared to Nahida's. She was miserable being forced to scrub and clean along with the Christian women, who didn't have the foggiest idea who she was or why she was there and made no secret of their discomfort with her presence. The barn and horses were off-limits to her because that was men's work. I had my own orders to stay in my room until Count Raymond decided what to do with me. So naturally we met at the stable the next morning.

"This is shameful. Do all Christians treat their animals like this?" Nahida combed the black horse's coat until it shone in the dappled sunlight. I didn't see the problem. The horses were inside, fed, and warm, which is more than could be said for most of the people. Nahida pointed to an unused comb and waved her hand like some princess at a servant. "You need to brush her. Her mane is all ugly and matted."

I picked up the metal device with two fingers as if it was an annoyed scorpion. Holding it the same way she did, I moved slowly toward my unnamed horse, who didn't seem any happier with the arrangement than I was. The plan was to start at her right rear flank, but she skittered away, and I remembered she didn't like to be touched there, so I moved to the front, giving her neck an awkward pat. I ran the comb down her neck, managing not to hurt either of us. The horse shook her head, slapping me with her mane, but seemed contented enough, so I continued brushing her with tentative strokes. When I realized I wouldn't get bitten or stepped on, I set to work with more confidence.

Despite her feelings of being enslaved, Nahida sang and gabbed away like a drunken crow. "Isn't it wonderful? They say Count *Raymond...*" she was making an effort to pronounce it in French, "...is leaving in two days for Tripoli. We'll be out of this awful place and I can go home."

I didn't share her enthusiasm. For one thing, I quite liked Tyre. It was smaller than Acre but had all the things a city needed: a crowded marketplace, constant activity, and lots of noise. There were plenty of people, which meant there was always something to look at. The city was interesting for other reasons, too. Tyre was an island, connected to the mainland by that wide stone causeway. It was surrounded by those multiple walls, which kept much of the city in shade except at noon. Because it was a smaller town, no matter which way you walked you were bound to hit water sometime and couldn't get too lost. I picked up the layout quickly, including the alleys and rooftops that might make for a quick escape, if it proved to be necessary. And in my experience, it always did.

I was unhappy about leaving with Count Raymond and being carted off to Tripoli. *How could Brother Marco just hand me off like that? Was he trying to keep me safe or did he think I couldn't be of any more use?* I thought of everyone trapped in the

St Lazar House, then of Gilbert, gibbering away to himself in the Hospital, and Firan and Fadhil and their family, and the rest of my friends. Could I really stay tucked away when they were in such danger? Even Sister Marie-Pilar was outside the city, vulnerable to God only knows what hazards. She expected me to go back home, she'd said as much.

Yet I was protected, at least for the time being, and well-fed. While my shame grappled with my relief, I let Nahida rattle on and continued working on my horse's chestnut coat. She was a much prettier beast than poor Droopy had been, to be sure. I still didn't like her as much.

"The road to Tripoli goes right past my village. I'll arrive with the Count and an armed escort, looking just like a princess, and my cousins will be so jealous and impressed. And my auntie will feed me real food, not the terrible stuff you Firangi eat." She paused, "I mean I'm grateful, but…all that pig meat."

I laughed for the first time since I could remember. "But bacon is so good. Why would God make something so tasty and then send you to hell for eating it?" She made a face and shook her head. "Yes, it is. It's salty and fatty and smells sooooooo yummy." She pretended to gag but the giggle gave her away, so I kept teasing her. "Can you imagine? I wish I were rich enough to eat it every day. What would you eat every day, if you could?"

The question was meant to be fun, but her smile dimmed. "My mother's lamb stew. Big bowls of it. The house smells for a week." This was the first time she'd mentioned her mother since that day in the mountains, and I felt the sadness

263

wash over her. She shook it away and kept a determined smile on her face. "She'd make it whenever Papa came home from a trading trip. He always said he could smell it all the way from Beirut." I tried to imagine how big *his* nose must have been but kept the thought to myself. I knew it was mean, and I was glad she couldn't see my grin. I'd have hated to explain what was so funny.

I moved to the other side of the mare and developed quite a good rhythm. My arms ached a little, but it felt good to be doing something besides sitting and fidgeting. I thought about all Nahida had endured and was surprised to realize I felt a bit jealous. She'd at least had something I'd never known, and no one could ever take those memories away. What did I have?

My life. I had my life, that was about all. The priests told me often enough I should be grateful—a lot of people were losing theirs every day. Families, homes, enough to eat—why couldn't I have what other people had? *Why didn't I deserve what other people had? Was something wrong with me?* The mare whinnied at me for brushing too hard, so I eased up and earned a grateful nose-nuzzle.

I took a break to observe Nahida working the comb over her black mount's withers. She appeared so much older and more confident than I did, concentrating on her work, running experienced hands over the animal. At that moment she looked very much like an adult and not a playmate. An unexpected lump in my throat, and I realized soon enough she'd be gone from my life like everyone else.

Reveling in the thought of going home, Nahida pretty

much ignored me and stuck to her work. I stared, motionless, until a nudge in the ribs from a brown head brought me back to reality. The horse seemed to think I could watch and comb at the same time.

As the girl reached across the horse's broad back, her dress pulled tight against her chest and I made out the tiny but unmistakable bumps of breasts. It was as if they'd suddenly appeared, although I knew that was ridiculous; they must have been there all along and I'd just never noticed them. I blushed and turned away.

Seeking a distraction, my brain bounced around from thought to thought until Nahida asked me, "Do you think you'll get married one day?"

"I... I don't know. I suppose so."

"Of course you do. Everyone wants to be married. You want children, don't you? You can't have children without being married." The Hospital orphanage was full of people who would have argued with her. Instead of correcting her, I shrugged.

I hadn't considered the possibility until that moment. Adults had children. People with duties and employment and a place in the world got married. You know who didn't? Priests. And knights. And nuns. While I had no idea what I was destined to be, it surely wouldn't be any of those things. So, what would I be?

Probably the same thing as I was now.

Nothing.

Nobody.

Alone.

She interrupted my sulking. "I think you'd make a good father," Nahida declared.

"What? Why?"

She bit her lip trying to conjure up a reason. "You take care of people. That's a father's job." She meant I'd taken care of her. "Don't you want a family?"

Only all my life. Only with every part of my heart. Yet all I could think of was Marco, sick and limping and isolated behind enemy walls, and Sister Marie-Pilar left to fend for herself in a hellhole camp while I hid safely behind Tyre's walls. Then I remembered Gilbert, who I'd last seen talking to himself and the shadows on his walls. I'd left them all behind. I could never do that to my own children if God blessed me with any. But it's what I did. I left people, at least the ones who didn't leave me first. No, I'd be a terrible father. Besides, the world didn't need more lice.

"I've never thought about it," I lied. "What will your husband be like?" I knew he'd be tall, which for some reason made me sad.

It seems she'd given this a lot of thought. "He'd be *Druzeh,* of course, and his mother would be kind to me, and treat me like a daughter instead of a daughter-in-law, and…"

I was waving flies away and only half listening. I realized she stopped talking and turned to see why she'd gone quiet. Her eyes were wide with fright, and her mouth hung open stupidly. For a moment I wondered what I'd done, but then a chill ran up my spine. She was staring behind me. Someone else's shadow dwarfed mine on the stable floor.

I turned slowly. With the afternoon sun behind him, it

took a moment to make out the huge, hulking figure standing between us and any way out.

"He said it was some brat from Acre. Didn't really think it would be you." Big Paolo shook his head. "You should have minded your own business, boy." I felt the small comfort of my knife in my sleeve. Unfortunately, he'd found a new blade since giving his old one to the poor drunkard back home. This one was newer, bigger, and sharper than mine. He bounced it in his huge palm like he knew what to do with it.

I took two long steps back, then realized I'd managed to back into a corner of the stall. That was the last place I wanted to be, even if it kept the packhorse horse between me and the Genoese thug.

Paolo took a couple of slow, shuffling steps. "I thought you, of all people, would know to keep your damned mouth shut and let things be. What in Christ's name are you doing here, anyway?"

Nahida hadn't said anything yet. I saw her pick up a hay fork and point its two rusty tines at Paolo. Instead of being intimidated, he just chuckled. The fear in her eyes turned to anger, and I knew nothing good would come from that.

"Let her go. She doesn't know anything." I was surprised at how calm I sounded. Nahida strode forward to take her place beside me. She never took her eyes off of Paolo and held the fork out in front of her. It would have looked more threatening if she wasn't shaking so much, but I was grateful for the help.

"Why are you helping him? Barseghyan? Why would you

turn against your own people?" I didn't care about the answer. I just hoped he couldn't stab and talk at the same time.

He took another step forward. "What people? The idiots who came to this godforsaken land to bake in the heat and die for a city we've no claim to? A bunch of priests and sodomite nobles? I don't give a rat's ass about Barseghyan. Or Jerusalem. Or Christ Almighty, for that matter. My people are home in Genoa, and all I care about is living long enough to see them again and having a little coin for my trouble."

He checked over his shoulder to make sure there was nobody about. "Barseghyan's going back to Antioch soon, where it's a damned sight safer than this cesspool. From there, it's home, with gold in my pocket." He took a side step, eliminating any room for us to get by him. "Unless someone gets in our way. D'you see my problem?"

My heart drummed against my ribs, and the blood sloshed around in my head. There was no way out, other than to fight, which was a lost cause. Nahida thought we had a chance, though. She poked her fork at him unconvincingly, which only made him laugh harder. She gritted her teeth and feigned another stab, but to no more effect than the first time.

I pulled my own small knife, making sure it sat in my palm exactly as Sergeant Jacques had taught me. I couldn't help but notice how puny and useless it was. Much like its owner. Still, it had saved me once before.

"You're brave, boy. Know I take no pleasure in this." The

corners of his mouth turned up the tiniest bit, belying the notion. The lights in his eyes dimmed as the humanity left them. My horse whinnied, smelling the fear in the room. She turned her nose to the wall, pulling at her tether but she couldn't get away. Her hooves shuffled and kicked up a cloud of flies and dust. Droopy had been willing to die for me. This cowardly beast turned toward the plank wall to avoid watching the slaughter.

I transferred my knife to my left hand and balled my right hand into as tight a fist as I could manage. Then I forced my eyes to meet his. My teeth ground together as I tried to look taller and stepped forward.

"You want to fight me, you crazy little bastard?" He slipped his knife into his belt and clenched his fingers into fists the size of melons. Then he patted his belly and spread his arms wide. "Come on then, I'll give you the first blow." He waved me forward.

"Lucca, no!" I ignored Nahida and willed myself to take just one more step. Scrunching my eyes shut, I pulled my arm back as far as I could. Then I threw the biggest punch of my life. I smiled when my blow struck exactly where I wanted it to, and felt the flesh give way under my hand.

As soon as my fist struck my horse's right rear flank, she let loose an outraged bellow and did what I hoped—but didn't dare believe—she'd do. She rocked forward the tiniest bit and then kicked both legs straight back. Those vicious hooves caught Paolo square in the chest, and by the time I risked opening my eyes, he was slumped against the far wall.

The big man's eyes looked like twin moons. He reached

back to push himself up, but collapsed, grabbing his chest. Panting, ragged breaths came through clenched teeth. "God's balls, that hurts." His eyes stabbed at me, but they were the most dangerous thing about him now.

Nahida stepped forward, the points of her fork leading the way. She had every intention of driving them into the wounded man. I didn't blame her a bit, and considered grabbing her weapon to do it myself. It turns out I didn't have to.

While Paolo flailed his arms weakly, he found a sword pointed at his chest.

Pierre's familiar voice barked, "Don't move, you whoreson. Lucca, are you all right?" He took his eyes off Paolo just long enough to check we were safe. "We've been looking for you everywhere, you silly little bugger."

"I told you he was a remarkable lad, didn't I?" Another voice drifted in from the broad doorway. Framed in bright sunlight were Count Raymond and Conrad de Montferrat.

"Indeed, you did, my lord. Are you all right, boy?" I nodded at the French nobleman. "And you, young lady?" It took Nahida a moment to realize he was speaking to her. She bowed her head meekly and nodded to the strange but imposing Christian. She was still clutching her weapon and almost impaled me with it before her shaking hands dropped it to the stable floor.

We could barely hear anything over Paolo's desperate gasps. Pierre bent over him, checking him out, none too gently. "His lung's collapsed on itself. Probably broken a few ribs, as well." He looked over to me. "Who is he?"

I may not have known how to fight, but I knew how to deliver a report. I assumed my straight-ahead-back-straight position. "His name's Paolo. He's a Genoan. From Acre."

De Montferrat asked the next question. "And why was he trying to kill two children?"

"It's what he does. He's for hire… Your Grace." I tried unsuccessfully to hide the shaking in my voice.

"And who hired him?"

I took a deep breath, "Lord Barseghyan, Your Grace. He works for the Armenian." I was proud of pronouncing it nearly right and for not calling him Eyebrows.

The noblemen exchanged an indecipherable look. Conrad de Montferrat nodded. "A most remarkable boy, indeed."

Chapter 21

Paolo continued groaning and uttering terrible oaths and curses with what little air he could suck into his chest. Pierre bent over him but didn't look like he knew or much cared how to heal him.

"Will he live?" I asked. I hadn't tried to kill him, and the full weight of what I'd done settled over me. I'd only wanted him to leave us alone. The last thing I needed was another ghostly midnight visitor to join al Sameen and Brother Idoneus. Pierre shrugged but saw the stricken look on my face, bit his lip, and reconsidered his answer.

"The air was kicked from his lungs. Sometimes it heals with time." *Sometimes. Sometimes not, then.*

"What has Barseghyan to do with any of this?" Montferrat's sharp question snapped me back to the present.

Count Raymond answered him, "It appears that the Armenians have an interest in discrediting me. I know who he works for. And why."

Paolo lay on the ground taking weak swings at Pierre between curses and gasps. Conrad de Montferrat snapped at the soldier, "Christ's balls, get him out of here. Take him somewhere we can question him properly, assuming he lives long enough. And find that cursed Armenian"

A single nod from Raymond ensured that the soldier and two of his cohorts got to work. Pierre took the Genoese by the shoulders, while the two guardsmen took his feet. With some effort, and a lot of curse words I'd never heard before but wanted to make sure I remembered, they removed him from the stables.

"Well?" Lord Conrad's impatience matched my own. None of this made any sense. Raymond looked for inspiration on the ceiling before explaining.

"As I tried to explain yesterday, I've not been blessed with natural children of my own—my wife, Eschiva, was widowed and her children are not my blood, although I've tried to do right by them. There is no proper heir to Tripoli. If my family chooses, they may pick my successor, but there's been no word, and no one thought there was any hurry." Raymond took a deep breath, which included a lot of straw dust and he began to hack and cough. Montferrat and I waited, not very patiently, until he caught his breath.

"In the event of my death, King Bohemond of Antioch is to appoint a regent. It will be one of his own sons. Good men. Capable, if too young for the responsibility."

Conrad wore a mask of impatient confusion. "I agree, Bohemond is good king, and no coward in a fight, I grant you. What's that to do with the Armenians?"

"A good man, a good friend, and a good Christian, your grace. At least he was. Three years ago he went mad and put aside his lawful wife, the mother of his heirs, and married a princess of Armenia—Sybilla." He spat the name out like it was moldy bread. "It's said she bewitched him. There is a rumor she'd like her own inbred, idiot son to rule in Tripoli. Armenia has long ago reached its own accommodation with Salah-adin and the Saracens. It's no secret she's in league with him."

"Am I the only man in Outremer who hasn't cut a bargain with the Infidel?" Lord de Montferrat demanded. "I seem to hear a lot of stories of people with their own agreements with that devil."

For the first time, some of the old Count Raymond flared up behind those defeated, watery eyes. "There is a difference between striking an honorable, temporary truce and being in the man's employ. As you well know, given your own flexible relations with Constantinople. I have a responsibility to the people of Tripoli. This just shows I must return. If I delay, or if I'm...I don't...something happens, Armenia will establish backdoor rule over Tripoli and we'll be lost to Christendom and of no help to anyone."

"And if you run for home now, you're no help to us anyway." The room fell silent save for the grinding of Raymond's teeth.

I tried mapping all this out in my head. If something happened to Count Raymond, the king of Antioch would get to choose the successor. And if this Queen Sybilla—*who must be the "Lady" Eyebrows was talking about*—had some hold over him, it would be bad. I didn't quite know why, other than Count Raymond was against it.

Raymond was sounding more like his stubborn self. "My people need me. I must prepare for the defense of Tripoli. It's already too late for Beirut."

Nahida shuffled her feet uncomfortably. She couldn't leave without permission but didn't comprehend much of what was happening. At that moment I wished I didn't understand it either. I knew I'd left Acre seeking both to get Raymond's help for my city, and to help him. I had achieved neither goal, from the looks of things.

Montferrat stroked his beard. "What is the situation in Tripoli? Have the local Syrians joined with Salah-adin? I presume so—or they soon will."

Raymond's eyes fell. "I have always done my best by the local population. I can only presume they've scented the wind and sided with Salah-adin by now."

"Not all of them." That voice was my own, rising unbidden and unwelcome. Conrad waved his hand in that "get on with it" way grownups have.

I complied. "There are bandits abroad, my lord. They hate Salah-adin and want to take over Tripoli for themselves now that Count Raymond is no longer…"

"Yes, damn it all. We know that." Raymond's lips curled in a snarl and his fists balled up.

I gestured to Nahida, who stopped fidgeting. "They— well some of them—killed Nahida's family. The *Druzeh* have no love for the Saracens and are still loyal to you. My lord," I added, to sound properly polite after that little outburst.

I felt Nahida squirming next to me as Conrad de Montferrat paid any real mind to her for the first time. "And why is an enemy girl in the stables at all?"

Count Raymond cleared his throat, "She's *Druzeh*, my lord…" That began a quick theological discussion I didn't even pretend to follow. Montferrat summed it up, though.

"But she's not Christian?"

"No. She's not."

"Then she's not our problem. And what is she doing here? That's the only decent horse in this stable. Was she planning to steal it?"

Getting Nahida accused of horse-thievery was not in the plans. "No, Your Grace. It's hers." I needed to convince him. "Really. It was a…" *What was the soldierish word?* "…spoil of war."

"And what war did she fight in, pray tell?"

"When we fought the bandits, Your Grace."

"What bandits? What in the holy name of Christ are you talking about, boy?" He asked for it. I gave it to him.

I related the story of our journey from Acre, not leaving out any of the good parts this time. In fact, I may have made them a bit better, unintentionally of course. Raymond listened to the story as if hearing it for the first time, although he'd heard it several times already.

Conrad de Montferrat stared through to the back of my skull. "I thought you said you didn't recognize Barseghyan as the man you saw with Taqi-adin."

I tried to suppress a grin at my own cleverness. "My lord, he asked me if I'd ever seen him before that day. And I hadn't. He didn't ask if I recognized him after." I thought that was obvious.

Raymond winked at me. Conrad was less impressed. "And why didn't you say anything when we were in council? You surely recognized him then."

"God's sake, Montferrat. Maybe he thought his life would be in danger. Which it evidently was," Raymond interjected, and earned himself an upheld finger to shush him. To my surprise, he allowed himself to be shushed. I didn't even think you were allowed to do that to a Count. Conrad continued his questioning.

"He's a smart lad. Possibly too smart for his own good. I don't suppose he knows how many troops are at Acre?"

I knew this one. Ali had told me, and I passed it on now, "Two companies, my lord. Stationed outside, although they're inside by now. The rest are on their way to Jerusalem to assist with the siege."

Both older men looked at me as if I'd summoned the devil. "How do you know?" they asked in unison.

"Brother Marco…and Count Raymond… They trained me to notice things."

De Montferrat turned to Raymond. "Brother Marco?"

"A knight of St Lazar. He's been our eyes and ears in that city for years. It's he who sent Lucca to us." *A good man, sick and perhaps dead, in danger every second you adults argue.*

"And he's still there?"

Raymond nodded. "As far as we know. He sent the latest word with Lucca, and we've heard nothing since."

Montferrat paced back and forth across the stable. "We can't rescue Acre without good information. Can we get word in or out?"

Raymond shook his head. "The city will be closed off. You saw the port blocked with your own eyes, my lord."

"What about the boy? Can't he go back?"

My heart swelled as I blurted out. "Yes."

At the same time I shouted my agreement, the Count offered a loud, "No." My heart fell to my kneecaps. "The lad was lucky to escape with his life the last time, and he's coming back to Tripoli with me. I've sworn it to him."

"Yet he made it out of a fallen city with a girl, a nun, and one bodyguard. Fifty miles, dodging bandits and Saracens along the way. It seems he's more resourceful than you give him credit for. Or maybe God has a greater purpose for him." That last sentence was meant for me more than Raymond, if I had to guess. The praise made me stand straighter and stick my chest out a bit. "One more time, boy, what did you see on the journey here?"

I told my story yet again, trying not to sound exasperated, because adults hate that. Conrad de Montferrat shook his head and said, "It's a shame. We could have used those horses."

Count Raymond shot him a poisonous look. In Arabic, he addressed Nahida. Even I'd forgotten about her, and she was taken aback. "I'm sorry for the loss of your parents. Your father was a good man, peace be upon him. And an honest one. You're right, I've failed your people. Please forgive me. I'll return you to your family. Your uncle Tazir, he still lives and is well?"

Nahida gave a quick nod. "*Inshallah*, he does."

"Speak like civilized Christians, damn you." De Montferrat stomped his foot like a petulant child. After a quick explanation, he said, "Infidels killing each other isn't our concern, but preparing a defense of the Kingdom is, even if I'm the only one who seems prepared to do it. Does this…horse trader, whatever his name is…have any decent horseflesh left to trade with us?"

Raymond thought long and hard before answering. "He may. They had the best stock in the Lebanon, although it sounds like raiders have bedeviled them. Because I wasn't there to stop them," he added, mostly to himself.

At some point in all this discussion, Pierre reappeared. He stood shifting his weight from one foot to the other, waiting for his betters to stop bickering so he could slip a word in sideways. "My lords, Ambassador Barseghyan is nowhere to be found."

De Montferrat spat a curse between his clenched teeth. "Well, find him! He has much to answer for. If Antioch is in league with Salah-adin, too…"

"Not Antioch. It's Bohemond's wife that…" Raymond tried to correct him, but the other man would have none of it.

"It's a sorry man who can't control his woman. Isn't there anyone in this pestilent place who remembers how to be a proper man, for Christ's sake?"

"We can't all marry empresses and leave them at our leisure." I had no idea what that meant, but de Montferrat's eyes nearly bulged out of his head at Raymond's impertinence.

Pierre shuffled his feet and looked like he wanted to say something, but held back from either fear or wisdom. They sometimes looked an awful lot alike. Raymond didn't see him, but Conrad did. There wasn't too much he didn't notice, it seemed.

"What? Spit it out."

Pierre waited until Count Raymond stopped another wet, nasty-sounding coughing jag. "You were asking about horses, my lord. There are some Druze horse traders—at least that's who they say they are—outside the gates. They've been asking for an audience with Count Raymond for two days now."

Count de Montferrat thought for a moment. "It might be a ploy—how do we know they haven't gone over to Salah-adin already?"

"The Druze have less reason to trust him than you do, Your Grace. The more fanatical among Salah-adin's people would kill them as heretics," Raymond answered, although his thoughts were clearly elsewhere.

While the two nobles went back and forth, Nahida stepped closer. Her eyebrows joined each other in confusion. She made out enough words to know it involved her, but not much more. Her brown eyes asked the question for her.

I whispered, "There are some horse traders outside who want to speak to…whoever is in charge." *Which is who, exactly? Was Montferrat now the power in what was left of the Kingdom?*

"Is it my uncle?"

"We don't know…" Before I had finished, Nahida brushed past me and addressed Count Raymond in that bossy-girl way of hers.

"*Effendi*, that must be my uncle. May I go see? He will have many horses for you. You know how good his stock is…"

Raymond held a hand up, translating to the other nobleman. "She wants to go see if that's her uncle. If so, it may be the first bit of good news we've had in a while."

If Nahida was going out there, it wouldn't be alone. "May I go, too?" Neither man spoke, so I kept pressing. "I can look around and report back. If that is her family, you'll want to hear as soon as you can, won't you?"

The way Raymond shook his head, he was about to protest. De Montferrat nodded. "Good idea. My Lord Tripoli, make sure they have an escort. A good one. And you…" He pointed at me. "We want a full report on everything you see out there. Understand?"

Out of the side of my mouth, I told a jubilant Nahida, "They're letting us go out to see." To Count de Montferrat, I simply said, "Yes, Your Grace," and tried not to look as excited as I was.

"He'll… They'll need a pass. I'll arrange for one right away." Count Raymond spun on his heel and left, muttering to himself.

"Signed by both of us, I should think," de Montferrat shouted over his shoulder. "And mounts. See if we can't find them mules or something."

"Your Grace, Nahida has a horse already."

De Montferrat nearly drooled over the black gelding but sighed. "Ah yes, the spoils of war." He nodded curtly, and Nahida gave him a quick salaam and me a brief hug before giving the horse's neck a much bigger one. I knew I had better catch up with Count Raymond, who was not pleased with me, although I wasn't entirely sure why. As I turned to leave, a large, somewhat soft hand grabbed me by the collar. "Boy, do you really want to go to Tripoli with Raymond? Or would you like to help rescue Acre and serve the kingdom?"

"Your Grace? Count Raymond has a letter…" *Letters are official. After all, they are in writing. Could you even argue with them?*

"Consider it carefully. And do tell me all you see out there, won't you? No matter how unimportant Tripoli may consider it. This will be our little secret. Hmm?" His too-calm manner removed any doubt about the answer.

I offered a non-committal bow and dashed off after Raymond and Pierre, while Nahida readied her blanket and bridle.

I hadn't really agreed to anything but felt like a traitor anyway. *After all, what kind of fool would want to go back to a defeated, fallen Acre if given the choice?*

Chapter 22

By the time I caught up to Count Raymond and Pierre, the Lord of Tripoli was in a full-blown rage. At first, I thought it was something I'd done. Perhaps the guilt of Lord Conrad's offer and my potential betrayal were plain to all. But it wasn't about me at all. In fact, Raymond never acknowledged my presence.

"That puffed-up, arrogant...cockerel. He's been here less than a fortnight and he presumes... Without the foggiest clue about what's at stake here...and the alliances..." He paused just long enough to hack up a gob of spit, which he shot into the street a good distance ahead of him. It was a good shot, for an adult—especially for a nobleman.

Pierre coughed into his hand. "Ummm, my lord..." He motioned with his head to indicate my presence. Count Raymond calmed down, although it took effort. At least he stopped ranting and raving. He let the steam quietly escape through his ears. All that energy must have gone to his legs because he walked faster, and I had to run to keep up.

He said not another word until we reached his dark rooms in the keep. After the bright sunshine, the room smelled musty, and it took a moment for my eyes adjust to the dim candlelight. It was like he was trying to make his comfortable room into a prison cell. "Take that girl to the horse traders. If they aren't her family, or you get the tiniest sniff that something is wrong, you get out of there. Understand?"

I nodded.

"What did I just say?"

I swallowed hard. "I'm to take Nahida to her family...if it is her family. If it's not, we're to get out of there."

"And if it is?"

That was a good question. Nahida would want to go with them. *Would they take her home? Would I see her again after today?*

Count Raymond mistook my hesitation for stupidity. He spoke as if I was a simpleton, slapping the tabletop with each word. "And if it is...find out how many horses they have and what they want. If they are who they claim to be, I'll come to them. Repeat it."

I did. It must have been sufficient, because it earned me a nod.

"Christ, I wish you could read and write. This would be so much easier. That's the first thing we'll see to when we get to Tripoli." He bent over his desk, grabbed a quill, and scrawled something on a small piece of vellum. Then he used his ring to embed a wax seal on it. He sprinkled a little sand and after a second held the sheet up to let the grit fall to the floor.

"Again."

I repeated my instructions.

He appeared satisfied. "I hope for everyone's sake this comes to pass. We need those horses. And for the girl, of course." That part came too late to sound sincere. He stared into the flame of his desk candle for a long time. When he spoke, at last, it wasn't to me. "Of course you'll need an escort. I presume you'll want that big Hospitaller along?"

As far as I knew he was sitting alone in his cell at the Hospital, being snubbed by his fellow soldiers. Apparently, word of his shameful condition had reached this far.

Count Raymond sat on his hard chair and expelled a long, slow breath. "I shouldn't be asking this of you. You're only a child. But I've run out of people I can trust." He rolled the parchment and wrapped a piece of string around it and held it out to me, When I reached for it he grabbed my wrist. "He'd be… He is…so proud of you. As am I. This is the last time, Lucca. Soon we'll be home in Tripoli, and I can keep you safe. Away from this madness. For a time, at least. You've done enough."

"Thank you, my lord." What else would I say? Tripoli wasn't home, was it? I managed not to say any of that out loud, and I'm certain he took my looking away as simple shyness or even overwhelming gratitude instead of shame. He smiled and waved me out the door. Pierre followed.

The afternoon sun sat right on top of the seawall, blinding us as we walked towards the stables. "Are you coming with us?" I asked him.

He shook his head. "No, but you'll be in good hands."

"About time. I vas getting bored. And Schatzie is ready to leave vithout you." Brother Gerhardt stood beside his big horse, beaming like the sun itself.

I grinned back. When he'd left me and returned to the Hospital, I wasn't sure I'd see him again. "They're letting you come with us? I thought they'd need you for…Hospital things." His smile dimmed.

"They aren't particularly fond of me there. Besides, I swore to Marco I'd keep you safe. As long as you keep insisting on doing foolish things like this, that'll keep me plenty busy."

Nahida led the black horse by the bridle. She'd combed it so the afternoon sun glinted off its coat like polished steel. It's what her father and uncle would expect. "It's about time," she said. "Let's get going." Her voice vibrated with excitement. She looked ready to just run off at any moment but somehow restrained herself. I couldn't blame her.

"I'm coming. Oh, should I get my mare?" I realized I hadn't given the poor packhorse a moment's thought since she'd saved my life earlier.

"Ride with me," Nahida said. She leaped up onto her mount, who danced and showed off for a second, then stayed still long enough for Nahida to reach down and take my hand. While she pulled, Brother Gerhardt placed his huge hand under my bum and almost tossed me up and over the horse entirely. I landed on her back haunches, wrapped my arms around my friend, and settled in. It felt a little embarrassing not to be on my own mount, and I'd have rather walked, to be honest, but the poor girl would have burst into flames if forced to wait another minute.

"Ready?" I asked her.

"Lead on." Brother Gerhardt mounted his own ride and waved her forward. Nahida shook the reins and clucked her tongue. The horse gave its black head an arrogant shake and took two steps forward when a firm voice commanded us to halt.

Conrad de Montferrat approached us at a determined, steady pace and when he was near enough, waved me over to him. To Nahida's annoyance, I slid off the back of the horse and approached with what I hoped was the right amount of deference. "Your Grace?"

The nearer I got, the taller he seemed. He wasn't an unusually big man, but like Count Raymond when I'd first met him, he carried himself with an authority that made him seem larger than he was. Knowing it was a sin, I thought how diminished my patron looked now compared to this man. Lord Conrad reached into his pocket and pulled out a big a ring with a seal on it; it looked like fishes and crosses.

"Raymond gave you a pass, I presume." I nodded. "Let me see it." I pulled it out of my sleeve. He nodded but didn't bother inspecting it. "You may have to go back and forth a few times. You'll need something that can take a bit more wear and tear." He handed me the ring. "In Constantinople we know a bit more about such things, you see. You have much to learn."

I gawked and fumbled with the heavy object as I tried placing it on my finger. I could have slipped it over two digits and it still would have been loose. "Your Grace?" I asked, unsure what he was asking.

"That will get you past any guard in the city. Naturally, I'll expect you to come see me immediately upon your return. We will discuss what you learn out there. Let's see how good you are at noticing things."

I was confused. He was asking me to report back to him separately from Count Raymond. Was that being disloyal? Weren't we all on the same side, fighting for Jerusalem?

I pulled Sister's crucifix from under my tunic and untied the leather thong. Then I looped one end through the ring and made a clumsy knot. The big clunky ring dangled from my neck and bounced against my chest accusingly. I placed it under my tunic, sure the bulge could be seen by anyone who cared to look.

"Good lad." He ruffled my hair. I know he had good intentions, but I hated when grownups did that. With great effort, I refrained from brushing it back into place. A moment later, I was back up behind Nahida and heading for the causeway gate.

Despite the growing throng of people camped outside the city, a large number had managed to gain access. Tyre's streets and lanes were over-crowded. We moved slowly enough that we ran no one over, but we couldn't escape the ugly, hate-filled stares. People understandably wondered why two Syrian children had such a fine horse and a holy escort. Not to mention how we even got into the city when so many worthy Christians languished outside. Poor Nahida just ground her teeth in frustration. I know what she wanted— to kick her horse in the haunches and run to her family as fast as that beast could go. If they were her family, of course. I couldn't bear to think of how she'd feel if it turned out any other way.

Approaching the gate, we were stopped by two old guardsmen with pikes held across their chests. There was the usual blustering about horse-thievery, a low growling threat from Brother Gerhardt, and a cursory inspection of my pass, which neither of them could read. Before Nahida's head burst into flames, the gates swung open and we left the safety of Tyre.

The wind on the causeway blew salty and cool. My hair, which was at least as long as Nahida's, whipped around my face, and the briny air stung my eyes. We rode upstream against the crush of people, garnering stares from those who couldn't imagine why anyone in his right mind would leave a city they themselves were desperate to get into. At points, the throng was so closely packed that Gerhard moved ahead of us to speed progress. The sight of a mounted Hospitaller parted the crowd like the Red Sea.

The closer we got to the mainland, the more the tension left Nahida's body. Being outside city walls relaxed her as much as being inside them made me feel safe. Eventually we reached the gate at the landward end of the causeway. There was more nonsense, but the guards weren't willing to fight to keep people in, so we passed onto the mainland without incident.

They came from the north, so they'll be that way somewhere," I pointed

"I know that," Nahida snapped, but her head swiveled back and forth anyway, desperate for some sign of her people. After another moment she turned her head as far over her shoulder as she could to look at me. "Uncle Tazir is a good man, and he has a big house. Maybe you could…come live with us?"

"Really?" So many people seemed willing to help me, and all I wanted to do was go home. I suppose I'd thought about it, the way you think about a big slice of melon on a hot day or a warm bed when you've been out in the cold, but far less seriously. "But I'm a Christian."

"Not a very good one," she laughed. She had a good point. "At least you could hide there for a while. Wouldn't it be better to stay with me than someone you don't know? And we could teach you about horses, and it would be so much better than being stuck in a dirty old city."

What would I do on a horse farm among people who were even more despised than I was? Still, being with her—and with a real family—was a pleasant enough daydream. I let her prattle on.

In the short time we'd been in Tyre, the camp of angry, hungry, frightened people had swollen even further. It was like a boil about to pop, and almost as poisonous. I could make out the stench of bodies and filth underneath the fresh sea air. People glared at each other over a few extra inches of elbow room, or one more spoonful of the watery soup they'd somehow pulled together. They gave us more than our fair share of hateful looks as we made our way on that beautiful black horse and headed in entirely the wrong direction.

I saw two very haggard, annoyed-looking guardsmen staring. I offered my best orphan-in-distress smile. "Excuse me, sirs. Do you know where we can find a family of horse traders? They arrived from the Lebanon a day or two ago. They might have been trying to speak to…"

"Count Raymond, yes, or Montferrat, or Saint Peter or

anyone else stupid enough to let the heathen bastards inside the gates. They're up there," he gestured vaguely north with the point of his lance. "Four of them and maybe half a dozen horses. They come by every few hours demanding we let them speak to who's in charge. Does it look like anyone's in charge here?" He had a point. "What's your interest in them?" he squinted at us with suspicion.

I loved lying to adults, and had a lot of experience doing it, so I puffed myself up properly. "They are my cousins. And Count Raymond is their patron, so nothing had better happen to those horses." I was a little worried that a cousin of Druze horse traders traveling with a blond giant Knight of the Hospital might raise uncomfortable questions. If they had doubts, they kept them to themselves. We were going away, and that made their lives easier.

"Then you'd best hurry. They aren't very popular, as you can imagine."

I could imagine all too well. I thanked them over and over until they waved us on, happy to be rid of us. Before we passed by, I had a thought and turned back. "Have you seen a nun anywhere? With a veil? She'll be with the sickest people."

"The Leper Nurse? That'd be east, near the cesspit. They call it St Jude's House because it's where we're keeping the hopeless cases. You've got some odd friends, boy." He was right about that, but I still would have given a smart-mouth response if Nahida hadn't lost her last shred of patience.

She clucked her teeth and snapped the reins, kicking her horse into a trot. We followed the guard's lance tip towards the north. I could tell the animal wanted to run. The muscles tensed along its flanks and straight up Nahida's spine, and I prayed they would both control themselves until we got where we were going.

After another five minutes, we heard the nervous whinny of horses. Our mount pricked up his ears, and Nahida sat higher over his neck, craning to see where the sound came from. Brother Gerhardt pointed, but his assistance was unnecessary. She urged the horse to move a little quicker, which caused a near-collision or two with people on the road, but it wasn't too much longer when we saw them.

Amid all the blankets and people and chaos was a circle of open space, like an invisible corral. Inside of that, four exhausted-looking men squatted with swords in their laps protecting half a dozen very nervous horses that were pegged to the ground. One man, with the blackest beard I'd ever seen and dressed in less-filthy robes than the others, stared defiantly out at the surrounding mob.

With that pitch-black beard and coal black eyes, he looked as fierce as any bandit could be, but his expression changed when he heard Nahida yell out—in Arabic and at the top of her lungs, which wasn't wise—"*Amm… Tazir amm.*" Hearing himself called "uncle," he lifted his head, shaded his eyes with his hand, and squinted into the afternoon sun.

I pointed. "Is that…" But I was speaking to the wind, as Nahida had already leaped off the horse to the ground, leaving me alone on top of the black monster. I slid off, just to be safe, and held the reins.

The scary man stood alert, hand on his weapon, then

dropped it, and that scowl became a big toothy grin.

"Nahida? What..." A flood of Arabic shouting and wailing began, with hugs and cheek-kissing, and all kinds of carrying on.

Nahida stood in front of the man for a moment at arm's distance, then collapsed into him, her shoulders bobbing up and down as he stroked her hair. His eyes lifted over her head to look straight at me. I avoided his gaze, concentrating on keeping the horse still. This wasn't my reunion. Not that I had anyone who'd care that much about me. I felt happiness for my friend while jealousy burned in my guts. Wiping my eyes and nose on my sleeve, I pretended to pat the horse's nose just for something to do.

So, it was her family after all. Part of me was a little surprised that her story turned out to be true—that part at least. I felt a little better knowing I'd been able to help. Count Raymond would be pleased, too. It looked like he'd get his horses. The clunky ring dangled at my throat like lead. But what of my other master?

"You vere a good friend to her." Gerhardt's rumbling voice interrupted my thoughts.

"She saved me more times than I saved her," I said.

"Friends don't keep score, Lucca." He smiled through his matted beard, and I thought he could use a good horse-combing.

"Just a moment," I told him. I led Nahida's horse over to one of Uncle Tazir's companions.

The old horse trader, ancient enough to be an uncle of the uncle, eagerly came towards me with his arms outstretched. I meant to hand him the reins, but instead, he wrapped me in a smothering hug, kissing me wetly on both cheeks over and over until I had to push him away. "Blessings upon you, my friend, for taking care of our Nahida. Tazir will want to thank you himself…"

I wiped his slobber off my cheek with the back of my hand and retreated a step. "I… I need to do something. Tell her I'll be back in a little while. There's something I have to do…" I offered the reins and he took them without question, giving the horse an appraising pat on the snout. "I'll be back…"

I spun around, ignoring both his praise and protests. Clenching my fists, I scanned the hills behind the camp. Then I set my jaw and marched east.

I heard Brother Gerhardt's voice over my shoulder. "Vat are you doing?"

"Seeing if I can find Sister. She's up there." I pointed towards the steep wall of hills. "I want to talk to her."

"Do you vant me to come with you?" I didn't, but I knew there'd be no shaking him. I nodded and tromped uphill towards the foulest-smelling part of the camp. The big man said his usual nothing and followed a respectful distance behind. Even as focused as I was, I found the tread of horse's hooves so close behind me comforting.

I didn't have to ask directions to the part of the camp named for the patron saint of lost causes. St Jude lay just on the other side of the smelliest place I'd ever been—and for someone with my experience, that was saying something. The clothing became more ragged, the eyes hollower, and the frowns deeper the closer I drew. Few people there stood. Most squatted or lay on tattered blankets as if strewn about by a windstorm. Families, mostly mothers and skinny, terrified children, huddled together for protection more than warmth. Every eye followed me as I made my way, shadowed by the huge soldier.

I scanned ahead, over the limp and prostrate bodies. Exhaustion, illness, and despair left most of the people here immobile. All except one small figure in a faded blue robe, carrying what looked like a bucket. She darted from group to group, offering a ladle of whatever was in there to people, always beginning with the children. I stood watching for a while. Some people shooed her away. The more pathetic-looking the person, though, the more meekly they accepted her help—in most cases a single scoop of water and a blessing.

One boy, a little younger than me, approached her a second time, and I saw that ladle circle above Sister's head like a cudgel as the lad scampered away in terror. I laughed, remembering the skill with which she wielded a wooden spoon to rule the kitchen at St Lazar. How many times had I been on the receiving end of one of those scoldings for filching food?

She turned in my direction only once. Even from so far away I saw the veil over her face was grimy and foul. She paused only to place her hands on her hips and stretch her back. Once, as Sister Marie-Pilar turned to face downhill, the sun caught her eyes and I could swear she smiled behind that awful mask.

My eyes and throat burned as I watched. The tears were only in part from the stench of the open latrine. Nobody who lived here for long would avoid pestilence, I knew that. Sister Marie-Pilar must have known it as well. But the knowledge didn't stop her. In fact, it drove her on to greater and greater efforts. She flitted from foul blanket to fouler blanket like a bee in a dying garden.

"Aren't you going to talk to her?" rumbled the voice from behind me.

I turned to Brother Gerhardt. "No. She has more important things to do." More important than me. Maybe more important than any of us. "Let's go back." I wiped my arm across my forehead to get rid of the sweat. Like Sister Marie-Pilar, I had a job to do, although mine wasn't as urgent or holy.

Count Raymond would get his horses. I needed to get back and tell him that. That was only half my job, though. I still needed something worth taking back to Count Conrad. If I could make myself useful...

But what was I going to tell him? There were thousands of sad, lonely, frightened, and sick people who'd die if they didn't find shelter? I doubted that would move him very much. What would Brother Marco expect of me?

I couldn't wait for inspiration to find me. It was time to get back. As usual, Gerhardt said nothing as we turned back towards the sun setting over Tyre and the sea. I cupped a hand over my eyes to get my bearings. Acre was far to the south. To the north, along the sea, was the road to Sidon and the Lebanon. Behind me were the mountains. Where had all these people come from?

I picked my way through the crowd, eyes sweeping side to side. I saw soldiers in tattered uniforms, some bearing the crests of their lords. I recognized the sigil of Acre. And Tripoli—some of Count Raymond's people were trapped out here; I was sure he'd want to know that. It was no great surprise to see those who'd fled Sidon, and Jaffa, and a dozen other small cities. A few soldiers appeared to have the crest of Jerusalem on what remained of their uniforms—were they survivors of Hattin, like me? There weren't a lot of priests to be found. It was heartbreaking, but it was just everyday misery. People lived, fought, stole from each other, and died of disease, hunger, and stupidity, as people always did. So many souls in such tight quarters made it worse than usual, but nothing a powerful man like Conrad de Montferrat would consider interesting in the least.

As we approached the Druze camp, I continued studying the scene in front of me. More banners and refugees. Haifa, Nablus. Two well-dressed soldiers from Antioch sat with some other men around the remains of a fire, while a few feet away a family tried to explain to a crying child why they couldn't go back to Sidon.

Soldiers from Antioch?

"Vere are you going?" My escort hissed as I veered off my path and stalked closer to where those troopers sat on rotten logs. There were two uniformed men, and two more dressed in rags. For some reason, one of the men sat with his head under a blanket even in the evening heat. *Look for what isn't there that should be or what is there that shouldn't be.*

They had two horses tethered outside the fire ring, nosing around in the dust for anything green to eat. One guard stood a half-hearted watch as the other three figures put their heads together, deep in conversation. The figure under the blanket sat directly opposite my position, on the other side of the dead fire. With his back to the sun, it was hard to make out any distinguishing features. The heat got the better of his discretion and he removed his makeshift hood to wipe the perspiration from his brow. That's when I got a good look at him.

In particular, his eyebrows stood tall and proud.

"It's Barseghyan," I hissed to Brother Gerhardt.

"Who?" He asked, far too loudly.

"The Armenian, the one they're looking for."

Gerhardt dismounted. His weapons and boots made a terrible racket, and his horse whinnied. "Pity's sake, I can't hear you, boy. Vat did you say?"

Even above the din of the camp, the noise drew the Armenian's attention. He looked up to see a giant Hospitaller and a very surprised little boy. A boy he knew. One he never expected to see again. Those giant eyebrows came together then flew apart as his eyes widened in shock and he jumped to his feet.

Startled out of their conversation, the Antiochian guards spun towards us, hands on their weapons. Out of the corner of my eye, I saw Brother Gerhardt pull his oak staff from his horse's saddle. He looked at the guards. The guards looked back at us. Then they pulled their swords.

The more senior soldier attempted to scare us off. "What

are the two of you looking at? Go on, keep moving." Instead of providing an answer, Brother Gerhardt took a step forward. The guards took a step backward, then regrouped and took two strides towards us. My eyes darted from the soldiers to Gerhardt to Barseghyan. The ambassador now stood and dropped the blanket from his shoulders. Under it were the fine clothes he'd worn in the council chamber. He inched away from the others and almost tripped over a small child playing in the dirt, because he was too busy keeping his gaze on us.

Gerhard took another step closer, swinging his staff in one arm, limbering up. The guards from Antioch were about to make an unfortunate mistake. As much as I'd have loved to watch the coming battle, I had to keep an eye on Barseghyan, who was sidling to his left—closer and closer to the horses.

The Armenian's compatriots now pulled their own weapons and for one ridiculous moment, I thought about pulling my knife. But I got distracted by a sudden movement. Barseghyan grabbed one of the horses and ripped the tether peg from the ground. He scrambled onto the bay's back and shouted to the others, "I'll go get help. Stop them." Then he kicked the unhappy animal in the haunches and took off, scattering a mass of shouting, angry people before him.

Without thinking about it, I took off after him on foot, leaving Brother Gerhardt to face three men. Barseghyan was heading for the main road, most likely to escape north. I ran in a diagonal across the camp as fast as I could, shouting, "Stop him. Wait, stop him. Thief! Thief!"

My path took me close to where Nahida's family was camped. She heard me shouting and ran towards me. "Where have you been? My uncle…"

I ran right by her. Looking back over my shoulder I yelled, "It's Barseghyan, he's getting away…," and kept running. I don't know what I was thinking. I was always quick, but there was no way a small boy with short legs could outrun a frightened man on horseback. Still, that didn't stop me from trying. My stupid limbs kept pumping, even as my breath got shallower and shallower. I saw and heard people scattering and screaming at the man on the horse, who was getting further and further away. At last, I could run no more. I bent with my hands on my knees, panting for air and trying my best not to vomit.

The ground shook under my feet, and I saw the hooves of a big black horse pull to a stop beside me. "Come on, we'll catch him." Nahida's hand reached down. I nodded and gripped it and she pulled me up on the first try.

I wrapped my arms around her waist, and between gulps of air, spat out, "He's getting away."

"No, he's not." Nahida gritted her teeth and kicked at her horse. Followed by a cloud of shouting and confusion, we took off after the ambassador from Antioch.

Chapter 23

Barseghyan had a long lead on us, but Nahida was determined to catch him. She laid her body flat against the horse's neck and urged it on with cries and ululations, while I bounced behind her, praying I wouldn't fly off each time my bum slammed into its spine.

The sun threatened to set into the sea now, and the world was painted bright orange, bathed in firelight. The shadows were long but fading—it would be dark soon, too dark to chase a man on horseback with a good lead. Luckily, the road was clear of travelers. The first wave of refugees had found the camp outside Tyre already, and those still on the road already had found shelter or at least a flat spot to camp for the night.

The onrushing darkness didn't seem to bother the horse any. Given the chance to run wild, the gelding was taking full advantage and seemed to enjoy itself nearly as much as Nahida did. The girl laughed and whooped, while I screamed and prayed and buried my face in her back. Occasionally someone shouted at us to slow down, and I waved apologies as we charged right past them.

Up ahead, the road curved and snaked in the way of shore roads. That meant I could see what lay two twists ahead when the bends were close to the ocean, but nothing straight ahead as a quick turn one way or the other meant we were flying blind. It was getting too dark to make anything out, and I had no way of knowing if we were gaining ground on our prey. I hoped we were—if only so the bouncing would stop.

Just before blackness engulfed us, we reached another bend. I managed to unsqueeze my eyes long enough to make out a fast-moving blur, perhaps a little more than a quarter mile away, that could only be a horse and rider. It wasn't moving nearly as fast as we were, but I'd been in gales that didn't move as fast as Nahida's animal. Either Barseghyan's horse was getting tired or he didn't think he was being pursued.

"That's him," I shouted.

"We've almost got him." She sounded triumphant. I was a little less excited as a question occurred to me.

"What are we going to do when we catch him?" I had the dead trooper's knife, but we were two children against a grown man—one who didn't seem to have any qualms about hurting us.

"You'll think of something. Heeeeee," she told the horse and gave another kick of her heels.

I will?

Before I could think of a brilliant plan, we entered another blind turn. The only sounds were the rumble of horse hooves on packed dirt over my own panicky breathing. Then there was something else. From somewhere up ahead came a terrible racket. In an instant, a man shouted, then a horse screamed in terror and the loud complaining bellow of an ox joined in. All that came to a crescendo with the sound of splintering wood and more screaming from more voices.

Nahida pulled the animal to a trot as we rounded the bend. Ahead of us was a scene straight out of hell, all shadowy forms and brain-scraping noise in the twilight. A horse shrieked and struggled to its feet while a big black ox lay on its side across the middle of the road, bellowing between panting gasps. Blood ran from its nose and its chest rose and fell in two parts; its ribs were shattered.

What remained of an oxcart and its contents—pots and pans and other household articles, for the most part—were scattered across the trail. A huge woman went back and forth between her two tiny children, checking them for damage, while her husband stood in the middle of the road with his hands in the air, cursing God and someone laying by the side of the road.

"You blind idiot! Look what you've done. Oh Lord Jesus, what have we ever done to you? I'll kill you, you bastard!" But he didn't move toward the other man. He stood looking around in shock. I followed the shouting to the side of the road, where a man lay groaning in the short, dry scrub.

Nahida jerked us to a halt to avoid hitting anybody, and momentum launched me onto the ground in a heap. She patted the horse's neck lovingly and jumped down. Brushing myself off and making sure all my pieces were still attached, I looked to the side of the road where a well-dressed man lay on the ground. He swore in Armenian—I recognized some of those words—and clutched his leg about halfway up the shin. In the moonlight, I could see his boot facing the opposite way from the rest of him. That leg was never going to heal right.

I heard the voices of people and animals around us as others came to investigate the accident. Questions and exclamations of amazement along with the cries of children flew all around as I stood with my mouth open. I stared at the havoc around me for a moment, then took two tentative steps towards the man on the ground.

Barseghyan lay flat on his back, rolling his head side to side in agony. Somehow, above his own groans, he heard my approach and lifted his head. At first, he thought rescue had come, but then those momentous eyebrows rose in surprise, then furrowed in outrage.

Glaring at me, he put his hands to his sides and tried to sit, then rise to his feet. He only managed to hoist himself a foot off the ground before crashing down in pain and fury. Lifting his head enough to watch me inch towards him, he hissed, "You did this, you little bastard."

I wasn't sure what to do or say. I was as shocked as he was to see my knife in my hand. I don't remember pulling it from my belt, but everything was unfolding as if I weren't involved. I felt more like a spectator than an actor. I know madness swirled around me, but somehow I shut it all out, keeping my focus on the wounded man. I took another step forward.

With more bravado than belief, I said, "I'm taking you back to Tyre." It came out much timider than it sounded in my head, and maybe that's why he laughed, despite his pain.

"No, I don't think you will." I hadn't expected that and had no response, other than to gawk at him. "What do you plan to do about that?" I had an old knife and a young girl for help, but nothing close to a plan, and he knew it.

Convinced I couldn't stop him now, he braced his good leg and once again tried to gain his feet. Keeping his eyes trained in my direction, he gave one more good grunt and raised himself almost to a hopping stand.

Out of nowhere, an arrow buried itself in the ground between his feet with a soft "thwunk." Shocked, the Armenian fell onto his backside. I spun around, as startled as Barseghyan. Nahida stood with her arms folded beside three fierce-looking Druze men on horseback. The one holding the bow was the older man who'd thanked me earlier.

Barseghyan's eyes trailed from the arrow between his legs up to the man who fired it. "Let me go. There's gold in it for you."

"No, we will take you to *Effendi* Raymond." Nahida's uncle said. His voice was flat and brooked no argument.

"Why help him at all? What's he ever done for your kind?"

"God alone protects us. But *Raymo* is an honorable man, and our family will stand by him as he's stood by us." Uncle Tazir nodded to his two companions, who leaped off their horses, pretty nimble for old men. They stood beside me, holding thin leather laces in their hands.

Barseghyan, like all Armenians, never gave up bargaining. "You'll be safer under Antioch. And when our Lady's son is your *effendi*, you'll be protected from Salah-adin for good.

And Armenia can be a very good friend—even to those who aren't Christian." I made a point of remembering that one. Count Raymond had been correct about the plot from Antioch's new queen after all.

The older uncle stood behind Barseghyan, reached beneath his armpits and hoisted him to a stand on his one leg. The other used the leather thongs to tie the ambassador's arms. There was no point tying his legs. He wasn't running anywhere—maybe ever again. It hurt to look at the flopping appendage. The horse Gerhardt killed looked healthier.

The crowd had swelled to more than a dozen people by now. Some were commiserating with the family about their oxcart. One or two surreptitiously eyed the household goods that were scattered on the road. The rest grumbled as the brown-skinned men wrestled a Christian onto his feet. Or foot.

The crowd went silent. "Vat have you done now, you little troublemaker?" I'd forgotten about Brother Gerhardt and was glad to see him atop his skinny, overburdened warhorse. The crowd looked from the knight to the Syrians and back again.

Uncle Tazir salaamed politely to Brother Gerhardt. "Well met, Sir Knight." The Hospitaller bowed his head in response. His cuirass was grass-stained, and there was a vicious bruise on his cheek, but he seemed otherwise in good health if a little confused.

"This is Nahida's uncle Tazir, and her...uh... Cousins? Uncles?" I looked to Nahida for help with the introductions.

"My uncles. All my uncles," she said. She laid a hand on

Tazir's arm. All three men bowed and offered effusive praise in Arabic about my bravery, which seemed to amuse the big man.

"So *Schatzie* found her family. God be praised." He squinted at the hopping figure. "Is this him?" He gestured to Barseghyan, who hop-shuffled on one leg, biting his bottom lip to stop from screaming.

"That's Ambassador Barseghyan. The one who sent Paolo after us."

At that, Gerhardt growled like a hungry bear. He pointed to Nahida's uncles. "Give him here. I'll watch him." Even if they didn't understand his accented French, there was no mistaking his purpose. He pointed at Barseghyan and then patted his horse's neck. He moved a little slowly getting off his horse, and I felt bad about abandoning him back at the camp. I also wondered what the Antioch soldiers looked like. Fierce and determined, he grabbed the ambassador by the arm and flung-hopped him onto the back of the warhorse, then climbed up behind, only kicking the man's broken leg once as he did so. That showed a lot of restraint.

"Ve should get going. Count Raymond vill vonder vhere you are. And I hear he's been looking for this one." I nodded. I turned to Nahida, happily chattering with her uncle, and had a terrible thought.

"Are you staying here?" I asked. Nahida nodded, but Uncle Tazir shook his head.

"She cannot stay in a camp with a group of men alone. And that place is terrible. Take her with you—Son of the Fleas—and when we meet with Count Raymond in the

morning to discuss business, we will take her home with us."
Son of the Fleas... I liked that. Ali called me that as well. The
Arabic language had its charms. I was happy to hear she'd be
coming with us. Happier than she was, but she accepted her
uncle's orders like an obedient niece.

The old archer got back on his horse, his bow strapped
behind him, and I reached out a hand to touch it. The horn
was smooth to the touch, and I saw it was considerably
smaller and lighter than the Frankish bows. It was the second
time in only a few days that an arrow had saved my life, and
I was drawn to the strange weapon, enthralled.

The old man pulled it down and gestured for me to take
it. I held it in my hand and used four fingers to give the string
a gentle pull. It took more strength than I thought.
Sheepishly, I handed it back to the old Uncle, who waved me
off.

"Take it, please. A gift for bringing back our niece, thanks
to God. For being such a brave young man." He smiled
toothlessly and nodded.

I shook my head. "Oh no, I couldn't..."

"Lucca, don't be rude. You can't refuse a gift." Nahida
was giving me that look of hers that brooked no argument.

I took the bow and salaamed gratefully.

Nahida held out her hand for me to join her on her horse.
Her uncle didn't think this arrangement was appropriate but
didn't want to fight with her any more than anyone else did
and held up his hands in surrender.

I climbed back on the sweaty, jittery creature. He danced
and snorted and didn't look at all happy to be going back to

the city. After salaams, bows, vows of friendship, and friendly threats about what would happen to me if anything befell Nahida, we headed back to Tyre. Gerhardt and his prisoner rode point, Nahida and I behind them, and Uncle Tazir and his men in the rear, keeping a watchful eye out for trouble.

The moon was bright and the road shone in front of us as we headed south. There wasn't a lot of conversation, just the clop of hooves on dirt, the occasional snort, and buzzing insects. The mosquitoes formed clouds around us, and it was my job to wave them away while Nahida guided her mount. Outside was too full of bugs, and I'd be glad to be back in the city. At least in town, the mosquitoes didn't travel in giant flocks, and cockroaches didn't sting or fly up your nose.

I didn't realize how fast we had traveled chasing Barseghyan, but we must have covered a lot of ground, because it took forever to make our way back. The sky was a lighter shade of blue by the time we arrived at the traveler's camp. One very nervous cousin had been left behind to watch the horses, and he was overjoyed to see the family return. There, Nahida parted with her uncles, promising to rejoin them when they met with Count Raymond the next morning.

Then the three of us—four if you count the silent and miserable Armenian—turned, bleary-eyed, through the camp and onto the causeway.

"Halt. Where do you think you're going?" The guard, who had a nose so round, pocked, and red I could see it even in the pre-dawn light, held up a mailed hand and demanded we stop. I'd have gladly run him over and gone straight to bed but wasn't up for the fight.

I expected Brother Gerhardt to say something, but he offered a mock bow and gestured for me to handle this. "You're in charge."

I mustered up my most adult voice. "We are returning a prisoner to Count Raymond." It sort of worked. The guard turned to examine Barseghyan, who moped and shivered in front of Gerhardt. "This is the man they've been looking for. From Antioch." I pulled the parchment pass from inside my tunic. "We have a pass."

I knew the guard couldn't read it, and I took great pains to point out Count Raymond's signature and on the bottom of the message. "That's his name, in case you can't read it."

Red-Nose horked up a phlegm-ball and spat. "A pox on Count Raymond. And Joscelin and the whole lot of them. The city would've surrendered to the infidels by now if it weren't for de Montferrat. Only real Christian man left in Tyre." My blood boiled, but I managed a superior grin anyway.

"Fine. Maybe this will make you happier." I pulled out the cross with de Montferrat's ring tied to it. Gerhardt gave me a funny look, but I didn't have time to explain. Red-nose took a brief, skeptical glance, then went white enough to glow in the dark.

"Let them pass," he yelled. With that, we made our way up the causeway and back inside the city walls.

Chapter 24

The sun was well up by the time I dragged myself to bed. Our return created a maelstrom of chaos and it took 'til dawn and then some to sort everything out.

Barseghyan was taken into custody, but not without controversy. The guards were uncertain where to hold him since Lords Raymond and Conrad issued competing orders and nobody was sure who to follow, at least at first. After a lot of questioning looks and silent pleading, they chose the wisest course and listened to the stronger, less weary man. They handed him over to de Montferrat's soldiers for safekeeping. People knew which way the wind blew now.

Count Raymond still had control of me, at least, and made a show of putting his hand on my shoulder. "Lucca, what am I going to do with you? I send you for horses and you come back with spies."

I grinned back, although I was so tired my face hurt. "Oh, we got those too, my lord. Six males, good, strong stock." *As if I knew good horses from milk cows!* "They'll bring them to you tomorrow. And there are more back at the farm. It *was* Nahida's uncle Tazir. They can't wait for your return, my lord."

That began another round of furious questions. How

were Tazir's kinfolk? How bad was the bandit situation? Did they still support him in Tripoli? Montferrat stood by, listening to my report and not saying a word, just looking me up and down and nipping at a persistent hangnail with his straight, white teeth.

"Anything else?" Count Raymond asked, at last. He sounded as tired as I was, and his cough wasn't getting any better.

"No, my lord." He nodded, as relieved to hear that as I was to say it.

"We need to find you a safer profession—an apprenticeship—when we get to Tripoli, hey boy? Get some rest." I turned away but remembered to look compliant. With a motion to his bodyguards, he offered a perfunctory bow to Lord Conrad, then left. I started to stagger after them but felt a far less gentle grab on my collar.

"Not so fast, lad." This signaled another round of questions, as grueling as the first. I'll say this for Conrad de Montferrat, he got his ring's worth. He wrung every ounce of information out of me. I may have made up a couple of little things just to satisfy his endless demand for more information.

At last, with my voice strained and my legs wobbling beneath me, he decided I'd had enough. He acted like he wanted to pat my head or something, but his hand wasn't quite sure what to do. Instead, he withdrew it and said, not unkindly, "Off to bed with you, Lucca."

"Thank you, my lord." I pulled the ring out from around my neck and began fiddling with the leather.

"Keep it. For the moment. I have a hunch you're not done with it." He saw the surprise on my face. "Oh, pity's sakes boy. Do you think I'm blind? You don't want to go to Tripoli, do you?"

"My lord? He has a letter from Brother Marco. He's supposed to keep me."

"Is this Brother Marco your father?"

Not really, at any rate. "No, my lord, but..."

"Then who is he to give you away like a mongrel bitch's runt? And what will you do there? An apprenticeship, he says. Yes, you'll make a fine tailor. Or maybe a blacksmith—that's work for a smart lad like you."

I stared down at my filthy feet. Was it that obvious I didn't want to go to Tripoli? That I yearned to return to Acre and rescue my friends? Yes, I'd be safe, but so what?

Nahida was returning to an uncertain fate in a country at war. Far from safe, but she was happy.

Sister Marie-Pilar was not safe—in fact, she was working herself to death—but I'd never seen her happier.

"Think on it, although I suspect you must make your choice soon. Just know I can always find work for a talented young man. Paid work, in fact. Unlikely as it seems, God may have a plan for you in regaining this place from the infidels. If he still wants the cursed place, of course, and only He knows why he would."

"Thank you, my lord." *A paid job. With money.*

I remember making it to my bedchamber. I fell deep asleep and for the first time since my return from Hattin, the usual ghosts didn't come calling.

"We live close to Tripoli. You can visit when you like. It will be fun. I'll teach you to ride properly." Nahida smiled when she said it, knowing I'd rather poke my eyes out or wrestle bears with one hand tied behind my back. Horses were always going to be a necessary evil, and I couldn't decide if they were more evil than necessary.

"That would be nice." I meant it would be nice to visit her. I didn't say anything about Tripoli. You don't lie to your friends. Not if it's really important.

I looked at her face for a long time. Then she held her arms out, and I held my arms out and neither of us moved for the longest time. I knew I shouldn't hug a Mohammedan woman, and she shouldn't touch an unbeliever. But she wasn't really Mohammedan, and what I was seemed irrelevant just then. We laughed and embraced briefly. It felt good. When we pulled apart, a huge teardrop was trying to make its way to the end of her nose, but that was an awfully long trip, and it dropped to the ground halfway there.

"Nahida, enough. Let's go," Uncle Tazir shouted. He'd given us as much privacy as decency allowed, but their business was done, and they had to get moving. It was a long, not very safe trip back to their farm. There were several more horses waiting, and some mares in foal they had to prepare for when *Effendi* Raymond returned home, assuming they could keep them out of marauders' hands.

After much wrangling and arguing, de Montferrat finally agreed that Count Raymond should return to his county, at least until the issue of succession was properly seen to and his wife safely returned, although Lord Conrad didn't see the urgency there. The rumor was he didn't take marriage very seriously, whatever that meant. The six Druze horses would stay behind to support the ongoing war effort and the rescue of Jerusalem. Count Raymond referred to that as "the price of his honor," when Lord Conrad wasn't around. For a while it looked like he would have to throw in Nahida's black gelding as well. Conrad de Montferrat considered it the only decent horse-flesh left in all of Tyre, but "spoils of war" and all that. Plus, he didn't want to tangle with Uncle Tazir. Or Nahida. Or me.

Nahida and her uncles rode slowly out of Tyre, ignoring the stares and dirty looks of the populace. There was grumbling about the four unbelievers on such beautiful animals. The black horse paraded as if on display just to annoy them, but nobody bothered them. I watched them ride away.

I wish I could say I had a peaceful parting with Count Raymond, but I couldn't face him to tell him I was staying in Tyre. There was talk of a rescue mission, and I needed to be part of that. To be honest, only Count Conrad de Montferrat talked of retaking Acre. Everyone else was too tired and beaten to argue with him.

On the day of his departure, I sat in my little room in the keep and watched from the window as the Count, his household, his guard, and my friend Pierre rode away. Raymond's wife was still a hostage in Tiberias, King Guy held prisoner, and Jerusalem besieged and likely to fall any day. All that was left of his life's work was keeping Tripoli in his hands and doing what he could for his people. All of his people. Slouched on his horse, he turned towards my window and held up a hand in goodbye. At least his arm was out of the sling.

I raised my hand, too, knowing he couldn't see me wave. But then he couldn't see me sniffing and welling up with tears either.

I turned back to examine my room. My room, provided by Conrad de Montferrat along with some coin in exchange for what information I could scrounge up for him. It looked like my cell at St Lazar, except it had a window that admitted bright, dust-mottled sunshine. I had a new set of clothes my new master provided, my knife, and the bow. It sat beside my bed, unstrung. Brother Gerhardt disapproved of archers, and Saracen bows in particular, but promised when I could string it myself, he'd show me how to use it.

I looked back at the companion who shared my room now. Brother Gerhardt loomed over me, and the hand that ruffled my hair could have snatched the head right off my shoulders, but I knew it never would.

"Ven do ve go back?"

"I don't know. Lord Conrad is still making a plan. And it all depends on what happens in Jerusalem. Do you think we can do it? Can we take Acre back from the Saracens?" I was surprised to discover I didn't even care that much about the city itself. Like Tyre, Acre was bricks and stones and too many people and rats. But my friends were there. Brother Marco and the people of St Lazar languished in uncertainty.

Gilbert argued with the walls and Fadhil and Firan and their family had nowhere else to go. Sister expected me to help, and I couldn't desert them.

"Who knows? It's all as God wills."

I nodded. We watched the last Tripolitan soldier ride out the gate. I knew he hated when I spoke Arabic, but it was the only right word to use under the circumstances. Arabic said some things much better than French.

"*Inshallah.*"

Obligatory Ending Stuff

Thank you for continuing with Lucca on his journey, especially since there was never supposed to be another book. Two things are responsible for the fact that this story got told, and there's another one in the pipeline.

First, *Acre's Bastard* was originally supposed to be a one-shot book, with no sequel. Really. I had a lovely epilogue with Lucca as an old man, wrapping up his life and looking back on his scampish adventures. My daughter, Her Serene Highness, hated it. In fact, she made the ultimate threat: "If you use that ending I'm putting you in a home when the time comes and never coming to visit." With an eye to the future, here we are.

The second reason is less personally compelling, but more serious to anyone who enjoys history. The Crusades kept going. Just because he got home in one piece, that didn't mean Lucca was safe. Acre fell within a week of the Battle of Hattin, and Tyre alone held out against Salah-adin's armies. So what was I going to do with him?

Every time I came up with a plot point, it didn't match the way the story actually unfolded. First, if you know your Crusades, you know that having Lucca wind up happily at Tripoli wouldn't be much help. Google "Raymond of

Tripoli," and you'll realize that what would have been a perfect happy ending just wasn't an option yet. (And did you really want one?)

Secondly, Conrad de Montferrat showed up, and I couldn't ignore him. With superhuman timing, this guy leaves Constantinople (where he was married to the Empress for a while) and tries to sail into Acre Harbor two days after the city's surrender, only to be turned back and sent to Tyre. From there he proceeds to bully and complain and scheme and be Mister Bossy-Pants until he winds up becoming King of Jerusalem—for four whole days until he was assassinated. Be careful what you wish for.

As for "The Lady," Sybilla of Antioch, she's shrouded in mystery, but the notion that she seduced King Bohemond and tried to insinuate her family deep into the machinations of the region are supported by multiple sources. There's also the rumor that she was in league with Salah-adin. Other than that, precious little is known of her. Of course, the records at the time were notoriously cruel to women and often accused them of licentiousness, stupidity, or licentious stupidity. It's not fair, but I could only go on what I had for sources. Oh, and there was a major "Three Musketeers" vibe I couldn't resist.

In truth, when Raymond of Tripoli passed in September of that year (if you haven't Googled it by now, it's too late for spoiler alerts) the County of Tripoli was inherited by Bohemond's son, (Count Raymond's godson and namesake) Raymond of Antioch. So I guess Lucca helped after all, now that I think about it.

As with all of my historical novels, I've tried to keep the major events as factual as possible. I've attempted to do right by the historical record when it comes to the famous people, timelines, and events. It matters that the events are supported by facts as much as possible. That said, a lot of Lucca's adventures won't be found in the official records. They must have gotten lost or something.

Everyone else is fair game and came from my imagination. For the record, Nahida may be my favorite character of all time, and I'm not sorry about killing that damned horse. I hope it hit you in the feels, and I laughed when I thought it up. I'm a terrible person. Sue me.

Getting a book out, even when you self-publish, is never a solo act, so here we go:

Thanks to The Naperville Writers Group for putting up with me for four years and three novels. By the time you read this I will have moved from Chicago to Las Vegas and no longer be hanging out with you on Wednesday nights. Please know that you will always be in my heart for your support, feedback, friendship and inspiration. And the laughs— mostly the laughs.

This group also provided most of my beta readers. Thanks to Ethan Pressley, Alicia Burns, Jorge Busot, Jeremy Brown, Eileen Kimbrough, Frank Fedele, Kelly-Lee Parry, and Her Serene Highness. You kept me honest and stopped me from indulging my baser writer instincts. This is a better book because of your help.

Copy editing was provided by Alicia Burns, who time and again saved me from myself, and any mistakes are those of the management.

Cover design and the look of the book is the work of the supremely patient Kelly-Lee Parry.

Finally, thank you for sticking with me. I'm gratified by the readers from around the world who have enjoyed Lucca's story and keep asking for more. It may seem ungrateful for me to say, "Don't tell me, tell Amazon," but it's true. If you blog, or use Goodreads, or have some other way of letting others know about books you enjoy (not just mine) please review them and spread the news. Getting the word out is tough, and you could really help a brother out.

Also, don't be a stranger. If you haven't already, visit my website at www.WayneTurmel.com. You'll find lots of interviews with historical fiction authors who deserve to be read, as well as news about what's happening in my world and even short stories and other pieces you might enjoy. And, of course, you can always find me on Facebook and Twitter @Wturmel. Seriously, it makes my day when I get a random email or tweet from a complete stranger who has enjoyed my work and almost makes it worth doing. Money is better, but this is nice.

There's a third (and I hope final) Lucca story in the works. Then I'll be free to tell some of the other stories I have rattling around in my skull. Until then, I am deeply grateful for each set of eyeballs that my work finds and wish you all the best.

Don't let the weasels get you down.

Wayne Turmel